12/14/15

HEART
of
GOLD

**Center Point
Large Print**

Also by Beverly Jenkins and available from Center Point Large Print:

Blessings Novels:
  A Wish and a Prayer
  Something Old, Something New
  A Second Helping
  Bring on the Blessings

Destiny's Surrender

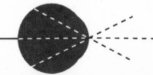

This Large Print Book carries the Seal of Approval of N.A.V.H.

HEART
of
GOLD

⮞ A BLESSINGS NOVEL ⮜

BEVERLY
JENKINS

CENTER POINT LARGE PRINT
THORNDIKE, MAINE

This Center Point Large Print edition is published in the year 2014 by arrangement with William Morrow Paperbacks, an imprint of HarperCollins Publishers.

Map of Henry Adams by Valerie Miller

The text of this Large Print edition is unabridged.
In other aspects, this book may vary
from the original edition.
Printed in the United States of America
on permanent paper.
Set in 16-point Times New Roman type.

ISBN: 978-1-62899-144-4

Library of Congress Cataloging-in-Publication Data

Jenkins, Beverly, 1951–
Heart of gold : a blessings novel / Beverly Jenkins. —
    Center Point Large Print edition.
pages ; cm
Summary: "In Henry Adams, Kansas, Zoey has tried to befriend a man who wants people to stay off his property by leaving him small offerings. When he dies, he leaves a saddlebag of gold to Zoey, who also has to deal with her parents' separation and troubled friends"
—Provided by publisher.
ISBN 978-1-62899-144-4 (library binding : alk. paper)
1. African American women—Fiction. 2. City and town life—Fiction.
    3. Large type books. 4. Domestic fiction. I. Title.
PS3560.E4795H43 2014b
813′.54—dc23
                                            2014011823

To Regina (Sarita) Jackson.
Her work with EOYDC positively impacts
the lives of children every day.
You rock, girl!

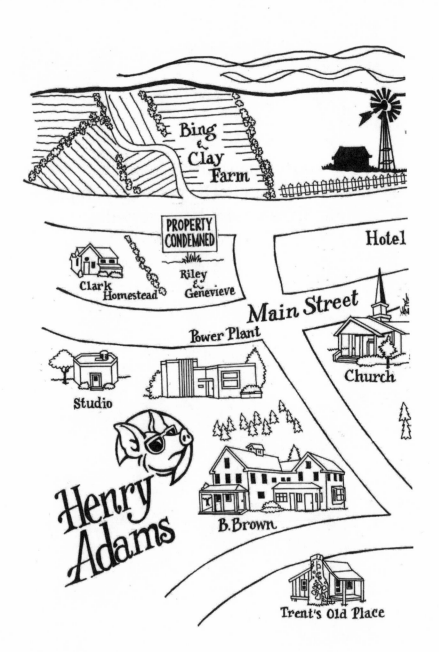

PROLOGUE

Autumn 1885
Kansas plains—outskirts of Henry Adams

Illuminated like a specter by the light of the full moon, Neil July sat his horse and voiced his doubts. "I don't know why you're burying the gold way out here. You're never going to find it again."

Griffin Blake tossed another shovelful of dirt from the hole he was digging. "Sure I will."

"We're on the plains of Kansas. No trees. No landmarks. Nothing to remember where it is when we come back for it."

Griffin paused. "We? This is *my* gold. I robbed that train."

"Well, yeah," Neil admitted a bit sheepishly, "but suppose Shafts and I need to bail you out of jail."

Griff glanced over at the big Comanche sitting silently on his mount. Two Shafts was Neil's half brother. He rarely spoke and didn't now, so Griff resumed digging. The three outlaws had been good friends for years, but the Julys, known as the Terrible Twins, were the physical embodiment of the mythical trickster Coyote. Griff trusted them about as far as he could toss them—

and considering Shafts's mountain-like size, that wasn't very far. "Since I'm not going to jail, you won't need bail. But if I come back and find this hole empty, I'm sending the Preacher to hunt you down."

The Preacher was another mutual friend, but also a gun-toting, Bible-quoting bounty hunter, and the only one of his kind ever to apprehend the Julys and turn them over to the law. Granted, they escaped less than a day later, but the Preacher still wore the crown.

Griff dug down another three feet. Convinced that the hole was deep enough to guard his cache of purloined double eagles from predators both animal and human, he tossed the leather saddlebag inside. The bag also contained a newspaper account of the daring robbery, complete with an artist's likeness of Griff, who thought himself far more handsome than the sketched rendering. But what was a wanted man to do?

With the hole now refilled, Griff used the sole of his boot to push a few rocks into the soil to mark the spot.

Neil shook his head. "You're never going to find it."

"Sure I will, and when I do, I'll buy you a drink."

"Nope. It's going to be dug up a hundred years from now by some farmer putting in fence posts for a pigpen, and you'll have been dead for so long, all you'll be able to do is curse him from hell."

Griff swung himself into the saddle. "Then I won't buy you a drink. Let's ride."

And with a slap of the reins three of the most wanted outlaws on both sides of the Mississippi rode off into the night.

CHAPTER
1

My Bonnie lies over the ocean.
My Bonnie lies over the sea.
My Bonnie lies over the ocean.
Oh bring back my Bonnie to me . . .

Traditional Scottish folk song

The present day
Henry Adams, Kansas

Saturday was Zoey's favorite day of the week. There was no school, no getting up early to be there on time, and the day was entirely her own. Sometimes she jumped on her bike and rode over to the garage to help Amari and his dad work on cars, or she rode over to the rec to see what town matriarch Tamar July and friends Miss Marie and

Miss Genevieve were up to. Or she hung out with her friend Devon, which was occurring less and less lately because he'd become a real pain in the butt. Usually her Saturdays were as idyllic as a ten-year-old kid could want, but this one was an exception. Her friend Crystal had run away from home last night. The seventeen-year-old had promised to text or call when she got wherever she was going, but hadn't, and Zoey was so worried that she'd tossed and turned all night, imagining any number of horrible outcomes. Crystal also made Zoey promise not to tell anyone, and so far she'd kept the promise, but the secret was weighing on her like an engine block around her neck. She was pretty sure Crystal's mom, Ms. Bernadine, was probably going crazy with worry, as would everyone else in Henry Adams once word got around. Being caught between her loyalty to Crystal and wanting to tell someone what she knew was a lot for someone her age to be carrying around.

After getting dressed, Zoey went downstairs for breakfast. The house was quiet and filled with morning shadows. Mama Roni was away on a concert swing through the West Coast but was due home later that day, and Zoey couldn't wait for her to return. She found Daddy Reg seated outside at the table on their big deck.

"Morning, Zo."

"Hi, Daddy. How are you?"

He held up his mug. "My coffee and I are doing fine. How're you?"

She shrugged. "I'm okay."

Something in her tone must've set off his inner dad alert because he looked at her real seriously. "You sure?"

"Yep," she lied. "Mama Roni still coming home today?"

"As far as I know."

"Good. I'm going to get me some cereal, then see if Amari and his dad will be working on the cars today."

"Okay, but make sure you check in with me so I know where you are."

She nodded and went inside. The kitchen's glass-door wall looked out onto the deck, so as she sat and had her cereal, she could see her dad's face. He looked really sad, and the reason behind that was also worrisome. Her parents weren't getting along. Mama Roni was a world-famous award-winning singer. Daddy Reg was a doctor. He was in the dumps because Mama Roni had been away from home a lot recently because of her career. Even though they'd built an awesome new recording studio in town so she'd be nearer, it didn't seem to make him any happier because he still missed her a lot. Zoey missed her too, but she and her mom had talked about it. Zoey understood that her mom's love of singing didn't mean she loved her daughter any less, and besides, Zoey knew how important the music was to her mom. Why it was so hard for Daddy Reg to understand that too was something Zoey had no answer for. When the adults did something the kids didn't get, Amari called it "grown folks business," so she stayed out of it, and hoped they weren't thinking about a divorce.

Done with breakfast, she put her dishes in the dishwasher and stepped back outside to give her dad a parting hug and a kiss on his cheek.

"I'll be here working on charts, so make sure you check in," he reminded her.

"I will."

"Oh, and I have some really sad news." He gently took her hands in his. "Crystal ran away last night, honey."

Zoey swallowed.

"No one's heard from her, and Ms. Bernadine's really worried, so if she calls or texts, make sure you let me know. Okay?"

She nodded and left him sitting on the deck.

After grabbing her green Danica Patrick jacket, riding gloves, and helmet, she went to the garage to get her bike. She felt really bad about not volunteering that she'd talked to Crystal before she took off, but she justified her silence by telling herself her dad hadn't asked. The promise she'd made to keep her mouth shut was becoming a major dilemma because she prided herself on telling the truth. But the moment she pushed her bike out into the sun, the dilemma worsened. Sheriff Will Dalton's police car was parked out in front of Crystal's house. Guilt rose. She needed to talk to someone. Ideally it would be her mom, but with the time difference between Kansas and California, Zoey wasn't sure if she was awake, or at the airport, or what, so she went with her second choice. Walking her bike next door, she parked it and climbed the steps to the porch.

Devon answered the bell, and before she could ask after his brother Amari, he gushed excitedly, "Crystal ran away from home last night. She's in so much trouble. Sheriff Will's at her house right now, along with all the adults and my mom and dad."

He reminded her of the gossipy old ladies at the church down in Miami, where she used to live. "Is Amari here?"

His eyes riveted on the patrol car, he answered with a question instead. "Where do you think she went?"

"I don't know. Where's Amari?"

"At Preston's. Crystal's going to have to paint Ms. Marie's fence a thousand times, I bet."

Once upon a time, Zoey had loved Devon as much as breathing. They'd come to Henry Adams as the youngest of the town's five foster kids and done everything together, but last year his adoptive parents, Ms. Lily and Mr. Trent, took him down south to visit his grandmother's grave, and he hadn't been the same since. He no longer wore his perennial black suit and clip-on bow tie and had given up on being the town's preacher, but she was liking the new version less and less.

"You want to hang out later?" he asked.

Zoey didn't like lying to him, but . . . "Um, let me find out if Amari's going to be working on the cars today first."

His face instantly soured. "I still don't get why you like doing that. All that oil and stuff is just nasty."

Zoey's newly found joy in all things automotive had become a major sticking point in their relationship. In spite of him being raised by the fiercely independent Ms. Lily, Devon had issues with girls working on cars.

Rather than say something mean, she left the porch. "See you later."

Amari was indeed at Preston's. The two teens were BFFs and in the house alone because Preston's adoptive parents, the colonel and Mrs. Payne, were in Florida for a marines reunion. "I need to talk to you guys," she announced, taking a seat on one of the armchairs.

They were playing *Madden* on the television. "What about?" Amari asked, controller in hand, doing his best to evade Preston's defenders.

"Crystal."

"What about her?" Preston asked, holding his own controller and not taking his eyes off the screen. "You know she ran away last night."

Amari added knowingly, "Fence painting in her future for sure. What a dummy."

"No, she's not!"

"Yeah, she is," Amari countered.

"She's just having issues."

"Uh-huh, like what?"

"She didn't tell me."

Both teens turned. "You saw her last night before she left?" Amari asked, searching her face. She nodded.

Preston, also known as Brain for his sky-high IQ, paused the game. "Okay, tell us everything, and don't leave anything out."

So she told them about visiting Crystal last evening and finding her packing in her bedroom.

"Did she say where she was going?" Amari asked.

"No, but she talked about hooking up with her old friends."

"That means Dallas," Preston concluded.

Amari exhaled a sigh. "Stupid. Have you talked to Ms. Bernadine yet?"

"No. Crystal made me promise not to tell anybody."

Once again Amari shook his head, "That's a helluva thing to do to a little kid."

Zoey wanted to argue that she wasn't little anymore, but both he and Preston were pushing fifteen and sixteen. To them a ten-year-old

17

probably was still a little kid. "You think I should tell her?"

"Yes!" they replied with one voice.

"But what if she makes me paint the fence for not saying something last night?" So far, Zoey was the only kid in town who'd yet to whitewash Ms. Marie Jefferson's fence as punishment for doing something dumb: Devon'd had a turn for lying and stealing money, and Crystal and the boys were busted last spring for creating a secret e-mail address in order to cruise the Internet in places they weren't supposed to be.

"I don't think Ms. Bernadine would do that, Zoey," Amari offered reassuringly.

Preston concurred. "Me neither. You want us to go with you?"

"No. I'll go by myself." She didn't want to go alone, but the need to get out from under the secret made it necessary.

"You sure?" Amari asked. "Might be good to have some support if the grown folks start yelling."

"I know, but I need to step up. Crystal said she was going to hitchhike."

"Double stupid," Amari declared.

It was hard for Zoey to defend Crys's decision to leave behind the good life they'd all been given with their adoptive parents. Before Ms. Bernadine came into their lives, Zoey had been homeless in Miami, Amari was in Detroit, stealing cars for fun, and Preston had been trying to survive the foster care system in Milwaukee. "Do you know whether Ms. Bernadine's heard from her yet?"

"No. We started texting Crys this morning as soon as we found out she'd taken off," Preston explained, "but she hasn't come back at us."

"But whatever happens, I'll bet she won't be gone long," Amari declared sagely. "She can't make it on the streets anymore. Kansas makes you soft."

Preston wasn't so convinced. "I don't know, man. She could be gone for a while."

"Then put your money where your mouth is. I give her two days, tops. If I'm right, I get your telescope. You win—I don't know. What do you want?"

"For you to stop tripping. No way are you getting my scope, but if I win, you do my chores over at the rec center and vice versa." Amari nodded, and they shook to seal the deal.

The bet aside, Zoey hoped Amari was right. Life in town just wouldn't be the same if Crystal stayed gone forever. Needing to talk with Ms. Bernadine before she lost her nerve, she got to her feet.

"You sure you don't want us to go with you?" Preston asked again, looking concerned.

"I'm sure, but thanks, Brain." She spoke to Amari. "Are you and your dad working on the car today?"

19

"Probably not with all this Crystal drama, but when you're finished talking to Ms. Bernadine, you're welcome to come back and hang here with us."

Brain nodded agreement. "Especially if you don't want to hang with Devon."

Zoey had been an only child in Miami, but now considered the boys family, and they were the best big brothers in the world. "Okay."

Feeling a bit braver, she left them to go talk to Ms. Bernadine. It was only a short walk across the street, but she kept saying "Please don't let them yell at me" the entire way.

Amari's grandfather, Malachi July, answered Ms. Bernadine's doorbell.

"Hey, Miss Z." Malachi owned the Dog and Cow, the town's diner, and was known to the kids as OG—hip-hop for Old Gangsta. He wasn't really a gangster but Amari had given him the title because he was so cool.

"Hey, OG." She took a deep breath. "I need to talk to Ms. Bernadine. It's about Crystal."

"We haven't heard from her yet, baby girl."

"I know—that's why I need to talk to her. Maybe I can help."

Sheriff Dalton was in the front room, talking to the Henry Adams adults: Amari's parents—Ms. Lily and her husband, Mr. Trent, who was also the town's mayor; Amari's great-grandmother, Tamar; Reverend Paula; Ms. Rocky, who

20

managed the Dog and Cow; and the town's schoolteacher, Mr. Jack James. All looked worried.

Ms. Bernadine walked over. "Hey, Zoey."

"Hi, Ms. Bernadine. I came over to tell you that Crystal might be in Dallas."

Every eye in the room swung Zoey's way, and she had to fight to not squirm under the scrutiny. "I—I talked to her last night before she left. She made me promise not to tell you. Do I have to paint the fence?"

Ms. Bernadine shook her head. "No, honey."

"Crys said she had friends where she was going. I told her hitchhiking was dangerous, but she didn't listen. A boy drove her away from the house."

The sheriff asked, "Do you know his name?"

She shook her head. "No, sir. But I memorized the license plate."

He grinned. "You just earned yourself a county sheriff's badge, young lady."

Trent said approvingly, "Way to go, Zoey."

Ms. Bernadine hugged her tight and kissed her on the top of her head. "You rock, missy."

Zoey felt a million times better. Crystal would probably call her a snitch when she got back, but at that moment Zoey didn't care. She'd deal with that when the time came.

"And free dessert for the rest of the week," Rocky told her. "On the house."

"Thanks! But you have to give some to Preston and Amari, too. They were the ones who figured out she probably went to Dallas."

"You got it."

Zoey recited the plate number for the sheriff, and he immediately got on his phone. Ms. Bernadine asked, "Did Crys say anything else?"

"Just that she wanted her old life back." Ms. Bernadine's eyes got real sad, so Zoey told her the next part. "I asked her if it was because she didn't like us anymore, but she said that wasn't it."

"Okay, honey. Thanks. That information helps a lot."

"You're welcome." She also wanted to tell her that Amari didn't think Crystal would be gone long, but she kept that to herself. She wasn't sure Ms. Bernadine wanted Amari's opinion. "Is it okay for me to go now?"

"Yes."

All the adults offered her thanks, and a relieved Zoey left.

CHAPTER
2

By late morning, Bernadine was finally in the house alone. After all the Crystal upheaval, she welcomed the solitude. Parts of her were angry, others disappointed, and others wanted to fall to the floor and weep. The signs had been there. In fact, as the summer waned, she'd sensed the storm on the horizon. Crystal had been despondent over her unrequited crush on Diego July and waxing nostalgic about her old life on the streets. Although Bernadine assured herself at the time that Crystal had too much to look forward to and would get over herself eventually, she'd been terribly wrong. And now, here she stood on her deck wondering if she'd ever see her child again. Thank God for Zoey, however. The information she provided on the license plate enabled the sheriff's office to track down the driver. As a result they'd learned that, one, Crystal had duped the boy into believing that Bernadine sanctioned the flight, and two, he'd dropped her off by the 183 South ramp. Sheriff Dalton's next task was to show Crystal's picture around at the local truck stops in the hope of finding someone who might have seen her or given her a ride. He also had a few law enforcement connections in the Dallas area, and he promised to e-mail her picture to them as well.

As had become her habit since this madness began last night, she took out her phone to check for messages. None of her texts to her daughter were being answered and all the calls had gone straight to voice mail. Why, Crystal? she wanted to ask. Why choose to run from such a blessed life? Bernadine took out the note she'd found taped to the front door last night and read it for what seemed like the hundredth time.

I have to go, otherwise I'm going to explode. Hope you'll forgive me one day.

Love you,
Crys

Sighing, Bernadine put the note back into her shirt pocket and prayed the nightmare might end soon.

When her phone rang, she startled. Hoping it was Crystal, she quickly viewed the caller ID and was crestfallen to see that it was her sister, Diane.

"Hey, Di. How are you?"

"Doing good. I'm at the airport. Can you send someone to pick me up?"

Bernadine froze. "What airport?"

"I think it's called Hays?"

Bernadine mentally pleaded. *Please lord, not today!*

"Are you there, Bernie?"

"Yeah. I'm here."

"How long will it take you to get here?"

Bernadine sighed. "I'll send a car for you. It'll take about an hour."

"An hour?"

"An hour. Are you on a layover?"

"No. Harmon and I are having some work done on the house, so I thought I'd come stay with you. Shouldn't be more than a week or two."

Bernadine felt a headache settling in. "Di, this isn't a good time."

"Don't be silly, just send the car." And she hung up.

Bernadine dropped into a chair. Head in her hands, she voiced an irritated and frustrated "Dammit!" then put in a call to her nephew, Harmon Jr., Diane's oldest son. "Why is your mother in Kansas?"

He chuckled. "Hello to you too, Aunt Dina. Is that where she is?"

"Yes," Bernadine snarled. Her sister was one of her least favorite people in the world.

"Well, it seems Dad's finally had enough of her minute-by-minute criticisms. He's divorcing her."

"What!"

"Yep. Served her the papers a few days ago."

"But why come here?"

"Probably no place else to go. She can't stay with me because she and Joan haven't gotten along since the day they met. Remember the drama at our wedding?"

The wedding took place seven years ago. When the preacher asked whether anyone had a reason the bride and groom shouldn't marry, Diane stood up and declared Joan too low-class to marry her son. It took half the church to restrain Joan's mother so she wouldn't leap over the pew and whip Diane's sneering behind. As a result, Diane and her son hadn't spoken for two years. "What about your brother Marlon?"

"He and his partner, Anthony, offered to take her in, but she said she had no intentions of living in an F-word household."

"Oh, good lord."

"I know. And since we all know my sister Monique is at the top of Mom's persona non grata list for marrying outside the race, you're it, Auntie."

"I'm so lucky," Bernadine declared sarcastically. "Okay. I suppose I don't have much choice. She is my sister."

"And remember, no good deed goes unpunished."

She laughed for the first time that day. "Anything else I need to know?"

"She and Dad are broke. He declared bankruptcy six months ago, and they moved into a one-bedroom apartment. I think the close quarters is what sent him over the edge. That, and the fact that she wouldn't stop spending. She called me yesterday, screaming that he'd canceled all her credit cards. I tried to explain to her that it went with being divorced, but of course she didn't want to hear it."

Bernadine's brother-in-law, Harmon Sr., was a good guy. He'd put up with his wife's tantrums and selfish, over-the-top behavior for thirty years. It saddened her to hear about his financial struggles. "Does he still have his dental practice?"

"Not sure. You know how closemouthed he can be, and with them being in Detroit and me in Austin, there's no real way to tell. He keeps saying he's fine, though."

She made a mental note to reach out to him just as soon as the Crystal situation was resolved —if it ever got resolved. "Anything else?"

"Not that I can think of. You okay?"

"Doing great," she lied.

"Good to know. Hope Mom doesn't make you too crazy."

"Me, too. If she does, I'll just bury her body where it can't be found."

"Sounds like a plan. Love you a lot. Later."

"Bye." After ending the call, Bernadine exhaled audibly in response to the continuing madness that had become her life. First Crystal, and now Diane. She had no idea what she'd done to be so deserving, but she needed it to stop.

She put in a call to her driver, Nathan, and asked him to make the airport run. A bit over two hours later the shiny black town car pulled up smoothly to the curb. She watched through the screen door as Nathan hustled around to let Diane out of the car. Her sister stepped out, swathed in scarves and wearing skinny black jeans and spike-heeled black leather boots. The expensive black handbag hanging from her shoulder looked large enough to hold a bowling ball, and her wrists were lined with gold bangles. She'd always had a trim figure, but there was trim and there was anorexic. Bernadine hadn't seen her since divorcing Leo five years ago, and Diane was skinny in a way reminiscent of aging women with old money bent upon reclaiming their youth. She was in her fifties now, and it was not a good look.

As usual, Diane was being short-tempered, giving Nathan grief for taking too much time wrestling not one, not two, but five pieces of green designer luggage from the trunk. His lips were set tightly in irritation. Bernadine stepped outside. "Hello, Di."

She turned. "Oh, hello, Bernie."

Bernadine hated being addressed that way, something her sister was well aware of but it hadn't made a difference when they were growing up, and apparently nothing had changed.

"Be careful with that bag. That's real leather," she railed at Nathan, who'd just set the last of her suitcases on the walk. "Be glad you don't work for me."

And Nathan, bless his heart replied, "I am, ma'am. Believe me."

The stunned look on Diane's face made Bernadine chuckle softly. He'd just earned himself a bonus, but she doubted all the money in the world would be enough to offset the mental distress he'd undoubtedly suffered during the trip.

While Diane's eyes spit flames, Nathan silently carried the safari's worth of bags up the steps. "Where do you want these, Ms. Brown?"

"Just put them inside the door, Nathan, please."

"She's not a nice lady," he said in a soft voice.

"I know, and I'm sorry."

"Yelled at me for driving too fast and then too slow. Every half mile she was complaining about something." When he brought in the last bag, he asked, "Can you find somebody else to drive her back to Hays, please? I know it's my job, but—"

Bernadine nodded. "I will certainly try."

"Thanks. Do you need me anymore today?"

"I don't think so. Roni's supposed to be in sometime this evening, but her text said she'd already made arrangements for the ride home."

"Okay, then I'll be going."

He passed Diane on the steps, acting as if she were invisible, got into the car, and drove off.

On the porch, Diane gave Bernadine a quick faux hug and an equally faux kiss on the cheek. "He should be fired for incompetence. So good to see you."

"Same here," Bernadine lied.

Diane moved past her and into the house. Before following, Bernadine took a moment to draw in a few calming breaths in an effort to convince herself that the visit would go well even though she knew it was a lie.

Inside she found Diane staring critically around at the living room. "Bernie, I don't like the way you have this room laid out."

"Then it's a good thing you don't live here."

"No, I'm serious. That blue chair would look much better over there, where you have that end table. And that gray lamp doesn't go with anything."

"Thanks for your opinion."

But instead of leaving well enough alone, Diane dropped her handbag on the sofa, walked over to the end table, and leaned over to unplug the offending lamp.

"Leave it be, Diane," Bernadine gritted out.

Diane stopped in mid reach and slowly straightened. "I'm just trying to help."

"Thanks, but I don't need it."

"Well, okay then," she replied, looking wounded. She took a seat on the sofa.

Bernadine blew out a breath. *And so it begins.* She'd always wanted a sisterly relationship with Diane, but it never worked out that way. Although Bernadine had refused to deal with the reality while growing up, she could now admit that her mother had favored Diane over both Bernadine and her now late sister Cecily. Diane had been the pretty one, the head cheerleader, the one with the Sweet Sixteen party. Had it not been for her father's tender loving care, Bernadine would've gone through her formative years feeling like an unwanted changeling left on the doorstep. When her mother complained about the difficulties inherent in shopping for her overweight eldest daughter (who just so happened to look exactly like her), or allowed Diane to make snide remarks about Bernadine's size and dark skin, her dad Emery would stick his head in her bedroom door and say, "Always remember two things, Dina—you're pretty, *and* you're smart. The grass out-side's got more brains than your mother and sister combined."

"In spite of the bad layout of your house, it's rather nice," Diane said, breaking into Bernadine's reverie.

"Thanks. I think so, too." Bernadine took a seat in the blue armchair. "So, what brings you here again?"

Diane waved off the remark. "Harmon and I are having an addition put on the house. A solarium."

"Ah."

"So I thought I'd come visit you, since I haven't seen you since the divorce. How is Leo, by the way?"

"No idea."

"Really?"

"Why would I keep tabs on a man I divorced?"

Diane shrugged. "I don't know—maybe for sentimental reasons. All that money, I'd be trying to get him back."

"I don't want him back, Diane. I caught the man screwing his secretary in his office when he was supposed to be meeting me for lunch—on my birthday."

"It's Diana now, remember?"

"Oh, right. I forgot." In high school, she'd decided to rename herself Diana, much as Diane Ross of Motown's Supremes had. *Well, so much for small talk.* "Are you hungry?"

"Famished."

"Okay, let's go get some food. My treat."

"I should hope so, since you're the hostess. Do you have someone to take my bags to the guest room?"

"No."

"No servants?"

"No."

"Didn't you get a fortune from Leo?"

"Yes, but why would I need servants?"

"Because you're rich now, Bernadine, and rich women always have them. Good grief, who's advising you?"

Bernadine knew from the moment her sister called that this visit wasn't going to go well, and it was already on its way straight to hell. "The guest room is down that hallway. We can move you in when we get back."

Diane replied with an impatient, "Fine. Where's your powder room?"

Bernadine gave her directions, and while Diane was gone, she picked up her keys and purse. She also prayed for strength.

On their walk out to the garage, Diane's steps slowed upon seeing Bernadine's Baby. "We're going to lunch in a truck?"

"Yep. Get in."

"Where's your driver?"

"Home by now." Bernadine made herself comfortable behind the steering wheel.

A huffing Diane settled into the passenger seat and slammed the door. Smiling inwardly, Bernadine started the engine, backed down the driveway, and headed her beautiful blue Baby toward town.

On the short drive, Diane said only, "Why in the world are you living way out here in the middle of nowhere?"

"I like it."

"With all your money, you should be living in Paris or some other upscale place."

"I have an apartment there, another in Madrid, and a time-share in Maui."

Diane eyed Bernadine with surprise.

Silence ruled for the rest of the ride.

As was usual on Saturday afternoon, the Dog and Cow's parking lot was packed.

"The Dog and Cow?" her sister asked, eyeing the sign dubiously. "What kind of name is that?"

"Long story. I'll explain later."

Inside, the place was bustling. The jukebox was blasting "We Are Family" by Sister Sledge, and there was a long line of people waiting for tables.

Diane took in the surroundings and, to Bernadine's amazement, smiled. "This is nice, Bernie. Love the music."

"And the food is as good as the atmosphere."

Rocky walked up and asked Bernadine, "Heard anything yet?"

She shook her head. "No." Thoughts of the missing Crystal returned, bringing with them a renewed sense of worry and melancholy.

"Okay. Hang in there. Should be able to seat you in a few minutes."

"Thanks, Rock."

As she drifted away, Diane asked, "Who's that?"

"Rocky Dancer. She's the manager."

"Pretty woman. What was she asking you about?"

Mal walked up and for that Bernadine was thankful. She had no desire to share what was going on with Crystal with her sister. "Hey, sweet thing."

"Hey yourself," Diane replied before Bernadine could respond.

Mal paused. He eyed Diane.

Bernadine plastered a fake smile on her face. "Mal, this is my sister, Diane. Di, Malachi July. He's the owner here."

"Hello, Malachi," Diane purred, sticking out a hand and eyeing him like a decadent piece of chocolate cake she couldn't wait to enjoy. "Name's Diana. Such a pleasure to meet you."

His features neutral, he shook her hand. "Same here."

When he attempted to withdraw his hand, she held on and purred again, "Mal, do me a big favor and get us a table so we don't have to wait. I'm really, really hungry."

His eyes met Bernadine's, and she shook her head. "We'll wait our turn like everyone else."

"Thanks, baby doll." He rewarded her with a kiss on the cheek and whispered in her ear, "You never told me crazy ran in your family." Stepping back, he said, "Shouldn't be long."

Diane's hungry eyes followed him through the crowd. "Wow. I'd move here in a New York minute if I had him to look at all day. Is he married?"

"No."

"Divorced?"

"No. He's never been married."

"Oh, lord. Please don't tell me he's gay."

"He isn't."

"Good."

Bernadine rolled her eyes. She held off on revealing that she and Mal were an item. It would never cross Diane's mind that fat old Bernadine would be hooked up with one of the finest men in the county.

They were finally shown to a table, and after settling in, their waiter, seventeen-year-old Eli James, came over with glasses of water on a tray. He set the water down and handed them menus. "Hi, Ms. Brown. Any news on Crystal?"

"Not yet."

"God. How can she be this stupid?"

"Now, Eli."

"She is, Ms. Brown, and everybody in town knows it. We'll be lining up to kick her dumb behind when she gets back."

Amused by his fervor but needing to change the subject before Diane got too interested in the conversation, Bernadine did the introductions. "Di, this is Eli James. Eli, my sister, Ms. Willis. Eli's dad is the town's schoolteacher."

"Hello, Eli."

"Hi, ma'am. You ever been to Henry Adams before?"

"No. Who's Crystal?"

"Ms. Brown's daughter. She ran away from home last night. Are you two ready to place your orders?"

Diane gave him a smile. "Let me check out the menu for a minute."

He nodded and moved off. The smug triumph on Diane's face warned Bernadine of the impending attack. Sure enough, her sister glanced up from the menu and asked, "Crystal's the girl you adopted, right? And she ran away?"

Bernadine nodded tightly.

"I'm so sorry. You must feel like a terrible mother."

Bernadine turned her head to the booth side window and focused on the view of the street so she wouldn't reach across the table and snatch her sister by the throat.

Without looking up from the menu, Diane added, "All those foster kids are on drugs anyway, you know. Maybe it's best that she's gone. I certainly wouldn't want that kind of drama in my home." She picked up her water and sipped daintily.

Bernadine decided a line needed to be drawn in the sand there and then. She asked quietly, "Is this the home that was foreclosed on, or the one-bedroom apartment Harmon threw you out of?"

Diane choked and began coughing. Eyes frigid, Bernadine waited.

Eli chose to return at that moment.

"You two ready?"

"Yes," Bernadine replied, smiling falsely. "What are you having, sister?"

Looking like a deer caught in poacher headlights, Diane quickly ordered a burger and fries. Bernadine had her usual. "The spinach salad with the house vinaigrette."

"Coming right up," he said, and left.

Bernadine picked up her water. Everything about her body language dared her sister to say another word. Diane's gaze went chasing off. Apparently she got the message.

Bernadine's phone buzzed. Praying it was Crystal, she quickly swiped it open. It was. Bordering on tears, her heart raced as she read: *I'm ok. Don't worry.*

Fingers fumbling excitedly, she typed, *Please call so we can talk. I love you!!!*

Bernadine waited anxiously for a response. It never came.

CHAPTER
3

After sharing a lunch of grilled cheese and tomato soup with Preston and Amari, Zoey helped the boys clean up and then remembered something. "Shoot. Devon and I are supposed to check the fish." Each month their teacher, Mr. James, assigned a pair of students to maintain the school's giant aquarium, and with all the drama surrounding Crystal, she'd forgotten. Technically Devon was supposed to help her, but apparently he'd forgotten as well. Since she'd had enough of his old-lady act for the day, she'd handle the task alone. While Amari turned on the big screen so the boys could resume their game, Preston handed her his lanyard with the key to the school attached on a ring, and she put it around her neck. "Are you going to be okay riding over there by yourself?" he asked.

She nodded.

"Be careful," Amari added.

Zoey laughed and drawled in her still-prominent Florida accent, "Y'all sound like my daddy."

"That's because if something happens to you, the first thing the adults are going to ask is,

'Why'd you boys let her go by herself?' " Amari pointed out. "Brain and I don't need that."

"I'll be okay. Promise."

"Text us when you get done."

"Good grief. Okay."

Smiling, Zoey left to retrieve her bike. Since she and the rest of the kids pedaled to school every day, she knew the way with her eyes closed. Up the road that led out of the subdivision, and then a right turn onto Main. The school sat between Mr. Trent's garage and the rec center. Using Brain's key, she entered the building. She was always amazed by how quiet the school was when it was empty. Her first task was to check the tank's temperature gauge. Seeing the numbers were within the ideal range, she slowly poured the premeasured food into the water and watched the sleek, colorful fish gobble down their lunch. Pleased, she locked the door behind her, put Brain's lanyard back around her neck, and headed back up Main Street for home. She was just passing the church when she saw Tamar backing her green pickup truck, Olivia, down the drive. Tamar beeped the horn and stopped. Zoey rode up to the window. "Hey, Tamar."

"Hey back. Where are you heading?"

"Home."

"Was real proud of you today."

The praise made Zoey feel good inside.

"Thanks. Has Ms. Bernadine heard anything yet?"

"Not that I know of."

That was disappointing.

"I'm going to check on an old friend and drop him off some groceries. Do you want to go? I can take you home when we're done."

"Sure!" She loved riding with Tamar. "Let me text Daddy Reg and Brain and Amari so they'll know where I am. The boys made me promise to let them know when I left the school. I had fish duty today."

"Glad they're living up to what brothers are supposed to do. Put your bike in the back and let's get going."

As they got under way and the open land of Henry Adams in autumn, with its spent fields of sunflowers and corn, rolled past Zoey's window, she thought about how much she liked her life. Back in Miami, she and her mom Bonnie had been homeless. Living on the streets and sleeping wherever they could had been difficult, and made even more so by Bonnie's addiction to drugs. Last night, when Crystal explained why she wanted to go back to her old life, she'd said living on the street had been sweet, but all Zoey remembered about those times was being hungry and sleeping on a smelly old mattress beneath the highway bridge. Nothing about it was sweet, especially not waking up the morning she found her mother dead, or the two nights after, when she was attacked by the rats.

Turning her mind away from that horror, she asked Tamar, "What's your friend's name?"

"Cephas Patterson."

"That's a funny name. Do I know him?"

Tamar shook his head. "He's the town hermit."

"Does he have any kids?"

"No kids or any other family, so I go out and check on him every so often to make sure he's okay. Ornery old cuss though."

"That's what my mom Bonnie used to call Old Man Barker back in Miami. Every day he'd be on the street corner, yelling and shaking his fist at the cars going by. He didn't have any family either. Bonnie said he yelled at the people in the cars because he was lonely."

"I imagine Cephas is lonely too, but he'll never admit it."

"I wouldn't want to be a hermit."

"Me neither."

As Tamar took the curve on the road that led past Mr. Clay's place on what felt like two wheels, Zoey grinned. One of the reasons she liked driving with Tamar was because she drove really fast, and a race car driver like Danica Patrick was one of the many things Zoey wanted to be when she grew up. "Did you ever want to be a race car driver, Tamar?"

Tamar glanced over and laughed. "I'd've loved

that, Zoey, but girls weren't allowed when I was growing up. Is that what you want to be?"

"Yep. And a singer like Mama Roni."

"Sounds like you're going to be real busy."

Tamar stopped Olivia beside a wire fence that hugged the edge of the road. There was an old weathered house set back a ways.

"Is that where your friend lives?"

"Yes, and he's kind of odd, so I need you to stay in the truck. Okay?"

Zoey had no idea what "kind of odd" meant and wanted to see for herself, but when she didn't readily agree, Tamar gave her a look.

"Did you hear me?"

Quelled, she responded, "Yes, ma'am."

Tamar got out and grabbed a bag of groceries from the bed. Zoey watched her walk through the rusty gate. Almost immediately an old man holding a shotgun charged out onto the porch and yelled, "Go away!"

Zoey knew the town's matriarch was fearless and that nothing in the world ever got the best of her, but worry for her safety made Zoey disobey Tamar's edict and leave the truck. Bending low so she wouldn't be seen, she hunkered down next to the front tires to watch. If she needed to call 911 for help, she had her phone.

The old man yelled again, "Not telling you again! Get out of here, you old bat, before I shoot you for trespassing."

Tamar called back, "You're not going to shoot me, Cephas, and we both know it. Be glad somebody comes out to make sure you're still alive."

"You're just after my gold!"

"Nobody wants your old gold. Are you taking your medicine?"

"What's it to you?"

"Not a thing, but since I'm the one who'll be burying you when the time comes, I thought I'd ask."

"Don't need your questions. Now git, 'fore I shoot you!"

To Zoey, Cephas looked like an old prospector from the westerns Mr. Bing, one of the town's senior citizens, liked to watch on the big screen at the rec center. Mr. Patterson was bald, had white whiskers, and was wearing a brown checked shirt and brown pants held up by worn suspenders. She didn't like the way he had the gun pointed at Tamar, though, and wondered if she should text her dad.

But Tamar didn't seem worried. "Do you have enough food?"

"Got enough of everything!"

Tamar set the big bag of groceries on the ground at her feet. "There's meat in here, so don't let it sit out and spoil."

Zoey's mom often left food for Old Man Barker in the spot where he slept behind an abandoned

44

gas station. He'd never thanked her, but it was always gone when she and her mom went to check on him the next day.

"Okay, Cephas. I'm going. I'll be back to check next month."

"Don't need you and your spies checking on me. The gold is mine!"

"What spies?"

He pointed with the gun. "That one hiding by the truck."

Zoey gulped, and on the heels of that heard Tamar call angrily, "Zoey!"

Chagrined, she stood and showed herself. Tamar didn't look happy. "Get over here."

Brimming with guilt, she walked over.

Cephas yelled, "You after my gold too, little girl?"

"No, sir."

"What's your name, so I'll know who you are if I have to shoot you?"

"Zoey Raymond Garland."

"Raymond? What kind of name is that for a female?"

Zoey opened her mouth to explain but closed it instantly in response to the flare in Tamar's eyes. Zoey wondered if she'd be painting Ms. Marie's fence for her disobedience.

"Get back in the truck," Tamar instructed coolly.

Zoey complied instantly and, listening from

inside, heard Tamar say, "Take care of yourself, you old mule. I'll be back."

"If you do, I'll shoot you."

Tamar shook her head and walked away. As she started up Olivia and headed back to town she asked, "What did I tell you to do?"

"Stay in the truck."

"Just wanted to make sure you haven't gone deaf."

"I was worried he was going to shoot you."

"I appreciate that, but next time I expect you to do as you're told."

"Yes, ma'am." After a few more moments of silence, she asked, "Why doesn't he have any kids or family?"

"He never married. His father died when we were in grade school, and years later his mother was in a car accident that left her paralyzed. He took care of her for the rest of her life."

Zoey found that sad. "Does anybody else come out to check on him besides you?"

"Trent, Mal, and Bing."

"Does he really have gold in his house?"

"He says he does."

"Did he tell you where he got it?"

"No. Some folks believe the outlaw Griffin Blake buried a bag of railroad gold near Henry Adams. Maybe Cephas found it. Who knows. Personally, I think the story's just an old myth." She gave Zoey a pointed look. "And if I catch you or the boys out here looking for it, you'll paint the fence every day from now until the snow falls—if Cephas doesn't shoot you first."

"Yes, ma'am."

Tamar's voice gentled. "Sometimes Cephas knows what's going on around him, and sometimes he doesn't. I don't want you hurt, okay?"

Zoey nodded. She didn't care about the gold. She was more worried that Cephas, like Old Man Barker, was lonely, especially living in that raggedy old house by himself. She knew better than to voice that, though, so she kept it to herself.

Crestfallen by Crystal's nonresponse to her text, Bernadine drove away from the Dog. Diane sat silent. Bernadine was pretty sure that being smacked with the truth about her foreclosed home had a lot to do with it, but Diane's feelings were the least of her concerns. Why hadn't Crystal responded? Bernadine was relieved to know the girl was alive, but that was all she knew.

Once they were back at the house, Diane said haughtily, "It was a long flight. I think I'd like to lie down."

No argument there. After helping her carry her luggage into the room, Bernadine watched and waited as Diane viewed the room's interior with a critical eye. "Do you need anything?" She hoped her sister had the sense not to complain about the placement of the furnishings or try to move stuff around.

"No."

"Have a good nap." Bernadine hadn't expected a thank-you for giving Diane a place to stay, and she didn't get one.

Even though she'd made a vow not to work on weekends unless it was absolutely necessary, she needed something to distract her from her worries, so she sat at the kitchen table and booted up her laptop. In her in-box were a few e-mails from Gary Clark. The new grocery store he'd be managing would have its grand opening next week. His e-mails assured her that all last-minute details like signage and painting were on schedule. Because of his focus and diligence, he'd proven to be a great choice to ride point on the town's newest business, and she was excited about the venture. The next e-mail was from her lawyers, giving her an update on the trial date for murderer and arsonist Odessa Stillwell, whose anger at Bernadine had resulted in a terrible fire that past summer. Two innocent people had lost their lives. She had no desire to ever see Odessa again, but would be testifying for the prosecution. She glanced at a few more e-mails, but thoughts of Crystal soon had her staring into space. Taking out her phone, she reread the short text. Still no reply. Shaking her head sadly, she went back to the laptop.

●●●

Sitting in the Kansas City airport, Roni Garland listened to the announcement updating her delayed flight. Sighing with disappointment, she called her husband, Reggie. "Hey, baby. How are you?"

"Doing okay. Where are you?"

Overlooking his slight accusatory tone, she explained, "Stuck in the Kansas City airport. The plane's having some kind of mechanical issues, so they're trying to find us another one. Zoey doing okay?"

"Yeah. She's been out on her bike most of the day, but she's up in her room now, watching NASCAR."

Roni chuckled. "That girl is something." When silence greeted that remark, she continued, "Um, it may be kind of late when I get in."

"That's okay. We'll be here."

"I've missed you."

"Same here," he said in a tone that lacked the love it used to hold.

She concentrated on keeping her voice light. "Okay. See you when I get there. Love you."

"Me, too."

The call ended, she slumped back against her seat. There were serious problems going on with her and Reggie. Although he wouldn't admit it, he was having difficulties with her career. She'd tried to fix things by commissioning an architect to build a state-of-the-art recording studio in town so she'd be nearer, but apparently that wasn't enough. He didn't like her being there any more than he liked her touring. This was his first taste of being married to a music woman, and although she'd anticipated having to make some adjustments in their life, she hadn't anticipated he'd not be supportive. Talking with him about it hadn't solved anything either. He kept trying to convince her that Zoey was the one suffering from her absence, refusing to own up to the reality that the problem was his and his alone. She sensed that his ideal solution would be for her to drop the music and be content with her former role of wife and mom, but he didn't have the balls to say it out loud for fear of her nuclear reaction. And deservedly so. She wasn't asking him to give up medicine and be with her twenty-four/seven. She hoped he wouldn't draw a line in the sand and demand she make a choice because everyone was going to be unhappy with the outcome. She loved her husband madly, and would walk through hell for him, but she wasn't going to toss aside her God-given gift just so he'd stop pouting.

When his call from Roni ended, Reggie placed the phone on the arm of the couch. The television was on, but he stared at it unseeingly. So Roni was finally on the way home. One would think that, having spent the better part of the month of August hunkered down in the studio, she could've passed on this five-day concert tour out west to spend some consistent time with her family. The CD was done, all the musicians she'd flown in were gone, and yet he could count on one hand the times they'd had dinner as a family since then. He missed his wife. He missed waking up beside her; missed her laugh, missed her smile, missed the way she snuggled next to him in bed. Hell, he missed everything about her that he'd come to love since they met at the hospital she was taken to the night a psycho gunned down one of her backup singers during a concert. Due to the trauma, she'd given up singing, and in the years that followed they'd married and been inseparable. But now, after they'd adopted Zoey, her musical flame had been relit, her career was on jam again, and he rarely saw her—at least that's how it felt. He had no idea how he was supposed to deal as a result. Yes, she'd had the studio built so she'd be closer to home, but it didn't make him feel any better—she was still gone. Granted, after the shooting he'd strongly encouraged her to get back into the studio, and now that she had . . . To her credit, she'd tried to get them to talk things out, but he'd rebuffed her efforts rather than confess to being insecure and unsure about his role. Another component of that insecurity was something else he didn't want to admit. Suppose, as a result of her resurgent fame, she no longer wanted to be married to a short, funny-looking, glasses-wearing nerd? To be honest, he'd never understood why she was attracted to someone like him in the first place. In his mind she was better suited for a man like her manager, Jason West, with his killer dreds, six-foot-plus height, and features that landed him on a list of the nation's finest men. Even though Roni had never given him any reason to believe she'd be unfaithful, the face he saw in the mirror each morning wouldn't make anyone's finest list. He sighed audibly. This was a mess, and so was he.

CHAPTER
4

Bernadine and Mal had a standing dinner date at her house every Saturday night, and she wasn't looking forward to her sister being a third wheel. But there was nothing she could do about it, so she began the preparations. Diane had yet to show herself after her nap. Bernadine hoped maybe she'd had second thoughts about the visit, climbed out of a window, and was on her way back to wherever. It was a ridiculous fantasy, but a girl could dream.

No such luck. Diane walked in and took a seat on one of the stools.

"You don't have to cook dinner on my account. I'm still full from lunch."

"This isn't for you," Bernadine pointed out as she seasoned the catfish and placed it in a dish. "Mal and I always have dinner together on Saturday night, but you're welcome to join us if you want."

"You and Mal? That fine piece of man from the diner?"

"Yes."

Her sister looked stunned. "Why would someone like that—" She stopped.

Bernadine finished the sentence for her. "Why would a man like that be interested in someone like me?"

Diane squirmed. "I mean, other than for your money, of course."

Shaking her head, Bernadine covered the dish with plastic wrap and stuck it in the fridge. She'd cook it later. "I'm sure if you ask him, he'd give you an answer."

Apparently that wasn't something Diane wanted to discuss anymore, because she changed the subject. "Who told you about the foreclosure?"

"Doesn't matter. I know about the divorce and the fact that you've alienated all three of your children."

"I had my reasons."

"All bogus."

Diane's eyes flashed angrily. "What would you do if your oldest son married a ghetto queen, your daughter married a man from Germany, of all places, and your youngest prefers men to women?"

"Try and be supportive."

"Bullshit."

Bernadine shrugged.

"Your adopted child's run away from home, so you're the last person to be judging me."

"Not judging. Just stating fact."

"And so am I."

Tension crackled in the air like summer lightning.

Bernadine sought the high road. "Di, look. I took you in because you're my sister. If you don't want to be here, there's the door."

"So how long have you and Mal been together?" Another subject change.

"A couple of years." Bernadine wondered if her sister would ever face the fact that the reason her life was such a mess could be determined by one good look in the mirror. Bernadine was the eldest of the three girls born to Ernestine and Emery Edwards. Cecily, who'd died of cancer in her twenties, had been the middle child. Diane, the baby, always acted like a spoiled only child. It hadn't been cute when they were young, and now that they were in their fifties, it was head-shaking sad. She would've given anything to have Di as a true sister. Bernadine and Cecily had always been partners in crime, and her death had torn Bernadine apart. With both their parents now deceased as well, she and Di were the only ones left. Bernadine would've loved sharing her travels and taking her shopping and buying her the fancy little baubles she knew Diane loved, but as it stood, she could barely stand being in the same room with her, let alone a nine- or ten-hour flight to anywhere.

Mal knocked on the door precisely at six. The kiss and long hug he gave Bernadine in greeting did much to salve the bruising day. "I really needed this," she told him while he held her against his heart.

"That's what I'm here for."

Arms wrapped around each other's waists, they entered the kitchen. "Di, you remember Malachi?"

"I do," Diane said, her tone tinged with flirtation. "Bernadine says you're eating dinner with us."

"She and I have a set date every Saturday night." As if emphasizing his commitment, he squeezed Bernadine's waist and gave her a quick kiss on her cheek. "What're we having?"

"Broiled catfish, rice, and a salad."

"Sounds good."

Diane's plastered-on smile looked so fake, Bernadine felt sorry for her, but the feeling lasted only until Diane asked Mal, "Did Bernie tell you about the time I stole her date for the prom?"

The pain of that memory seized Bernadine by the heart and twisted.

"No," he replied. "She's never told me anything about you."

"Oh." For a moment she appeared stricken by that but quickly recovered. "Well, let me tell you what happened. It was really funny."

"No thanks." He pointedly turned his back on her and, looking down into Bernadine's pain-filled eyes, asked, "Anything I can help you with, babe?"

She shook her head. "No." Her voice was far quieter than she'd intended. Diane had pulled some cruel stunts back in the day, but convincing James Headly that it would be more fun to take her to the movies than honor the commitment he'd made to Bernadine for her senior prom had been at the top of the list. "Would you like some coffee? We could take it out on the deck."

"I'd love that."

Patently ignoring Diane, he stood silently while she went about the prep, and once the coffee was ready, the two of them stepped outside and closed the door.

Bernadine took a seat. She couldn't ever remember seeing Mal so outraged.

"Are you sure she's blood?" he asked, standing by the deck's rail.

"Wonderful, isn't she?"

"Was she like that growing up?"

"Yes. And yes, she did leave me without a date for the prom."

"And your parents let her get away with it?"

"They knew she was going out that night too, but they didn't know it was with my date until he showed up. Neither did I." She ignored her coffee as the awful memory rushed back. "Had on my new prom dress. Had my hair done—the whole bit. It was my first real date, and I came down the stairs from my bedroom feeling like a princess until I saw the confusion on my parents' faces, and Jimmy standing there looking all sheepish, with Diane hanging on his arm. And she says to me, 'Oh, I forgot to tell you, Jimmy and I are going to the movies.'

"My parents stared at Diane, and I'm not sure if it was the smug glee in her eyes or the horror on my face that made my mother slap her so hard you could hear it across town. It was the first time she'd ever chastised Diane for her behavior." She paused for a moment as the chaos of the next few minutes replayed itself in her mind. "Daddy was yelling at Jimmy about honor, and threatening to call his father. Mama was yelling at Diane, and she's holding her face and screaming like someone had chopped off her head."

"And you?"

"I went back upstairs, took off the dress, put it back in the box so Mama could return it to the store. Then I got into bed, pulled the covers over my head, and cried."

"Aww, baby."

Bernadine shrugged and sipped. "Hated her."

"But you're letting her visit?"

"No, *stay* with me, temporarily. Crazy, right?"

"Uh, yeah."

"Her husband's divorcing her. Over the years she's managed to piss off all three of her kids. She lied to me to get me to take her in, but truth is, she has no place else to go." The reality of that saddened her, even though there was no good reason it should. "She's my sister, Mal. I knew from the moment she called me this wasn't going to be fun, and I was right, but—"

"She's your sister."

She gave him a small smile. "Now, granted, I may have to kick her out eventually, but until then she's welcome."

"No good deed goes unpunished."

"That's exactly what my nephew—her son—said to me when I spoke with him earlier."

"Maybe you should send her over to stay with Tamar."

Bernadine laughed. "That would be something, wouldn't it?" Bernadine's phone rang. Seeing DALLAS POLICE DEPT. on the caller ID made her heart race, and she quickly answered. A woman on the other end identified herself as Sergeant Sandra McCall and asked if she had a daughter named Crystal. Bernadine's racing heart jumped into her throat. "Yes, I do. Is she okay?"

The next voice she heard was Crystal's, asking through what sounded like tears, "Mom, can you send me a bus ticket or something so I can come home?"

Elation soared through her blood. "Oh my god! It's so good to hear your voice."

"I'm so sorry," Crystal cried. "I'll understand if you don't want me back."

"It's okay. We'll figure this out. Are you okay? You're not hurt or anything?"

"No, I'm fine. I just want to come home," she said softly through her sobs. "And can you have my phone turned off? It was stolen, along with some of my other stuff."

Bernadine was struck by that. "Okay, honey. Don't worry, I'll take care of it. Let me speak to the officer again." She turned tear-filled eyes to Mal.

"Good news," he whispered.

She nodded in agreement. After making arrangements for the pickup, the call ended and Bernadine stood and walked into his waiting arms. "I'm so happy!"

"So am I."

"I need to call Katie and have her fire up the jet."

"You want company?"

"Of course."

"What about your sister?"

"We leave her here and hope she doesn't rearrange all the furniture while we're gone."

He looked puzzled.

"I'll explain later."

Stepping back inside, she explained the situation to Diane, who blessedly kept her vitriol under wraps. "I'm so glad it worked out," she said, although her withering tone made it plain that she didn't mean a word.

"We're going to fly down and pick her up."

"That little bitty airport has planes going to Dallas this late in the day?"

"No idea. We're taking my jet."

Diane's jaw dropped.

Bernadine smiled. "You don't know a whole lot about me these days, do you?"

"I guess not." She continued to stare. "Let me grab my handbag."

"Just Mal and I are going. We'll be back later tonight."

"Oh. Okay."

She looked hurt, but Bernadine didn't care.

While Mal did the driving to the Hays airport, Bernadine rode shotgun and sent texts to the Henry Adams family to let them know Crystal was coming home. The replies she received made her smile. From Lily: Whoopee! From Jack

James: Excellent news! From Rocky: Tell her her apron is waiting! From Amari: Brain loses bet. Details at 11. From Eli: About time! Forming line of butt kickers. From Marie: Give her my love. From Reverend Paula: God is Good. All the time. All the time!

Bernadine agreed.

Upon landing at the Dallas airport, she and Mal were driven by a hired car service to the police precinct. When they entered the bustling station, she identified herself to the desk officer. He pointed across the room. On a bench sat a wet-eyed Crystal, who immediately flew into her arms. Bernadine caught her up and rocked and cried. "Oh, baby," she whispered. "I'm so glad you're okay. So glad."

"I'm sorry," Crystal replied as she wept. "I'm so sorry. This was so stupid."

"It's okay. Don't worry about it. Are you ready?"

Using the crumpled wad of tissue in her hand to wipe her eyes and nose, she nodded. "Yeah." Upon noticing Mal for the first time, she walked into his outstretched arms and let him hold her tight.

"Thank you for coming to get me."

"Thank your mom."

Bernadine stared down at Crystal's feet. "Where are your shoes, Crys?" She was wearing an old pair of fuzzy, mismatched socks.

Her lips tightened and her eyes flashed angrily.

"Stolen by the same people who took my phone and the jacket I got in LA last year."

"Wow. Okay." Bernadine was real interested in hearing about this adventure, but she wanted to get home first. She threw a comforting arm around her child, and the three left the station for the return trip to the airport.

On the flight, while Crystal slept, Bernadine snuggled against Mal's side. "Somebody stole her shoes? You think they pulled a gun on her?"

Mal shrugged. "Hope not, but either way it would be enough to make me call home."

She smiled. "I'm thinking this is going to be quite the story if she actually tells me about it."

"She probably will. I saw those eyes flash when she talked about her stuff being taken. She looked too mad not to talk about it. I'm more worried about her being around your crazy sister."

"Crystal can handle herself—she'll do okay."

"As long as Diane doesn't steal her shoes."

When they entered the house, Bernadine was so glad to be home that it took Crystal to point out the obvious.

"You changed the furniture around?"

Bernadine stared.

"I kind of like it," Crystal told her.

Bernadine hated to admit it, but she did as well. The room flowed much better. Score one for Diane, she thought grudgingly. "It's my sister Diane's doing. She's staying in the guest room, and may be with us for a while." She'd have to thank Diane in the morning. "You go on up and get into bed. We'll talk details after church."

Crystal asked warily, "You're not mad at me?"

"After having my heart ripped out, of course I am, but I still love you, so go on upstairs and get some rest."

"Thanks again for letting me come back."

"This will always be your home, Crys. No matter what."

"Do I have to go to church?"

"What do you think?"

"But everybody's going to be looking at me."

"Yeah, they are. Better to go and get it over with now, don't you think? Aren't you the cross bearer tomorrow, too?"

She sighed heavily, "Yeah. I'm on with Zoey and Devon."

"Then there you go."

Crystal looked over at Mal, who'd been watching silently, but seeing no support there, she offered a departing nod and slowly climbed the stairs.

Bernadine met Mal's eyes. "Was I supposed to lie to her about my feelings?"

"No. The truth's always the way to go." He walked over and gave her another strong hug. "You go on upstairs, too. I'll see you tomorrow."

"Thanks for being you."

"Told you when we met we'd be a good pair."

"Yes, you did, and you were right."

"Love you, girl."

She leaned up and gave him a kiss. "Love you too." After walking him out to his truck, she came back inside, turned out the lights in her rearranged front room, and climbed the stairs.

When the hired driver pulled the car up to the Garland home, it was almost two a.m. Roni saw lights shining from behind the drapes in the living room windows and from the bedroom window upstairs. She hoped that meant Reg was up and waiting to welcome her home. The driver helped her bring in the luggage and, after receiving his tip, drove off.

The interior of the house was hushed. Even though she was anxious to see Reg, the urge to see her daughter was stronger. By the soft glow of the race car night-lights that had recently replaced the ones featuring Barbie, Roni stood beside the open door and watched her daughter sleep. It was good to see her. The West Coast gig had been only five days, but she felt as if she'd been away much longer. Who'd've ever thought she'd be mother to such an awesomely bright and inquisitive child? Zoey was also a child of incredible strength, and it was that strength that had taken Roni by the hand and led her back to singing, and to life, something Roni would always be grateful for. And in exchange

Roni promised to keep her safe and love her unconditionally for as long as she drew breath.

Zoey continued to sleep with Tiger Tamar and the night-lights, but Roni didn't care. Had she been overrun by rats the way Zoey had been, she'd sleep with every light in the house turned on. At least her nightmares from the attack seemed to have subsided. It had been almost a year since the last time Zoey woke up screaming and crying. Roni liked to think that the love of her new parents was helping the healing process along.

As if sensing Roni's presence, Zoey's eyes opened. As they focused, she shot out of bed and ran for her hug. "Mama! You're back!"

Roni bent low and held her close. "I am. Missed you so much. How are you, Miss Lady?"

"I'm good."

They grinned at each other in the shadows. "I see the NASCAR pj's I sent you fit." The shirt and pants were covered with cars and sponsor decals.

"Yeah, but they're boys'. They have a hole in the front of the pants. See?"

Roni chuckled. "I know, babe. They didn't have any for girls."

"Well, that's messed up."

Roni loved her southern accent. "I thought so too, but I figured you'd still want them."

"I did. Do you think if I sent Danica Patrick an e-mail, she'd make girl pajamas?"

"No idea, but an e-mail sounds like a good idea." Roni shook her head at her tweenage force of nature. "Let's get you back in bed."

Hand in hand they walked the short distance, and Zoey climbed in. Roni covered her up and sat down on the edge of the mattress.

"Did you hear about Crystal running away?" Zoey asked.

"Yes, Ms. Bernadine sent me a text. That was really sad."

When Zoey looked away as if something was bothering her, Roni asked, "What do you need to tell me, Zoey?"

So Zoey told her all that had happened, from the promise she'd made to Crystal to being encouraged by Amari and Preston to spill the beans.

"I wanted to talk to you about it, but I didn't know if you were in rehearsal or sleeping or at the airport, so I talked to them."

"And sounds like they gave you some straight-up good advice."

"I felt bad about not saying anything last night."

"And next time what will you do?"

She shrugged. "I don't know. Tell, maybe."

"Either way it's water under the bridge. I got a text from Ms. Bernadine, saying Crystal was home."

"Dad told me. Do you think she'll be mad at me?"

Roni shrugged. "No telling, but if she is, I doubt

it will be for very long. You did the right thing by coming forward, Zoey. The truth will always set you free."

Her answering smile warmed Roni's insides. "Now, you and Tiger Tamar need to get back to sleep. We have church in the morning."

"One more hug, please."

Roni obliged her and let the feel of her thin little arms fill her with even more joy. Zoey scooted back beneath the bedding, and Roni placed a light kiss on her cheek. "Night, baby girl. Love you."

"Love you, too. I'm glad you're back."

"So am I."

Buoyed by the visit, Roni entered the bedroom she shared with her husband and found him asleep as well. "Reggie," she called softly. "Wake up, your baby's home."

He didn't move. He'd left the light on in the bathroom so she could see her way around, and she was thankful for the small act of kindness. Moving quietly, she eased open a dresser drawer to extract a nightgown. Leaving her discarded clothes on a chair and wishing he'd turn over and say hi, she made use of the bathroom and turned off the light. She crawled into bed. She waited for him to pull her close. Nothing. The measured cadence of his breathing never changed, so she whispered, "Night, baby," and hoped sleep would take away the pain.

CHAPTER 5

At church on Sunday morning, while the congregation raised their voices in the processional hymn, Crystal held the large cross aloft. Acolytes Zoey and Devon, carrying their lit torches, walked solemnly at her side down the center aisle. Zoey was pretty sure Crystal was mad at her because she hadn't said a word while they were in the basement putting on their vestments. Usually Crystal would straighten the necks of their white cottas to make sure they weren't all crooked, but this morning she and Devon had been on their own. Now, as she and Devon reached the altar and stuck their torches in the wall holders and took their seats, Crystal sat too, but never made eye contact.

When the hymn ended and Reverend Paula began to recite the opening prayer, Zoey took a discreet look out at the sea of faces spread out over the sanctuary. Nearly every eye was on Crystal. Some faces wore smiles, others appeared relieved. She couldn't tell how Tamar felt, but something about her expression made Zoey think their collective great-grandmother was none too happy with the town's oldest teen. But no matter the congregation's mood, Zoey was glad she was home; she just hoped Crys didn't stay mad at her forever.

It was good having Mama Roni home too, and as always she was dressed up for church. She had on a pretty green suit and one of her big matching hats. Zoey had expected Daddy Reg to be happy about her being home too, and that breakfast would be filled with smiles and them making google eyes at each other as they always did. Instead the kitchen was silent, and they acted like strangers at the table. She wanted them to act like they used to, but being a kid, she couldn't say anything, so she finished her bacon and eggs and went up to her room and waited until they called her to leave for church. All the kids had been told that if something was bothering them they were to go see Reverend Paula and talk to her about it. Zoey wondered if the adults had been given the same advice, because although her parents were sitting next to each other, Momma Roni was staring straight ahead, and so was Daddy Reg. She loved them both, and it made her sad to see them so unhappy.

After the service Zoey followed Devon and Crystal down into the basement to take off their vestments and hang them up in the acolyte's closet. So far, Crystal still hadn't said a word to either of them, and she looked kind of down.

Zoey put her black cassock on the hanger and placed the cotta on top. Because she wasn't tall enough, she handed the hanger to Crystal, hoping she wouldn't yell at her. She took it without a word and did the same for Devon. Zoey mustered up her courage to ask if she was mad, but changed her mind when Tamar walked in. Zoey and Devon shared a quick look. Neither had any idea why she was there, but the way her eyes were focused on Crystal made them take a small step backward to get out of the way.

"Hi, Tamar," Crystal said.

"Hello, Crystal. Everyone's glad to have you home, and so am I."

"Thank you," Crystal replied softly.

"So, how do you feel?"

"Dumb, stupid. All of the above."

Tamar nodded as if she understood, but with Tamar one couldn't be too sure. She walked closer to Crystal and, to Zoey's utter surprise, opened her arms, and Crystal, eyes filled with tears, stepped into the embrace and let herself be enfolded. She and Devon shared another look. Zoey couldn't ever remember seeing Crystal cry.

Tamar placed a kiss on her forehead and asked quietly, "No place like home, right?"

"Right."

Tamar gently released her hold. "One day you're going to fly away and soar so high you'll make this whole town proud. It just isn't time yet."

Crystal nodded and grabbed a couple of tissues from the box that always sat on the table next to the closet. She wiped her eyes and nose.

"You and Bernadine make your peace?" Tamar asked.

"Not yet."

"She loves you a lot."

"I know, and I feel awful worrying her like I did."

"That's why the Spirit gives us youth, so we can do dumb stuff, learn from it, and move on."

Crystal offered up a watery smile. "I guess."

"Anyway. I just came down to say welcome home."

"Thanks," Crystal whispered.

Tamar's eyes swept over Zoey and Devon, and Zoey's heart froze in her chest, but Tamar didn't say anything. With a swirl of her hems, she was gone.

Devon exhaled a sigh of relief, and Zoey released the breath she'd been holding in, too.

Crystal turned to her. "Sure wasn't expecting that."

"Me neither."

Devon crossed his arms and said self-importantly, "She's probably going to make you paint the fence anyway."

Zoey glared. "Shut up."

"Bet you ten dollars."

An exasperated Crystal pointed at the open door. "Go!"

"You can't make me," he threw back.

Crystal did her best imitation of Tamar and walked up real close. "Sure I can. Want me to show you?"

That was all it took.

After his exit, Crystal asked, "What is wrong with him these days?"

"He is such a pain in the behind. Been crazy ever since he went down south."

"Never thought I'd want him back in his suits and those stupid ties again."

"I know." She regathered her courage to ask, "Are you mad at me?"

Crystal shook her head. "Mad at myself for being so stupid, but not at you."

"I memorized the license plate when you left and told Sheriff Will. I'm sorry."

"Nothing to be sorry for. I was the one who screwed up." She stared off and was quiet for a moment before confessing softly, "Nothing turned out like I thought it would."

Zoey wanted to ask what that meant, but having already used her daily allotment of courage, she kept the question to herself. "I'm glad you're back."

"Me, too. Give me a hug."

Zoey went gladly, and when the hug was over, they both smiled.

Zoey said, "Rocky's giving me free dessert. You want to go to the Dog later and split a sundae?"

"No, I need to go home and talk to my mom."

"Oh. Okay. Then I'll see you at school tomorrow."

"Yep."

Zoey gave her a wave and left to find her parents for the ride home.

Bernadine couldn't remember ever seeing Crystal so solemn. As they drove home from church, she didn't press her for details about the two-day adventure in Dallas, even though she dearly wanted the full story. As requested, she'd had her purloined phone turned off, and whoever had it was now was free to do whatever thieves did. Diane had not accompanied them to church. In fact, she hadn't even shown her face that morning. Once again, Bernadine fantasized about her sister running away, and a smile curved her lips.

"What's funny?" Crystal asked.

"Just imagining my sister climbing out of a window and disappearing before we get back."

"You don't like her?"

"Let's just say we don't see eye to eye."

"Why not?"

"Because she's selfish, mean, and a first-class witch."

"Oh. She older or younger?"

"She's the baby."

Crystal nodded understandingly. "I don't know

73

if I have any brothers or sisters. I mean, the kids here are sorta that, but no clue whether I have any real sibs."

"We could get in touch with your aunt, if you'd like, and ask. Might be nice to get a definitive answer if it's something you've been wondering about." Crystal's aunt had been instrumental in exposing the true identity of Crystal's no-good father, Ray Chambers, who'd come to town masquerading as a handyman.

"Maybe."

By then they'd reached the house. Bernadine pulled Baby into the garage, and after the door lowered behind them, they sat in the shadowy silence. When Crystal didn't make a move to get out, Bernadine turned off the engine and waited, watching her child staring out the window at something only she could see.

"Diego was right," she finally said.

"About what?"

"About me being a princess now, not knowing how to be on the streets anymore."

Bernadine thought back on Crys's meeting with the twenty-one-year-old, motorcycle-riding bad boy Diego July that past summer. She'd convinced herself that Diego was in love with her. She'd been wrong.

"I so wanted everything in Dallas to be exactly the way it was when I left."

"And it wasn't?"

"No."

"Time doesn't stand still, honey."

"I know that now. Even my best friend Kiki was different. I figured we'd pick up right where we left off, party, go to the clubs—but she has twins now. She doesn't do the club thing anymore. Just takes care of her kids."

"Having children can make you grow up."

"I thought maybe she could get a babysitter, but she just laughed. Said she didn't have the money, and even if she did, she wasn't going to waste it on going out."

Bernadine thought she liked this Kiki.

"I told her about my life with you and how nice you are and all the places we've been, and she wanted to know why in the world I'd wanted to come back to Dallas."

"What did you tell her?"

"I tried to explain how slow it is, that there's nothing to do. She started yelling at me like she'd turned into Ms. Lily."

Bernadine let a small smile show.

"So I told her she didn't understand, and she was like, right—she had no idea how it felt to have someone take her in and give her all the stuff you've given me, and that she definitely preferred living on food stamps with two babies and no life."

Bernadine was liking Kiki more and more. "Is she with the father of her twins?"

"Yes. His name's Bobby. He's working two jobs and trying to get his GED so he can start his own business. Something to do with pimping out cars."

"Good for him."

"They're really struggling, though. Their apartment is tiny, and one of the windows was cracked and they drive an old beat-down van you can hear coming a mile away."

"Is that the life you want?"

"No. I wish they didn't have to have that life either." Crys looked her way. "I know I have no business asking for anything after what I did, but can they live here with us?"

Bernadine was taken aback.

"I don't mean in our house, but in town someplace. Bobby wants to work on cars, and Amari's dad has the garage, which would be perfect. And Kiki's a hairdresser. Be nice not to drive all the way to Hays to get our hair done."

"You've been thinking about this, haven't you?"

"Just last night, after I got back and looked at all the stuff I have, and how Kiki would love to have even just a little bit of it."

Bernadine knew Crystal had a good heart, but this was surprising. "How about we talk about it again in a few days."

She nodded.

"So tell me what happened with your shoes."

76

She sighed. "All I wanted to do was go to the club, and Kiki's cousin Ross offered to take me. So I went. Thought I could hold my liquor. I couldn't. Had too much. Passed out and woke up so sick I thought I'd never stop throwing up."

"Oh, Crys."

She shrugged. "Then I realized my purse was gone along with my phone, my jacket, and my shoes. Kiki warned me to watch my back around Ross. I should've listened."

"But why would he take your shoes?"

"Wasn't him. It was his girlfriend. She kept saying how cute they were and wanted to know where I got them and if she could try them on."

"What?"

"Yeah, after I got through throwing up, I had to walk all the way back to Kiki's in the freezing rain, barefoot." She retreated into silence again, and when she looked at Bernadine, there were tears in her eyes. "I was so cold and my feet hurt so bad," she whispered.

Like any mother, Bernadine's heart ached for her child.

"I lasted one day. One! I tried to get a job as soon as I got to Dallas, but I didn't know my whole social security number or have an address, so I couldn't even finish filling out the application."

Bernadine wondered what had gone through Crystal's mind when she realized she didn't know as much about how the real world rolled as she thought she did.

"Tamar told me at church that I'll get the chance to fly away when I'm ready. Can I still go to college?"

"Is that what you want?"

"Yes. I want to finish my triptych for that art show in LA next year, too."

"Okay."

"I promise to never do anything this dumb again. Ever."

"Going to hold you to that. Your mom is way too old to go through this again." Bernadine thought back on who Crystal had been when she first arrived, with her tats, ratty gold weave, and urban attitudes. In the years since, she'd grown and blossomed and made incredible strides. She hoped the maturity would continue to grow so that when she did fly away, the wings would be strong and true. "Anything else you want to discuss?"

"No."

"Then let's go in and see what Diane's been up to."

Inside, Bernadine made the introductions. Diane eyed Crystal up and down. "You should be grateful my sister took you in, instead of running away and causing her trouble."

Crystal's mouth tightened, and angry tears filled her eyes. Bernadine said to her softly, "Go

78

on up to your room, Crys. I'll see you later."

Crys nodded and left quickly.

Because Bernadine didn't bother veiling her anger, Diane responded with, "What? I'm not supposed to call her out? Apparently somebody should. She needs to know how blessed she is."

"How do you know she doesn't?"

Diane's chin rose in challenge.

"This is her home, and I'm not putting up with you bullying her. You don't know a thing about her or her circumstances."

"Why are you defending her? Have you had her tested for drugs?"

"You have two seconds to shut your mouth or get out."

"I'm going to my room."

"Not yet. How long are you planning on being here?"

"I hadn't really thought about it."

"Then do, because if you're going to be here more than a week, you'll need to start looking for employment."

"What? Why?"

"Because you're a grown woman."

"But I'm also your sister."

"So that means you get to loll around and not contribute to the food you're eating and the bills."

No response.

"Yes, you are my sister, but you're also single,

and single women have to take care of themselves, especially financially."

Diane's face was as sullen as a teenager's.

"Or you can leave."

"You know I have no place else to go."

"And why is that?" Bernadine asked gently.

More silence.

"Sometimes the hardest thing to do is to look in the mirror and acknowledge truthfully what you see."

"Thank you, Iyanla Vanzant. Or is it Dr. Phil?"

Bernadine held on to her temper, reminding her sagely, "You're the one with no place to go." The underlying message of Reverend Paula's sermon that morning had been about choosing to be kind over being right. Bernadine was trying to use that philosophy with her sister, but Diane didn't seem to be appreciating her restraint. "So figure out what you want to do and let me know."

With nothing more to say to the sulky-faced Diane, Bernadine headed upstairs.

Two doors down at the Garland house, Roni ended the call with her manager Jason West and set the phone aside. For years she'd wanted to do a tribute CD for the musical matriarchs like Billie Holiday, the great Ella Fitzgerald, and Sarah Vaughan. Securing the rights to the songs had proven difficult, but Jason had finally worked things out and was ready to get back into the studio. Although she was equally ready, she knew Reggie wouldn't be happy with this, so she'd asked Jason to hold off on the project for the time being. He wasn't pleased, and truthfully neither was she, but marriage was supposed to be about compromise. Never mind that she was the only one compromising, or at least that's how it felt. Why had she gone through all the trouble of having a studio built in town if she wasn't going to use it? Swallowing her resentment, she walked into the study, where Reggie seemed to be retreating more and more. "Hey. What're you doing?"

He glanced up from papers in his hand. "Checking out this medical conference I'm going to in Seattle on Tuesday."

"Really? How long will you be gone?" This was the first time he'd mentioned leaving. Had they grown that far apart?

"Be back on Saturday. There're some great lectures on the agenda."

"Do you need me to take you to the airport?"

"No. Trent has a meeting in Hays that day. He said I could ride with him."

"Ah." She paused for a moment to think about how to phrase what she planned to say next, but decided to hell with it. "Jason wants to go back into the studio."

His eyes flared.

"But I told him I'd like to take a break for a month or so."

He visibly relaxed. "Good. Zoey will appreciate that."

The knowledge that this had nothing to do with their daughter almost made her lash out. Instead she swallowed the urge to set him straight and changed the subject. "So, did you find an assistant for your office?" The college student who worked for him quit to move to Topeka. He'd just begun advertising for her replacement when Roni flew out to the West Coast.

"Not yet. Hoping to hire somebody soon, though. My practice isn't that busy, but having someone handling the paperwork is helpful."

Roni felt as if they were two strangers conversing. In spite of her having voiced interest in what was going on with him, he'd not reciprocated. How they were going to close the chasm between them and get back to the love they'd once shared was anyone's guess. There was no guessing about how much this was hurting her, though. None.

"Anything else?" he asked.

She wanted to ask why he'd pretended to be asleep last night. She knew that to be the case because Reggie snored. In fact, some nights he snored so loudly she had to place her pillow over her head to muffle the sound so she could sleep. There'd been no snoring last night. But instead of asking, she answered his question with a shake of her head. "Nope. I'll let you get back to your reading." And she withdrew.

Upstairs she looked in on Zoey. "Whatcha doing, shortcake?"

Zoey grinned, but her eyes never left the flat screen on the wall. "Watching Danica Patrick." The room was loud with the drone of race car engines.

"Can I join you?"

"Sure!"

Roni walked over to the bed, where the thoroughly enthralled Zoey sat cross-legged in the center, and settled her hip on the edge. Cars were zooming like crazy around the track. "Now which car is she in again?"

"The green one. Number ten. The Godaddy.com car." She pointed at the screen. "See, there she goes. She's driving a Chevy SS, but sometimes she's in an Impala."

Roni had no idea if that was significant, but she was impressed by Zoey's knowledge.

Zoey's eyes were going around and around with the flow of the race. "She's the only girl to ever come in third at the 500. And the only one to win the pole."

"Wow." Roni's sports were football and basketball. NASCAR was a whole 'nother world.

"And she started driving go-karts when she was ten. Same age as me."

When Zoey looked her way, Roni chuckled and

asked, "And you're telling me this why—like maybe I don't already know?"

"I really want to drive go-karts."

"Do you now?"

"I really, really do."

"Is there a go-kart track somewhere near town?"

"I think so. Amari's dad takes him all the time."

"Okay. Let me talk to your dad and Trent, and I'll get back to you."

Zoey beamed before refocusing on the race.

Temporarily setting aside her inner fears that Zoey might get hurt driving go-karts, Roni took a moment to glance around at the changes in Zoey's room decor. Gone were the Disney princess posters and all the Barbie stuff. Instead the walls were now graced with the likes of a smiling Danica Patrick holding her helmet on her hip and members of the WNBA in various basketball poses. Serena Williams, bent at the waist, fist balled up in triumph, held court on the wall by Zoey's closet. And her prized green-and-black Patrick leather jacket hung on a hook on the wall next to the flat-screen. Everyone knew green was Zoey's favorite color—it was the color of her late mom's eyes. Roni glanced over at the framed picture of the smiling Bonnie on Zoey's night-stand and wondered if it was Patrick's signature color that had initially drawn her to be a fan, but thinking about that, she decided probably not.

This was all Trent and Amari's doing. The day Trent allowed Zoey to help him and Amari at the garage, her little girl's life changed. She'd become confident, more self-assured, and car crazy. The shy little girl they'd adopted three years ago and thought mute because she didn't speak now had so much confidence that Roni'd be willing to bet there wasn't anything in this world Zoey didn't think herself capable of doing. Unfortunately, being at the garage had also altered her relationship with her former BFF, Devon. "How're you and Devon doing?"

Zoey made a face. "If he'd stop being so fussy all the time. He acts like an old lady."

"That's who he was raised by, honey."

"No kidding. He thinks he knows everything. If he tells me one more time that I'm not supposed to like working on cars, I'm going to punch him."

She thought back on the fight they'd had last year. "No punching allowed—we've already been through that once, remember? And you might want to cut him some slack."

"Why?"

"Because we all change as we get older, and maybe he's not sure who he wants to be or how to be it."

"He's a pain in the ass."

"Zoey," Roni warned.

"Sorry, but he is."

Now that Zoey was speaking—thanks to the

intervention of Reverend Paula—every now and then she let a few curse words slip out. Roni attributed that to her having been raised on the streets of Miami—and to hanging out with Crystal, Amari, and Preston. Roni slipped every now and again too, so she added herself to the list. Reggie, of course, had never let fly a curse word, at least not since she'd known him. He was from a very traditional upper-middle-class family who never cursed. His father was an architect and builder, and his mom had stayed home to raise Reg and his two younger brothers, which could be the reason he was having issues with her career.

"Why do you look so sad?" Zoey asked, cutting into her musings.

Roni played it off. "I'm just tired, babe. That's all." She knew Zoey didn't believe her. Her daughter was old enough and astute enough to sense the vibes in the house, but Roni didn't want her worrying, so she reached over and gave her a hug. "So what else have you been doing?"

"Tamar took me to visit one of her old friends yesterday. His name's Cephas Patterson, and he's real ornery."

Roni chuckled at the descriptive wording. "Really?"

Zoey told her about the visit, the shotgun, and the gold. "I don't think he was really going to shoot her, and she said the gold is just an old myth."

"Gold or not, he sounds pretty scary."

"He's just like Old Man Barker."

Roni listened while Zoey explained who Barker was before steering the conversation back to Mr. Patterson. "My mom and I checked on Old Man Barker every day, but Tamar only goes to see Mr. Patterson every now and then. What'll happen if he gets sick or something, and he's all by himself?"

Roni had no answer for the earnest question in her eyes and tone. "I don't know, but Tamar's pretty smart. If she thinks he's okay out there alone, you'll have to go with that."

Zoey appeared to think that over and asked, "Is it okay if I ride my bike to check on him? I can even take him some of my lunch or some fruit and leave it by the fence. I won't get shot."

"No." She appreciated Zoey wanting to see to the man's welfare, but not if he was waving around a shotgun. What if it went off accidentally, or worse, he shot her on purpose? No!

"But, Mom—"

"No." She didn't raise her voice. "Too dangerous."

Pout. "Okay."

Roni placed a kiss against her brow. "I'm going to lie down and see if I can't shake this jet lag."

"When you get up, can we go to the Dog for dinner?"

"Sure can."

"I'm glad you're home."

"Me, too."

After her nap, Roni found Reggie seated outside on the deck. She leaned around the door. "Zoey wants to do the Dog for dinner. What time's good for you?"

"Go on without me. Got some charts I need to go over."

She kept her disappointment hidden. "You sure?"

"Yeah."

"Want us to bring you something back?"

He shook his head. "I'll make a sandwich."

"Okay." She closed the door and pressed her back against it until the sting subsided.

"Dad's not coming?" Zoey asked as they got in the truck.

"No. He has some work to catch up on."

"Oh."

Feeling Zoey's disappointment match her own, Roni chose a light tone. "It'll be girls' night out. How's that?"

"Yay!!"

So they went to the Dog and had burgers and fries, and after dinner, Zoey received her free dessert—a huge sundae big enough to share. They talked about Roni's West Coast trip, whether Roni had talked to Amari's dad about the go-karts yet, and what Zoey might say in her e-mail to Danica about the pajama problem. They had fun, but Roni worried about Reg, and Zoey worried about her mom and dad.

CHAPTER
6

Monday morning, Zoey joined Amari, Devon, and Preston out in front of her house for the bike ride to school. They all watched with envy as Eli James backed his car out of his driveway. As he slowly drove past them, he rolled down the window and called out as he did every morning, "Hey, Amari! Wanna race?" Grinning, he rolled the window back up, stopped at Crystal's house to pick her up for the ride to school, and drove away.

"That is so unfair," Amari groused.

Zoey strapped on the Danica Patrick helmet that matched her jacket. "You say that every morning."

"That's because every morning it's unfair. How come he gets to drive, and we have to ride our bikes?"

"Because he has a car," Preston pointed out.

"Ah. The reason we call you Brain."

They pushed off and started up the street. Devon and Zoey rode at the front, while Preston and Amari brought up the rear.

"I still don't think it's fair," Amari said again.

"But it isn't going to change anything," Preston

pointed out, sounding exasperated. "We're former foster kids. We know life can be unfair sometimes."

"When I get my car, I'm not giving him a ride either," Amari declared, as if that would settle the matter.

But Preston begged to differ. "He'll be in college by then. He won't care."

"Thanks for the support, my brother."

Devon piped up, "And Dad told you to quit fussing about Eli and his car anyway. He said there's always going to be somebody getting to do something you can't."

"Who asked you to be in this conversation?"

"I can talk when I want to. It's a free country. Right, Zoey?"

"Name's Bennett. Not in it."

"Now that, America, is a smart girl," Amari crowed. "Take notes, Devon."

"Shut up. You take notes."

The two brothers went back and forth for the rest of the ride. Zoey turned to look at Preston. He replied with a shrug of his shoulders as in, *What can you do?*

After reaching the school, they parked their bikes in the rack out front, removed their helmets, and went inside. The Marie Jefferson Academy was a big, beautiful brand-new building, but because there were so few students, Mr. Jack James, the only teacher, conducted class for everyone in one room. Zoey had recently discovered the old TV program *Little House on the Prairie* and thought their classroom a lot like Laura Ingalls', except Laura's school didn't have computers, water fountains, or a fish tank.

They always started off the day with the Pledge of Allegiance and the singing of the Negro National Anthem, "Lift Ev'ry Voice and Sing." Zoey and Devon alternated accompanying the song on the piano, and it was his turn that week.

When the last notes had faded away and Devon returned to his seat, everyone took out their math books. Math was always the first lesson. Zoey was much better in the subject than she'd been in the past—she chalked this up to working in the garage, where she had to use socket wrenches of varying sizes, which helped her with her fractions (a five-eighths socket was larger than a half-inch one)—and she often helped Amari do the stocking, so she knew that a gallon of something like paint or oil was larger than a quart. As she began working on the assignment, she realized she'd learned a lot of things from being in Henry Adams. From Amari she learned: Never to steal the OG's truck. From Devon: Never steal money from anyone—especially not Crystal. And most recently: Never try to trick your parents so you can visit bad places on the Internet, like Eli, Preston, Amari, and Crystal tried to do. Thinking of Crystal made her look over discreetly. If anybody in class had something smart-mouthed to say about her running away from home, they were keeping it to themselves, which made sense; no one in their right mind wanted to earn what Amari called the Wrath of Crystal.

But to her, Crystal looked more distant than wrathful. Since she'd been back only a few days, no one knew anything about the circumstances that made her come home. Had something bad happened? Did she get homesick? Zoey didn't know. Putting her questions aside, she refocused on her lesson.

As always, they ate lunch outside. In another few weeks it was going to be too cold, so Zoey planned to enjoy it as long as the fall weather held. Crystal was seated at the big kids' table, along with Eli and his girlfriend Samantha Dickens. Megan Tripp, Sam's supposedly BFF, was with them as well, but no one liked Megan, so Zoey pretended she wasn't there. Amari, Brain, Leah, and Tiffany had a table of their own, and she and Devon had theirs, but she was tired of eating with him, and this was the day she planned to do something about it.

So she walked right past her old table, where Devon was getting his sandwich out of his bag, and set her lunch down about a half foot away from Amari. Whatever he and the rest had been talking about suddenly stopped when she took a seat. Refusing to make eye contact, she dug in her bag for her sandwich, cookies, and apple. She and Tiffany hadn't gotten along since their run-in at the football game last Thanksgiving, when Zoey pointed out Tiff's lack of dance skills, so of course she had something to say.

"What are you doing at our table?"

"Leave her alone," Amari warned. Zoey kept eating her sandwich and smiled inside. Amari always had her back. Always.

But Tiff ignored him. "This isn't a table for little kids."

"Then what are you doing here?" Preston asked before popping a few grapes into his mouth.

Tiffany glared but kept her opinion to herself.

Everyone's smug smiles faded when Devon walked up. He calmly placed his lunch on the table and sat down across from Zoey, which earned her an impatient look of censure from Amari, which sent her urge to sock Devon sky-high.

Amari opened his mouth to protest. Devon cut him off. "If she can eat here, I can too."

Amari's mouth snapped shut. Shooting daggers at his little brother, he gathered up his stuff and stalked off. When he got about ten feet away, he plopped down in the grass and ate alone.

"You know you're giving your brother the blues," Preston pointed out.

"So what," Devon replied disinterestedly.

Zoey cut him a look and once again fought off the urge to say something mean.

• • •

Over at the Power Plant, which held the town's administrative offices, Bernadine settled in for her Monday-afternoon visits. Because there was always something going on in and around Henry Adams, she'd instituted a specific day for folks to stop by and fill her in on whatever they felt she needed to know. Having a dedicated time cut down on people just dropping by and interrupting her daily workflow.

First up was Sheila Payne. As VP of social affairs, she was responsible for pulling together the upcoming Friday-evening soiree celebrating the opening of the new grocery store. The ribbon-cutting ceremony would take place bright and early Saturday morning.

"I have everything in place," she reported while checking her notes. "Siz and Rocky will handle the catering, Siz's band will provide the music. I told him to stick to the jazz, no hard rock stuff, and Tamar and her crew will help me bling out the gym."

While she continued to lay out the budget, the menu, the guest list, and the rest, Bernadine thought back on the old version of Sheila who'd arrived in town with a spine made of spaghetti and a husband every woman wanted deep-fried in oil. This new version had one of the steeliest spines around and was now a regular contributor to what made Henry Adams such a great place to be. The colonel treated her better as well.

Sheila finally finished rattling off logistics, and the pleased Bernadine replied, "Sounds like we're good to go."

"Thanks. Now, I'm thinking about having a townwide Thanksgiving."

Bernadine had no idea what that really meant. "Okay."

"We derive so many blessings from one another around here that I think we should celebrate it. I know I'm thankful for Henry Adams and all it's done for my life. And I want to open it up to our out-of-town relatives. I know you have a sister, so maybe see what she and her family are doing for the holiday."

"I know what she's doing. She's bunking at my house for now, unfortunately."

Sheila cocked her head. "Problems?"

"Many. But nothing I can't handle."

"Okay. So you think this might be a good idea?"

"I do. We've never done anything like this on my watch, and you're right about us having much to be thankful for as a town."

Sheila seemed pleased by the verbal support. "Need to pick my brain about anything else?"

"Not for now."

"How was Barrett's reunion?"

She rolled her eyes. "Unless you were a member of the unit, a boring time was had by all.

He may have to go to the next marines reunion alone. Crystal settling back in?"

"She seems to be. I'm just glad she's home."

"So am I." She gathered up her things and stood. These days, she was always in a hurry. "I'll keep you in the loop on Thanksgiving."

"Okay. Thanks, Sheila."

With a waggle of her fingers she was gone.

Two seconds later, Lily Fontaine July, administrative assistant extraordinaire, appeared in the doorway. "You're not going to believe who's here to see you."

"Who?"

Too late. Austin Wiggins, the toupee-wearing mayor of the neighboring town of Franklin, bypassed Lily and approached her desk with a grin on his pumpkinesque face and his hand extended for a shake. "Hi, hon."

Bernadine sat back in her navy leather chair, crossed her arms, and eyed him coolly. His calling her "hon," repeatedly disregarding her requests that he not address her in that manner, had gotten old. "What can I do for you, Mayor *Hon?*"

He turned beet red.

Bernadine noticed Lily cut him a scathing look before exiting.

As always, Bernadine didn't offer him a seat. If she had her way, he wouldn't be there long enough to need one. But as always he stood there looking uncomfortable for a moment, then sat down. He'd traded in his usual shiny-with-age black suit for an orange-and-brown-tweed sport coat with gray leather patches on the elbows. She heard he'd given a two-hour seminar on small government at the community college a few weeks ago, so she guessed he now fancied himself a college professor. The pants were a cheap gray flannel, and on his feet, brown penny loafers, complete with pennies. He hadn't ditched the roadkill that passed for hair on his head, however.

"I hear you're throwing a wingding on Friday to open the new grocery."

"We are."

"That store will be direct competition for the store over in Franklin."

"And?"

"Are you trying to put us out of business?" he asked with a smile as fake as the possum on his head. "You have the new school, all our seniors are members of your senior center, and lots of Franklin people come to your movies on Friday nights."

"So you want us to put up signs saying, 'No Franklin Residents Allowed'?"

"No!" His eyes were wide.

"Just checking. Why are you here, Mr. Wiggins?"

"I'm wondering why I didn't get an invitation

97

to the shindig on Friday. Seems like everyone else in the county did."

"Think about it."

His eyes met her steely regard. "You can't still be mad about that Big Box misunderstanding?"

Bernadine fought to remember if she'd taken her blood pressure pill that morning. "Misunderstanding," she echoed doubtfully.

He offered a fake laugh. "Sure it was."

"The way I remember it, you took me to court on a bogus claim that made Judge Davis so angry I'm surprised she didn't remand you straight to Leavenworth."

He quickly broke eye contact. The lawsuit had been so ridiculous the judge promised him jail should he ever waste the court's time with such foolishness again. "So why would I invite you?"

"To prove there's no hard feelings?"

She shook her head at his audacity.

"Look. I know we've had issues in the past, but consider inviting me as a way to bury the hatchet for the sake of our two communities."

She didn't bite.

"How's it going to look if the mayor of your neighboring town isn't in attendance?"

"Why's being invited so important?"

"Because I should be at your side, showing the rest of the county how progressive we are here in Henry Adams."

"We?"

"Well, you, the area. You know what I mean."

Bernadine had no idea what he was up to, but she'd rather keep him in sight than behind her back, bent on something sneaky. She also reminded herself of Reverend Paula's sermon. *Kindness over rightness.* "Okay. In the spirit of local cooperation, I'll have an invitation sent to your office. You should have it in hand before Friday."

"Thanks, Ms. Brown. I appreciate it." He stood. "I'll let you get back to your afternoon."

She nodded. He exited. She wondered what he was up to.

Trent July and Barrett Payne entered a short time later. Barrett had become the town's operations manager. He maintained the street lighting and the network of surveillance cameras installed after the devastating fire set by Odessa Stillwell. He also acted as the fire marshal and handled everything else along those lines, which in turn freed Trent, the town's mayor, to concentrate on coordinating the town's ongoing construction projects. She'd racked her brains for years to come up with a way to keep the retired marine busy, and his new position was turning out to be a perfect fit.

"Gary and I just finished the walkthrough of the store with the state health inspector," Trent began. "He's signed off on the paperwork, and said Gary can start stocking the store whenever he's ready."

"And I did a preliminary run on the store's surveillance cameras," Barrett added. "We finally have them positioned properly so that the entire store, from the milk coolers to the checkout lines, is covered. Should help if Gary has to deal with thefts—which he probably will."

Bernadine agreed. There wasn't a store in the nation immune from people with sticky fingers, and she knew theirs wouldn't be an exception.

"He'll need some extra hands to help stock the shelves and coolers, though," Trent pointed out. "I'm going to volunteer Amari and his crew. We also have some workers being sent over by a temp agency, but pretty much anyone willing to lend a hand is welcome."

"Good. I'll have Lily send out e-mails and make some calls to see if we can't get as many people involved as possible." Like everyone else, Bernadine was looking forward to being able to shop in town instead of having to drive all over east-west hell to get what she needed. "Does he have his employees ready to go?"

"Far as I know."

"Okay. Anything else on the stove right now?"

"Nope."

"Trent, you'll need to do a short speech about the store at the reception."

He nodded. "No problem."

"Then I believe we're done. Thanks, gentlemen."

They filed out.

Alone again, she turned back to her laptop. She'd set up college funds for both Eli and Crystal, and she was checking the numbers to see how much interest they were drawing. If all went well, both would be leaving the nest come fall to pursue the next chapter of their lives. Eli and his dad, Jack, had moved from California to Henry Adams two years ago, so he wanted to get back to the West Coast and had applied only to schools there. Crystal had sent applications to institutions on both coasts, and to all the top art schools. Bernadine was so glad the teenager had come to her senses and not thrown away her future just because she missed the smell of hamburgers.

Lily stepped in. "We finally got the bill for Bing's hospital stay. Here's what his Medicaid didn't cover."

Bing's leg had been broken by flying debris from the Odessa Stillwell fire. The doctors had put it in a cast and sent him home, but he wound up having surgery when complications set in from tiny slivers of metal embedded in the skin that were somehow missed during the initial diagnosis.

Bernadine looked at the surprising total, then up at Lily, who cracked, "Being elderly in this country can put you in the poorhouse."

The bill reached into the thousands. "Okay. Just send the payment."

"Will do." Lily dropped into one of the chairs. "What did Squirrel Head Wiggins want?"

"To be added to the guest list for Friday's reception."

"Why?"

"To further cooperation between our communities, or some such nonsense."

"You told him to take a long walk off a short pier, right?" When she didn't reply, Lily declared, "You're way too nice."

"I know, but I'm trying to work Paula's sermon into my life. Besides, if Wiggins is up to no good, I'd rather have him out front where I can see him."

Lily crossed her arms. "True, but still way too nice. And our Crystal? You two talked yet about her grand adventure?"

Bernadine told her what she knew and how remorseful Crystal seemed to be.

"Do you think she learned anything?"

"If nothing else, she learned that trying to be grown up means you need to know your social security number."

Lily chuckled, then asked, "So is your sister coming to the meeting tonight? Can't wait to meet her."

In response to the area men forming a support group they called Dads Inc., the women had recently formed a group of their own. It had no name yet, but they were hoping to come up with something at Tamar's this evening during the first meeting. "She's coming. I'm hoping all the strength and purpose in the room will rub off on her."

"That's kind of cryptic. Is something wrong with her?"

"To be fair, I'm going to let you form your own opinion."

"Uh-oh. She must have issues."

"Not saying another word."

"Bernadine, if she's crazy we should know in advance. You know Tamar keeps her shotgun loaded."

Bernadine laughed. "Go back to work."

"As the kids say in text speech: IJS."

"Which means."

"I'm just saying."

"That's what that means? Crystal will text me that sometimes, but I've had too much adult pride to ask what the heck the letters stood for."

"IKR. I know, right?"

Amused, Bernadine asked, "How do you know this stuff?"

"Amari and Preston. To stay one step ahead, I have to keep up."

"I guess. Well, thanks. I learned something today."

"Any time."

When Lily exited, Bernadine was still marveling over her newfound knowledge. "IJS. Who knew?"

Zoey usually spent Monday after school helping Amari and his dad at the garage. Devon helped out as well, but only because Mr. Trent gave him no choice. But on this particular Monday, Zoey had other plans. She'd been told by Tamar and her mother not to visit Mr. Patterson, but her urge to make sure he was okay outweighed the directives. If she got caught and had to paint the fence, so be it.

So after school was dismissed, rather than pedal with the July boys down the street to the garage, she told Amari she was going to the rec instead.

He nodded. "Okay. See you in the morning."

He and Devon pushed off for the garage, and as Preston and the Clark sisters, Leah and Tiff, pedaled toward the new grocery store, Zoey rode toward the rec. Hoping no one inside would see, she rode by it and over the open grass towards the road that ran in front of Miss Marie's place. When Amari got his new bike over the summer, Zoey'd convinced him to give her the old one because unlike her Barbie version, his was a scaled-down mountain bike. It was designed to handle the uneven open field, and although she was bounced around, the tires on it were awesome.

Pedaling fast because she knew she had to get back to town before anyone got suspicious, she hooked a left at the famous Jefferson fence and rode on. To her left was the mound of rubble that used to be Ms. Genevieve's home until Cletus the hog trashed the place and it had to be condemned. Passing it, she hung a right. She was pretty certain Mr. Bing and Mr. Clay were in town, so she skirted their empty pens and kept going. Her legs were tiring. Mr. Patterson's place hadn't seemed this far when riding with Tamar in Olivia, and she wasn't looking forward to having to ride all the way back, but finally the old house came into view. When she got close enough, she got off the bike and gently laid it down. Taking the apple she'd saved from her lunch, she repositioned the napkin around it and, walking quickly, set it down in the spot outside the fence where Tamar had placed the grocery bags. She was glad to see that the bags weren't there, which meant he'd taken them inside. Backing away now, she thought she saw him watching her from behind the curtains in the front window, but she didn't want to peer too closely. Mission accomplished, she hopped back on the bike and pedaled like mad toward town.

CHAPTER
7

"How do I look?"

Bernadine surveyed the voluminous gold scarf draped around her sister's neck; the pricey red sweater peeking from beneath the midriff-cut black leather jacket; the matching leather pants; the stiletto boots, and the gold in her ears and on her wrists. "You look fine, but this is a pretty casual affair we're going to."

"So I'm overdressed?"

"Just a bit."

"Good. Then I'll make a good impression. I don't want your friends to think I'm poverty-struck."

Bernadine glanced over at Crystal, seated at the kitchen table looking through a new cookbook that had come in the day's mail. Crystal rolled her eyes and went back to viewing recipes.

In the truck on the way over, Diane had questions. "So are these women farmers' wives?"

"No. Most are retired from one thing or another. Roni Moore lives here too, and she'll be there."

"Roni Moore the singer?"

"Yes. She and her husband are adoptive parents."

"And they live here?"

"Yes."

"I'm impressed."

Bernadine was glad she'd found something impressive about Henry Adams—besides Mal, of course. "She and her husband are nice people."

"I wonder if she adopted because she can't have kids of her own?"

"I don't know."

"Maybe I'll ask her."

"Don't."

"Why not? Inquiring minds want to know."

"It's none of your business."

Diane didn't seem to care for that, so Bernadine broke it down. "Suppose a stranger walked up to you and asked why Harmon filed for divorce?"

"I'd tell them the truth—that he's having a midlife crisis and will be begging me to take him back within six months."

Bernadine stared. "You really believe that?"

"Of course," Diane replied, as if the question had been a stupid one. "Harmon can't cross the street or tie his shoes without my help. He'll come to his senses soon."

The reply made Bernadine wonder just how deep Diane's denial went. "What if you're wrong?"

"I'm not, so end of conversation."

When they reached Tamar's, all the cars parked out front seemed to suggest everyone had already arrived.

"Why are you meeting in this old place?" Diane asked. "Who lives here?"

"Mal's mother, Tamar."

She perked up. "Will he be here, too?"

"No."

Inside, Bernadine was immediately bombarded with questions about Crystal. "I'll get to that in a minute. Let me introduce my sister, Di, first."

After the introductions were done, Diane said, "My real name is Diana, and I'm so pleased to meet you. Thank you for being Bernie's friends. She didn't have many when we were growing up."

Everyone froze.

Roni raised her wineglass in mock tribute. "Wow. We didn't know you had such a neat sister, Bernadine."

Apparently the sarcasm sailed right over Diane's head, because she replied, "Thanks. I was head cheerleader back in high school and had a ton of friends. I really felt sorry for her."

"Lots of friends and a big heart. How interesting." Genevieve added, "You must be so proud of yourself, Diana."

"I am."

Bernadine removed her coat, placed it on the chair with the others, and headed straight for the wine set up on a card table on the far side of the room. She needed a drink.

"Are you married, Diana?" Sheila asked. By

then Diana was standing beside Bernadine and eyeing the selection of beverages. She showed Sheila a false smile. "No. I've recently divorced my husband."

Bernadine paused in midpour. She turned her sister's way, but Diane was focused on reading the label of the wine bottle in her hand. Her face pained, she leaned over and whispered to Bernadine, "Where on earth did these country bumpkins get this no-name wine?"

Bernadine whispered back, "From my cellar. It's a 1966 Petrus Bordeaux. Bought it at an auction for a thousand bucks." She loved the startled expression, but by then she was too through, so she stalked off to claim one of the empty chairs.

Lily came over and stood at her side. "Opinion formed."

Bernadine watched Tamar walk over to Diane and strike up a quiet conversation. "And your verdict?"

"Like Roni said, wow."

"I know." Apparently Diane wasn't liking whatever Tamar was saying. She tried to move away, only to find herself gently taken by the arm.

Roni drifted over to where Bernadine was seated too. Apparently she, like everyone else in the room, was discreetly eying the interaction between Tamar and Diane. In a singsong voice reminiscent of the kids, she offered quietly, "Somebody's in trouble."

Bernadine nearly choked. "Go away before you make me spill this thousand-dollar wine." As she'd mentioned to Lily earlier, she thought Diane might benefit from rubbing elbows with their friends. Instead, she'd set them on edge straight out of the gate. Opinion formed.

Since it was Sheila's idea to form the ladies' group, she opened the meeting. "My reason for wanting to found this organization is so we can get together and relax."

"And drink Bernadine's fabulous wine," Marie cracked, to much laughter.

Bernadine watched her sister finally move away from Tamar and take a seat. Diane's stormy face mirrored the way the kids sometimes looked when Tamar called them out for their behavior. On the other hand, Tamar, who'd taken a seat on the sofa, didn't appear the least bit upset. Then again she never did.

On the heels of the laughter, Sheila said, "Tonight we need to come up with a name, elect officers if we want to go that route, and talk about what we want to achieve going forward. First, though, we need Bernadine to fill us in on Ms. Crystal."

Bernadine relayed what she'd been told of Crystal's doings in Dallas. When she'd finished, there was head shaking all around. The ladies had a few more questions about the stolen shoes and the role played by the police. When those were answered, she added, "Crystal asked if the couple she stayed with in Dallas could move here."

Reverend Paula asked, "And your response?"

Bernadine shrugged. "According to her, they're struggling big-time, but I was impressed by the common sense they seemed to have."

"We're all about opening our hearts here," Lily reminded everyone.

"And it might be nice to have some babies in town," Sheila added.

"Babies?" Genevieve gasped. "We may have babies here?"

Everyone laughed, and Lily cracked, "Better them than me, because lord knows I'm not having any, regardless of Devon's constant nagging for a little brother."

Roni laughed. "Aw, come on, Lily. Forty-plus isn't too old."

"Then go for it, Roni. Me, I'm done. Amari and Devon are more than enough for this old woman, thank you very much."

Diane interrupted. "You mean you're seriously considering letting these strangers live here?"

Bernadine replied, "Sure. Why not?"

"But you don't even know them."

Rocky quipped, "Before Ms. Money Bags over there bought the town, many of us in this room didn't know one another either. Worked out fine."

111

Mumbles of agreement and glasses raised in toast followed that.

Diane had shock on her face again. Bernadine wondered if it might stem from not having known about her poor, friendless big sister's ownership of Henry Adams. She'd never told Diane about purchasing the town on eBay because her sister's only interest was herself. "Let me get some more info on the couple, and then we can have a serious conversation about the pros and cons."

That seemed to suit everyone except Diane, who looked disgusted, but no one paid her any attention. Sheila moved on to the next item on her agenda.

On the drive home, Bernadine glanced over at her silent sister and wondered what she might be thinking. "So, did you enjoy yourself?"

She shrugged. "I suppose. Didn't like Tamar, though."

"Why not?"

"She had the nerve to tell me I shouldn't have said what I did about you not having any friends. And apparently Malachi told her about the prom date story, and she didn't like that either."

"Ah."

"Do you really own the town?"

"I do."

"You couldn't come up with a better way to spend your settlement?"

"After the divorce I needed a new purpose in life, and this was it. Had no idea how things would turn out, but it's been a blessing all the way around. That old religious saying about casting your bread on the water has really proven true. I can't put a price on what this town and the people here have given me in return."

Diane stared out her window at the passing darkness.

"You might want to think about finding a new purpose in your life, too," Bernadine added.

But Diane didn't respond.

When Roni got home, Reg was in their bedroom, packing for his trip to Seattle the next day. "How'd the meeting go?" he asked.

"We had fun. We decided to call ourselves the Henry Adams Ladies Auxiliary."

"Sounds pretty old-fashioned."

"That's the point. We're patterning ourselves after those old school groups. Zoey still up?"

"Yeah. She's watching TV."

She picked her words carefully. "I talked to Paula. She said she'd be willing to sit down with us to try and help us sort out whatever this is we're going through."

"No."

"That was quick."

"The only thing wrong was you being gone all the time. Now that you aren't, we're good."

"That why you faked being asleep when I came home Saturday night, because we're good?"

He stiffened.

"We're both adults, Reggie. If you don't want to be married anymore just say so."

He met her eyes, then went back to his packing. "I need to get this done."

"You do that," she replied icily, and left the room.

On the heels of her departure, Reggie sighed and dropped his head. He didn't want their marriage to end, but talking to a counselor, even someone he knew and admired like Paula, wasn't something he was comfortable with. More than likely folks around town had already picked up on the fact that he and Roni were having trouble, but thankfully no one had said anything out loud. Going to see Paula would be to openly admit they were having issues, and he didn't want to air their dirty laundry. It was his hope that now that Roni was home, the tensions between them would miraculously dissolve. Although he didn't believe that, he clung to it anyway because he had no other solution.

In light of that, he thought his first step back to normalcy would be to patch things up with Roni before leaving for Seattle in the morning. He had been feigning sleep, and although he didn't want to discuss the reasons behind it, he did owe her an apology. She was down the hall in Zoey's room and they were watching *Leave It to Beaver*.

Zoey glanced up at his entrance. "Did you watch this when you were little, Dad?"

"I don't believe it was still on TV when I was growing up, but I do know about the show."

Roni's soft smile gave him hope, and he offered her his own in reply.

"Why does Mrs. Cleaver wear high heels and dresses all the time?"

Roni chuckled. "That's the way some women dressed back then."

"Is she just getting home from work on every show?" The confusion on her face made them both chuckle.

Roni said, "I'm not sure whether June had a job, babe."

"So she walked around the house all day in dresses and high heels, just because?"

Roni nodded.

"That's dumb."

Reggie tried to explain it better. "Zoey, back then a lot of women didn't work. They stayed home and took care of their families."

"Was it some kind of law, like when they wouldn't let Black people vote or drink out of the water fountains?"

He could see Roni waiting for the answer. He swore she was laughing at him. "Well, no."

"What did the dads do?"

"They went to work and took care of the family."

"That doesn't sound fair. That sound fair to you, Mom?"

"On the surface, no, but things were different back then. Men sorta ran things."

"Why?"

"Well, a lot of them didn't think women were smart enough to do stuff."

"What?"

When Reggie cut Roni an impatient look, she responded with, "You explain it to her, then."

He'd come into the room with the intention of trying to iron things out, only to find himself caught up in a dilemma not of his making.

"I need to finish getting ready."

As he headed for the door, he heard Zoey say, "They should've called Martin Luther King. He'd've fixed that."

Roni entered their bedroom a few minutes later. "That child of ours is something else."

"Yes, she is. Martin Luther King."

"Women's roles back then probably confuse a lot of the girls these days."

"Probably, but I didn't like having to defend my entire gender."

Her flinty-eyed response to that made him instantly regret the words and, more importantly, his snappish tone.

"It's kind of hard defending the indefensible, isn't it?" she asked coldly.

He exhaled an angry sigh. "I'll be leaving

116

before Zoey gets up in the morning, so let me go say good-bye."

She shot him a terse nod.

He left.

"Hey Zoey," he called, sticking his head back in through her open door again. The TV was off, and she was sitting up in bed, reading. "What're you reading?"

"The book you ordered for me." She'd found it on Amazon a few weeks back and had to have it. It was titled *Car: The Definitive Visual History of the Automobile.* It chronicled the history of automobiles and was filled with great glossy pictures.

"Enjoying it?"

"A lot."

"I'm going to Seattle in the morning. Just came to say good-bye."

She put the book aside and scooted over so he could sit on the edge of the bed, as he always did at the end of their day. "Is this the medical conference you were telling me about?"

He nodded.

"How long will you be gone?"

"Should be back Saturday afternoon." From the first time they met, she'd been the daughter of his heart. He'd always remember the evening Bernadine announced the matching of foster parents to kids. Zoey had been slated for Sheila and Colonel Payne, but instead she'd walked over to him, grabbed his hand, and staked her claim. "I'm going to miss you while I'm away."

"I'll miss you, too."

This trip would mark their first prolonged separation. During Roni's descent into the studio they'd formed quite a bond, with their nightly checkers games, their fishing trips to Tamar's creek, and him watching her working on the cars with Trent and Amari. "Take care of Mama Roni while I'm gone."

"I will. Are you getting a divorce?"

That threw him. "No. Now that Mom's home, things will be better."

"She's going to record again, right?"

"Would it be so bad to have her here all the time?"

"Like Beaver's mom?"

"Maybe?"

"She'd be sad without her music."

He knew that to be true, but he didn't want to talk about it. "She won't turn into Mrs. Cleaver. Promise. And we're not getting a divorce either."

"Good."

He leaned over and kissed her brow. "Another twenty minutes, and then lights out."

"Okay. Did Mom talk to you about me driving go-karts? I really want to."

"She hasn't said anything, but how about we talk about it when I get back from Seattle?"

"But that's a long time from now."

"When I get back." Reggie smiled and left. *Go-karts.* When he entered their bedroom, Roni wasn't there. He noticed her pillow was gone from the bed, as well. In the empty space lay a note: *Don't want you to have to fake being asleep. I'll use the guest room. Have a safe flight.*

He dropped his head. As he got into bed, he could hear the faint strains of the piano being played downstairs. Feeling like a world-class jerk, he turned out the lights.

On the ride to the airport with Trent the following morning, Reggie thought back on the note. "Why are women so complicated?"

Trent looked over. "That rhetorical?"

"I don't know. Probably."

Being the good friend that he was, Trent didn't press him to explain. He just drove and remained silent.

"Why is it so wrong for me to want my wife to be at home?" Reggie asked.

"Is that what's going on with you two?"

He nodded. "I don't think it's fair to Zoey for her to be gone as much as she is."

"Zoey or you?"

"Zoey."

"Ahh."

Reggie knew that was a lie. "Who am I kidding? I feel like the colonel."

Trent chuckled. "I don't think the town can

handle two Neanderthals, Reg. Although Barrett seems to have seen the light."

"My mom didn't work outside the house, and she was fine."

"Was she a Grammy Award–winning superstar?"

He didn't respond.

"Music is her life, man. You knew that when you married her, right?"

"When I married her, music was on the back burner."

"Lily always says, 'Husbands and children don't like change.' What if Roni asked you to give up your practice?"

"She wouldn't do that."

"But it's okay for you to want her to give up hers?"

"No, but—"

"But what?"

"Honestly, I liked things better when she was home and I was the provider."

"Back to Neanderthal mode."

"I guess."

"Have you talked to her?"

"Can't defend the indefensible."

"True, but it's either try to or get with the change."

Reggie sighed audibly.

"How's Zoey handling the undercurrents?"

"Asked me if we were getting a divorce. I told

her no. She wanted to know if I was going to turn Roni into June Cleaver."

Trent laughed. "Roni will become June Cleaver the same day my Lily does."

"Yeah, I know."

"Talk to her, man. Put all your cards on the table and start there."

"I need to do something. I started this ball rolling, but I had no idea it was going to roll back and flatten me like somebody in one of those old-school cartoons."

"Then you need to fix it."

Reggie knew Trent was right, but he wasn't sure it was fixable. Roni had never slept in the guest room before. This morning when he was moving around, getting ready to leave, he kept hoping she'd show up to see him off, but she hadn't, and he supposed after faking sleep the other night, he was getting what he deserved. Why he thought there'd be no ramifications for hurting her feelings the way he had was tied to the Neanderthal thinking. He'd wanted to prove to her that he held the reins and to show his displeasure, and now those same reins were around his neck, slowly choking him and their marriage to death. "Zoey asked me about go-kart racing. I know you used to take Amari all the time. Do you think she's too young?"

"No. There are girls at the track who are younger. The boys sometimes give them a

121

hard time, but I know she can handle herself."

Reggie agreed with that. "Okay. I'll talk to you about the ins and outs when I get back."

"No problem."

Trent let him out in front of the terminal doors.

"Thanks, man. And thanks for listening."

"You're welcome. Have a safe trip and a good time."

"Gonna try." But as Reg went through the doors, he conceded that having a good time was going to be easier said than done.

CHAPTER
8

After hearing Reggie leave, Roni lay in the echoing quiet and wondered what her life might be like a year from then. Would she still be Mrs. Reginald Garland? If she couldn't convince him to confront the demons riding his back, the answer could be no. She dragged her hands down her eyes. Sleep had been fleeting. She'd tossed and turned, but didn't chastise herself for opting for the guest room. Why share a bed with a man who pretended to be asleep rather than deal with his wife? His behavior of late was so out of character for the guy she thought she'd married, she wondered if maybe there was something wrong medically. Granted, this distancing hadn't happened overnight; they'd been drifting apart for nearly a year now, and no matter how she tried to fix things, the breach continued to widen. It was frustrating and maddening. Her seven-year marriage was slowly slipping away like sand through her fingers, and all she could do was watch.

A glance at the clock on the nightstand showed 7:00 a.m. The urge to call her brother Tommy was strong. Although he was two years younger, no matter what she was going through she could always count on him to help her find clarity, and he was a good listener. She wasn't sure which version of him she was in need of at the moment, but since they hadn't spoken in weeks, she thought she'd check in.

When the call went through, his first response was a groggy "Big sis, you'd better be dead or on fire. Do you know what time it is?"

She laughed softly. "You're a schoolteacher. You're supposed to be up by now."

"Boiler issues. School's closed."

She felt terrible. "Oh, I'm sorry for waking you up. Go on back to sleep. We'll talk this evening."

"No, no. I'm good."

She could hear him sitting up.

"So, how're things?" she asked.

"Good. Denise is in St. Louis for a conference. Your niece and nephew have apparently gotten too grown to call their old parents—unless it's for money. But since neither has shown up at the door saying they've been kicked out of school, I guess they're okay."

Her niece Danida was in her sophomore year at Spellman. Her nephew Tommy Jr., the football phenom, was in his freshman year at Notre Dame.

"How're things with you?" he asked. "Zoey and Dex good?"

Roni had two brothers, and both referred to Reggie as Dex—short for Poindexter, because of his short stature, thick glasses, and intellect. "Zoey's good. Reggie and me, not so much."

"What's going on?"

For the next half hour, Roni spilled her guts and finished with, "Any thoughts?"

"Only that when men don't want to talk, it's usually because they're holding on to something dumb or scary."

"Scary?"

"Yeah. Although men don't want to admit it, being in a relationship is terrifying sometimes. We wonder about screwing it up—not measuring up, being replaced. Basically, beneath all the chest-beating and posing, we're a bunch of insecure little babies."

She chuckled. "Seriously?"

"Seriously—but sorry to hear you two are going through this. You want me to give him a call?"

"No. Might make things worse."

"Might not."

"I don't want to take that chance." And she didn't. Things were already bad enough between them.

"Understood. So are you coming this way for Thanksgiving?"

Usually she and Reggie and Zoey went to his parents one year and to Tommy's the next. She and her brothers lost their musician parents in 1991 in a plane crash outside Tokyo. At the time she'd been twenty-two, Tommy twenty, and Randy seventeen. "We're having a townwide Thanksgiving this year and inviting our families. Hoping you and yours might want to come up."

"Wow. Maybe. Let me talk to Denise and get back. Is Randy coming?"

Baby brother Randy was one of the busiest and best studio musicians in the business. "Haven't talked to him yet. Has he checked in with you lately? He was in Amsterdam when he called a few weeks ago."

"Talked to him on Monday. He's in London."

"Okay."

"But put us down as a strong possibility. Denise and I have been wanting to come out to see your little Mayberry, so this might be perfect."

"I'd love to see you."

"Same here. And hang in there. Hopefully Dex will come to his senses, and you guys can get this worked out."

"I hope so."

"You will. Give Zoey my love. Dex too, when you talk to him."

"Will do."

"Love you, girl."

"Love you more." She ended the call.

Although Tommy hadn't offered any eureka-type advice, talking to him had made her feel better. It also made her wonder if his assessment of men held any truth. Considering all Reggie's successes, she couldn't imagine him being insecure about anything, stupid or otherwise.

Leaving the bed, she forced her feet into her slippers and headed for the bathroom. She wasn't the type to wallow, so it was time to get the day under way.

As far as she knew, there were no boiler problems at Marie Jefferson Academy, so after taking care of her morning needs she padded down the hallway to make sure Zoey was up.

She stuck her head in the door and paused with surprise at the sight of her daughter standing in front of her mirrored vanity table, lifting small blue hand weights. "Good morning."

Zoey quickly placed her hands behind her back, as if Roni had suddenly gone blind and hadn't seen what was in them.

"Why're you lifting weights, Zoey? Did Dad say it was okay?"

Silence.

"Guess the answer is no. Tell you what," Roni said, coming into the room and taking a seat on one of the chairs. "How about you put the weights down and let's talk about this."

Zoey stood there for a moment, looking over at Roni as if trying to decide if she was in trouble and if so how much, but finally placed the sky-blue weights on the bed, stood beside it, and waited.

"And you can sit on the bed, too. It's okay."

She climbed up.

"So, tell me why you're secretly lifting weights."

"I asked Dad, and he said I was too young—my body wasn't ready yet."

"So, what, you didn't believe him?"

No answer at first. "I believed him, but—"

"But you wanted to do it anyway."

Shame-faced nod of agreement.

"Okay. So tell me what is so important that you dissed your dad's advice—who's a doctor by the way. You do know that, right?"

Zoey whispered, "Yes."

"Just making sure. So give me the reason you blew off what he said."

Once again, there was silence and much staring at the lap. "I want to be strong enough to lift Rocky's motorcycle."

Roni stared, confused. "What?"

"Rocky said I could learn how to drive her

motorcycle once I was strong enough to lift it."

Roni folded her arms and studied her remark-able child. "You know, if I ever catch you on a motorcycle, both you and Rocky will need a burial plot."

Silence—then, "Do I have to paint the fence for disobeying Dad?"

Roni shook her head. "No, but we need to talk about this after school. In the meantime, you get ready for breakfast. I have a taste for blueberry waffles. You want to split a few with me?"

Zoey's eyes widened, and her face beamed bright as the sun. "Yeah!"

"Then I'll meet you downstairs." On her way down the steps a humor-filled Roni called out, "Lord give me the strength to raise this child!"

As they sat down to eat, Zoey forked up a bit of waffle and said, "These are so awesome."

"Why thank you."

"Are you and Dad getting a divorce?"

Roni choked on a swallow of orange juice. Once she recovered, she said, "No."

"Good. Dad said the same thing."

"That's good to hear."

"I told him I wouldn't want you to be like Mrs. Cleaver and that you'd be sad without your music."

"I would be." She wondered how Reg reacted to that bit of wisdom.

"If you get divorced, I might turn into a pain in the behind like Tiffany, and nobody has time for that."

Roni chuckled. "You are so right." She met the bright eyes of her child. "Thanks for having my back."

"You're welcome," she replied, and went back to her waffles.

Once breakfast was done, Zoey and her crew rode off for school, and Roni drove to the Dog for a talk with Rocky. She was pretty certain Rocky would never put Zoey in harm's way, so there had to be more to the story about the motorcycle.

Inside the Dog the morning rush was over, so the place was rather quiet. She waved at Mal, who was bringing breakfast to Marie, Genevieve, and Clay Dobbs, but the sight of Bernadine and Lily sitting in a booth was surprising. "What are you two doing here? Aren't you supposed to be at the Plant, doing the Power Rangers thing?"

Bernadine answered. "We're waiting on Gary so we can tour the store."

Lily moved over so Roni could join them.

Once seated, Roni asked Bernadine, "So how long is your sister visiting?"

She replied over her cup, "Too long. She's going to be with me for a while."

Before Roni could inquire further, Rocky came over to the table. "Morning, Roni. Can I get you something?"

"Yes, coffee—but let me ask you something first. I walked in on our mini me lifting weights this morning. She said you told her you'd let her drive your bike when she got strong enough to lift it. Is that true?"

Rocky shook her head and blew out a breath. "It was the only thing I could think of to get her to stop pestering me about wanting to learn. No way is she old enough, and no way is she strong enough. I even have trouble getting that Shadow upright."

Roni understood now. "Okay, gotcha. Girlfriend doesn't take a no real well."

"Tell me about it. Isn't she too young to be lifting weights?"

"Yes, and apparently Reg told her that, but—"

Rocky finished the sentence. "Girlfriend doesn't take a no real well."

Lily cracked, "Knowing Zoey, she'll probably make those muscles appear overnight out of sheer will."

"Well, she'll have to lift in her dreams from now on."

Rocky moved off to get the coffee, and Roni returned the talk to Diane. "So how long is your sister staying?"

"Maybe until the Second Coming. And her comments to the contrary, my brother-in-law divorced her, not the other way around."

"Oh."

"And I told her if she plans to stay, she needs to find a job."

Lily asked, "What's she qualified for?"

"Other than trying to make me look bad? She headed up her husband's dental office for a few years, so I guess she could do that, somewhere."

"Reggie's looking for a new office manager," Roni offered, hoping that info might help. "Do you think she'd like to interview?"

Bernadine replied, "She doesn't have much choice. I'll let her know."

"He left for Seattle this morning. Be back Saturday."

"Okay, good."

Rocky returned with the coffee and she poured the hot brew into Roni's cup. "I know you just finished the new CD," she asked. "What's next?"

Roni gave her a quick explanation about the tribute CD she wanted to do. "But I told Reg I'd stay away from the studio for a while."

Her disappointment must have been plain because Lily asked gently, "Still having issues?"

"Yeah. If I could just get him to talk about it, maybe we could figure it out, but he won't."

"How about a sit-down with Paula?" Bernadine asked.

"I suggested that and he said no so fast you'd've thought I'd asked him to run naked down Main Street. Frustrating."

Gary Clark arrived on the heels of that. "Morning, ladies."

They all greeted him in turn.

Bernadine gathered up her things and asked Roni, "You want to come along? You're welcome, you know."

"Thanks, but no. I'll stay and finish up my coffee."

Lily appeared worried. "You sure?"

"Yeah, I am. I'll see you all later."

After their departure, Roni sat in the booth alone. She sipped and thought about Zoey's championing of her cause, which made her smile. Again she wondered how Reggie had taken it. Realizing she might never know, she finished her coffee and stood. Leaving the money for her bill beneath her empty cup, she slipped out.

On her way back to the house she swung by her recording studio. From the simple exterior, it was impossible to tell its purpose. It was one story, had a hexagonal shape, and its kelly green bricks were her tribute to Zoey. She used her key to let herself in and turned on the lights. They were dimmed like she preferred, and for a moment she simply stood there, taking in the booth where she laid down her tracks and the huge electronic board where Jason sat and worked his audio magic. The studio wasn't blinged out with lights and chrome like some of the places she'd recorded in, but it had the best acoustics and equipment her money could buy. Just the sight of the place made her want to put down her purse, step into the booth, and sing. Would Reggie ever understand that what went on in this building was as vital to her life as their love for each other? The pain of their discord rose again, but she beat it down and came to a decision. If Reggie didn't want her, fine—her music did. Locking the door behind her, she walked to her car, took out her phone, and hit the speed dial for Jason. Whether Reggie approved or not, her gift was calling, and she planned to answer.

Over at the school, Zoey was doing her best not to stare too much at the new kid. He'd joined their classroom that morning, and his name was Wyatt Dahl. She didn't know how old he was, but from the work he was assigned, she assumed him to be no more than a year older. He was about Devon's size, which meant he was skinny, and he had black hair like hers and green eyes like her mom Bonnie. According to Mr. James, Wyatt and his family recently moved to Franklin from Chicago. She had no idea why somebody would leave a big city like that to live in Kansas, but she supposed it had to do with his parents. When he looked over and saw her watching him, she quickly dropped her eyes to her book, but she took peeks at him for the rest of the morning.

At lunch, he came outside and stood for a

moment, as if not sure what he was supposed to do, so Devon went over and brought him back to the table. Everyone introduced themselves. When it became her turn, she said, "I'm Zoey Raymond Garland."

Devon groaned. "God. Why do you always say 'Zoey Raymond Garland'?" he asked in a mincing voice. "Why don't you just say 'Zoey Garland'?"

"And why don't you just shut up?" she shot back. Amari and the older kids watched with amusement.

Ignoring the mini argument, Wyatt sat. "Hi, Zoey Raymond Garland."

She grinned. "Hi."

Leah led the gentle interrogation of Wyatt, and when she was done, they'd all learned he was an only child living with his grandmother. He had no dad, and his mom had been killed last year in Afghanistan.

"She was in the army," he explained. "She stepped on an IED."

The others seemed to know what that was, but Zoey didn't. She planned to Google it when she got home.

"Sorry for your loss," Leah said quietly, and everyone else offered condolences as well.

"I miss her a lot," he added.

Amari said, "Zoey lost her mom, too."

Devon added in a disapproving voice, "But she died of a drug overdose."

Preston snapped, "What are you, the *National Enquirer*? Damn, Devon. What does that have to do with anything? Shut up for a minute, would you?"

Wyatt looked over at Zoey, but she concentrated on eating and wanting Devon struck by lightning. She wondered if Wyatt now thought she was bad. She wasn't sure why it mattered, but it did.

Amari spoke up. "Zoey's a nice person."

There seemed to be general agreement on that. Yes, Tiffany rolled her eyes, but the support made Zoey feel good and not care that Devon appeared mad about the verbal smack-down meted out by Brain.

When the time came to go back inside, Zoey walked her trash to the container. Wyatt got there a step later. He tossed his trash in and said, "Nice to meet you, Zoey Raymond Garland."

She gave him a nod. "Nice to meet you, too." As they returned to the classroom and took their seats, her heart was beating really fast. Cute boys were usually on TV or in magazines, but for the very first time she knew one in real life.

CHAPTER
9

After touring the store, Bernadine returned to the Power Plant. On tap was a review of the architectural drawings for the rebuilding of the old Henry Adams hotel site. Because neither she nor the town elders knew what they wanted the site to become, she'd had her architects sketch out a few possibilities.

Opening the e-mail and its attachments, she saw that the first one was for a hotel. It was small—in keeping with the size of the town; no one expected Henry Adams to be hosting conventions. It was only two stories, but its edgy design would go well with the other new buildings in town. The next drawing was of a one-story strip mall holding six shops. The architect had added plantings and a fountain to give the building some character, but she wasn't sure her town needed such a thing. The shops were labeled "Beauty Shop," which brought to mind Crystal's friend; "Hardware," which would give Mayor Wiggins fits because he owned the hardware/feed store in Franklin; "Bakery," of which there were none within fifty miles; "Bookstore," which every community needed, in her opinion; and, for the last two, "Bikes," which garnered a shrug, and the smile-invoking "Bernadine's Bangles," a jewelry store. Granted, the businesses were named just for the rendering, but she kind of liked the idea of the bookstore, beauty shop, and bakery; hardware too, maybe. If the places were to be profitable, they'd have to be patronized by more than the handful of local residents, though.

That being the case, she turned her mind to something she'd been trying not to deal with—more residents. For Henry Adams to survive, growth was essential. Without new arrivals to sink familial roots and raise their children, the town would once again be on a fast track to death. Thanks to her wise investments there was still plenty of money available to fund whatever might be needed, but after her demise there'd eventually come a time when the town would have to go its way alone, and the only way that would happen was if it had enough of a tax base to keep the dream alive. She'd provided a school, a solid infrastructure of roads, homes, and lighting, a recreation center, and a church. It was a great beginning, but the town needed more people.

Her computer held the names and addresses of at least fifteen families who wanted to move in, yet she'd placed the requests on the back burner because she wasn't sure how it might affect the town's ideal. Henry Adams was a family. For all intents and purposes, everyone got along—Riley Curry being the exception, but he and that hog of his were in Hollywood and out of the town's hair for the time being. Her concern was that opening up residency might kill that spirit. There was also the issue of how to go about picking new residents. Should there be a lottery, or should she just throw open the gates to anyone who could afford to move in? Granted, not everyone was going to want to live in a historic Black town, but it was her wish that everyone who did, no matter their race, would respect its traditions and want to participate in things like the August First celebrations, not look down their noses at the idea.

She rose from her chair and walked over to the windows that looked out onto Main Street. The once-crater-filled dirt road was now paved, and there were sidewalks and streetlights where there hadn't been when she first arrived. To the north, open fields of autumn-kissed grasses stood between town and the land owned by the Julys and the Jeffersons. That open acreage belonged to her, and she'd become so accustomed to its pastoral beauty that it was hard to envision it taken over by shops, homes, and the like. Preserving as much open land as possible was paramount, but whether she embraced the idea or not, more residents would have to be brought in. They were needed to ensure the future.

With her decision made, she went back to the

drawings. She needed to prep a presentation concerning all this for next Monday's town meeting, so she opened a new file on her laptop and began.

An hour later she had a detailed outline that met with her approval. She'd be relying on her core group of residents to aid her in refining the plan, pointing out the things she might have overlooked, and giving her the valuable feedback she'd come to expect.

Her watch and grumbling stomach let her know it was way past lunchtime. She supposed she should swing by the house to see if Diane wanted to join her at the Dog, so she grabbed her purse and keys. She also wanted to alert her sister to the possibility of employment with Reggie. It might not go well, but Bernadine didn't care. The woman needed a job. Those thoughts led her back to the sadness she'd sensed in Roni that morning. Bernadine cared for both the Garlands, but it wasn't her place to choose sides. Nothing kept her from hoping their issues were ironed out, though, for the sake of their marriage, for Roni's music, and, most importantly, for Zoey.

"Lord, that man is fine!" Diane gushed, watching Mal interact with a couple seated on the far side of the diner.

Bernadine did her best to ignore the remark and concentrated on eating her salad.

"You know, if I wanted to have him for myself, I could."

Bernadine met her sister's superior stare and responded nonchalantly, "Really?"

"Yes."

She gave Diane an eye roll. "Yeah, right."

"I could, you know."

"What are you, twelve?" Bernadine asked, mildly irritated. "This isn't junior high. You need to start living in the real world for a change."

"You're the one not living in the real world. If I wanted him, there's nothing you could do to stop me."

Time to draw another line in the sand. "How about I call him over, so you can run that by him and see what he says?"

Panic flashed on Diane's face, but was quickly replaced by composure. "I've no problem with that."

"You sure?" For all the bravado, her sister now looked real uncomfortable.

"Yes."

Bernadine waved him over.

"What can I do for you, doll?"

"Di wants to run something by you."

He waited.

When Diane seemed more interested in the french fries on her plate than stepping up, Bernadine asked encouragingly, "Well?"

The silence lengthened. Mal glanced between

them. "Is this a test to see if I can read minds, because I have stuff I need to be doing."

Still nothing from her sister, so Bernadine said to him, "Go on, babe. I'll call you later."

A confused Mal shook his head and departed.

Diane stared unseeingly out the window flanking the booth.

Having too much class to gloat, Bernadine went back to her salad.

On the drive home, Bernadine told Diane about Reggie's job opening. "He'll be back on Saturday, so unless you're leaving town before then—"

"Why did you do that?" Diane asked.

"Do what?"

"Call Mal over?"

"Because you asked me to. Why would you even challenge me on something so stupid?" In a singsong voice she mimicked, " 'I can take your boyfriend.' Who does that? We're grown women now. You don't get to hurt me and laugh about it anymore. Sorry."

"Well, I can certainly do better than the owner of a countrified diner in the middle of nowhere."

"Then why are you here? This is the reality. You're an over-fifty divorced woman with no means of support. End of story. I've been willing to help you, but apparently you still think you're in your Queen Bee days."

"I was a Queen Bee."

"And now—you're not. Grow up, Di. I'm not Mama. My job is not to hand you rose-colored glasses to see through."

"You're just jealous because I was her favorite."

"True, I wanted her love more than anything in this world, but where was her favorite when she was dying? Every day she asked, 'Is Di coming today?' And every day I lied to her and said, 'Yes, Mama. Di's coming.'"

"You know I never liked being around sickness."

"She was our mother, you silly witch! How dare you deny her the only thing she wanted before God took her home! You couldn't take a day away from doing nothing to visit?"

"I was busy."

"Right." Bernadine pulled up to the curb in front of the house. "Go on inside. I need to get back to work."

Looking wounded, Diane exited the truck and stomped up the steps to the door.

Bernadine had steam pouring from her ears as she drove away. She wanted to grab her sister by the throat and shake her until she got a clue. Hot tears filled her eyes. After the ravages of diabetes left their mother, Ernestine, blind, crippled, and unable to care for herself, Bernadine had taken her into her California home. She'd footed the medical bills and paid for the aides who came each day to assist Bernadine with bathing and feeding. Throughout it all, Di had been the one she'd asked for. As a grown woman, she knew she should put the issue behind her and move on, but she'd wanted the recognition and love of her mother so badly that the resonating pain continued to hold her in its thrall. Diane's visit was ripping the scabs off old wounds that had always been in the back of her mind but lay hidden beneath the accomplishments and duties of daily life.

That Diane failed their mother when she was at her lowest was one of the few things Bernadine and now ex-husband Leo were agreed upon. He too saw Diane as a selfish conniving bitch and that her claims of being too busy to visit were nothing but crap. First she claimed she didn't have the money to fly to California, but when offered a first class ticket, another excuse took its place. Then it became a matter of her children's needs, and then Harmon's dental practice. The only excuse she hadn't cited was having to wash her hair, which may as well have been invoked for all the water the many excuses held. When Ernestine passed on, Bernadine honored the request that she be buried at Woodlawn in Detroit, next to their father, Emery, and of course Diane showed up for the funeral. Decked out in black, her show of grief could've won her an

Oscar—had anyone believed it. From throwing herself over the casket to keening as if her heart was broken, she hit all the notes. Bernadine remembered Leo leaning over and whispering in her ear, "Can we find someone to shoot her and put her out of her misery?" He was from the state of Bullshit, and he readily recognized a fellow citizen.

Bernadine pulled into the lot of the Power Plant, wiped away her tears, and asked herself again why she was offering her baby sister a hand.

The answer remained the same. She was blood.

After school, Zoey toyed with the idea of riding out to check on Mr. Patterson, but with her mom waiting to discuss the business with the weights, she figured she'd better go home.

As she entered the kitchen, her mom met her with a smile. "How'd your day go?"

"Okay. You want to talk about the weights now?"

"I do, but you can put your backpack and stuff in your room, and we'll talk when you get back. Did Mr. James give you homework?"

"Always."

"Okay."

Zoey trudged up to her room. Her mom didn't look too angry, and since she'd already been assured there'd be no fence painting, she figured she could handle whatever the punishment turned out to be. After hanging up her Danica jacket, she took her school books out of the backpack, and Wyatt Dahl came to mind. She wondered if she could talk to her mom about her feelings about him. Punishment first, she reminded herself, so, gathering up her courage, she went downstairs.

Mama Roni was in the kitchen, shaking tortilla chips onto a paper plate to accompany the bowl of salsa on the table. Zoey liked salsa and chips after school. That her favorite snack was being offered lowered her anxiety a bit.

"So," her mom began once Zoey had gotten a plate and dug in. "I talked to Rocky, and she said the reason she told you what she did was to stop you from pestering her about the bike."

Zoey froze in midbite and met her mom's eyes.

"She's fully grown and can barely lift that bike herself, honey."

Zoey remained silent.

"I know this may be hard to take, but when someone, especially an adult, tells you no, you need to go with that."

Zoey thought about riding out to see Mr. Patterson and swallowed guiltily. "Okay, Mama."

"And as for the punishment, I'm leaving that up to your dad, since he was the one you blew off and dissed."

She concentrated on using a chip to lift up some salsa.

"But until he gets back, there'll be no TV or DVDs."

Her eyes went wide, and her jaw dropped. "But Danica's racing Friday."

"And?"

Zoey sighed inwardly. "Okay."

"Laptop for homework only."

Another inward sigh. She'd hoped to skirt the television ban with her computer. Guess not.

"Anything you want to say about this?"

"Just I'm sorry for not listening." She was a kid. She knew her lines.

"I appreciate that, and I'm sure your dad will too when he gets back."

"Can I still go to the garage with Amari and Devon?"

"Yes."

That was something. "Think I'll go up and start my homework now."

"That's fine."

Upstairs a sad-faced Zoey carried her books to her desk and plopped down into the green desk chair. Life sucked. She hadn't meant to pester Rocky. She just wanted to be able to ride her Silver Shadow motorcycle because it was the coolest thing on earth. And now that she thought about it, it was a really big bike. No way would she be able to grow enough muscles to lift it, and she was dumb to even think she could. *Grow up, Zoey Raymond Garland!*

Considering all the begging she'd done, she supposed she should be glad Rocky hadn't told her to beat it and get the hell out of her face. Not that Rocky would've talked so mean, but Zoey knew from life in Miami that not everyone was nice. More than once she and her mom had been cursed at for begging on the streets or threatened with the police for getting caught going through a restaurant's trash, looking for stuff to eat.

The picture of her mom that she'd gotten from her aunt Yvette in Toledo sat in a little frame on her nightstand. Getting up, she walked over and picked it up. The face was younger than when Zoey had known her, but it was her mom, and she still missed her an awful lot. Mama Roni said that was okay because it showed how much Zoey loved her. She wondered how her life might have turned out had Bonnie not died. In a perfect world, she'd've gotten off all the drugs, and the two of them would be happy and living in a house just like the one she stayed in now. However, like the other kids in town, she knew the world wasn't perfect. It was filled with sad stuff, people who hurt your feelings, and rats. She promised herself she'd never do drugs because she didn't want her own kids to be homeless or eat out of trash cans. Life in Kansas was much better than the one she'd had in Miami. She just wished her mom was there to share it. Giving the picture a solemn kiss, she walked it back to its spot and started on the homework assignment.

Downstairs, Roni hadn't let Zoey's glum face bother her or give her a case of the guilts for doing her job as a parent and trying to raise her up right, as the old folks called it. Life would hand her a lot of no's as she grew older. She wanted Zoey to get with the program now rather than later, when the consequences could prove greater. She debated whether to call Reggie and let him in on what was happening. Last thing she needed was his fussing about her having interrupted whatever he might be doing at the moment, so she opted not to. There were already enough bad feelings between them. She didn't want to add another piece of kindling to the fire, so she started on dinner instead. Her phone sounded. Caller ID showed it to be Reg. Surprised and, yes, pleased, she answered.

"Hey." She kept her tone neutral.
"Hey back. How are you?"
"I'm good. You?"
"Good, too. Conference is kinda cool."
"Nice to know."
Silence.
"How's Zoey?" he asked.
Roni told him what was going on.
"I specifically told her she shouldn't be lifting

weights. Did you put her on some kind of punishment?"

"I figured, since you were the one she disobeyed, I'd let you—"

"So I get to play the bad guy?" he demanded before she could explain fully.

She held on to her temper. "Can I finish before you rake me over the coals? Again. Please."

"Sorry." His voice was tight.

"I figured, since you were the one she disobeyed, I'd let you decide her punishment. In the meantime, I've revoked her TV privileges, which means no Danica on Friday night, and her laptop is allowed only for homework. Does that meet with your approval?" This wasn't going well.

"Yeah, it does. Sorry again."

"Thanks. And so you'll know, I called Jason today. We'll be working on the tribute CD, starting a week from today."

"But we need to discuss this first."

"Why?"

"Because of how it's going to affect Zoey."

Roni's anger flared. "Stop laying this on Zoey. It isn't fair, or the truth, and we both know it."

"Look, I'm not going to argue with you on the phone. We'll talk when I get home."

"Fine. Bye." She ended the call.

Zoey crept back up the stairs, as silent as a cat. She'd come down to ask her mom what they were having for dinner, only to be frozen in place by Mama Roni's raised voice. Torn between staying out of grown folks business and desperately wanting to eavesdrop, she now wished she'd immediately gone back to her room because she had confirmation of something she'd been speculating about all along. The mess with her parents was her fault.

CHAPTER
10

During breakfast the following morning, Zoey did her best to mask her misery. She wasn't sure what to do about the feelings pulling at her insides. Talking about it with Reverend Paula was probably the best way to go, but she wanted to talk to Crystal first.

As she put her dishes in the sink, her mom said, "Ms. Bernadine needs everybody to help Mr. Gary with getting the store ready for the opening this weekend, so I'll meet you there after school."

Zoey nodded.

Concerned, Roni asked, "Are you okay?"

"Yeah." She hoped her mom would attribute her mood to the punishment she'd been given.

Sure enough, she did. "Not going to apologize

for putting you on punishment, honey," she said quietly.

"I know."

"If I didn't love you, I'd let you raise yourself."

"I know that, too. I'm going to get my stuff and meet the boys."

"Okay."

Once Zoey had her backpack and coat, she returned to the kitchen. "I'll see you later."

"Have a good day, baby."

"You too, Mom."

As the school day began, Zoey's mood lightened a bit when she saw Wyatt enter the classroom. He smiled a greeting. She acted as if cute boys smiled her way all the time and gave him a royal nod.

After opening the day with math, Mr. James moved them on to world studies. There was a test on tap for Friday, and to prepare them, he divided the class into two teams. Amari, Zoey, Devon, and Wyatt were joined by the two Clark sisters. Crystal, Eli, Brain, and the Franklin girls, Samantha and Megan, made up the second team.

"The goal is to see how many countries you can identify in the Middle East. The winning team will get ten extra points added to their test score."

Zoey liked the sound of that. They'd been studying the history and culture of the area for the past two weeks, but she wasn't sure she knew where all the little countries were positioned.

Mr. James went to the computer and displayed a big map on the board. It had shapes but no names.

"You have fifteen minutes to confer with your team members, and then I need one person from each team to be your representative."

As Zoey's group began their huddle, Wyatt spoke up. "I know all those countries."

Everyone paused.

"My mom did two tours there. I have this big map in my bedroom with pins in every place she was stationed."

Amari asked, "Are you sure?"

"Positive."

Tiffany wasn't buying it. "He's going to mess up. He wasn't even going to our school when we started studying this."

To which Wyatt replied testily, "So what? I know what I'm talking about."

Seemingly impressed by Wyatt's comeback, Amari asked Leah, "Well, do we let the new kid represent?"

"If he says he can do it, I say let him go for it."

Tiffany remained unconvinced. "I really need those ten extra points." She was not the best student.

"So do you want to represent us instead?" Leah asked coolly.

Her sister huffed out an impatient breath that everyone took as a no.

Devon spoke up for the first time. "You sure, for real, Wyatt?"

"For real." And he looked over at Zoey. "What do you think, Zoey Raymond Chandler?"

She hadn't expected to be asked and was caught off guard. "Um. Sure. I vote yes."

And with that, Wyatt stood.

Because only a few minutes had passed, Mr. James eyed him curiously. "Your team's ready, Wyatt?"

"Yes, sir."

Crystal called out in a voice laced with irritation, "But we're not, so take a seat."

He didn't.

Pleased, Amari elbowed Leah. "I like the new kid."

Laughing, she concurred. "I do too."

Crystal's team chose Brain as their champion. Zoey was certain Wyatt would be creamed.

Mr. James opened the contest. "Wyatt, since your team was ready first, you get the first country." The map showed his stylus pointing to an island in the Persian Gulf.

"Bahrain, sir."

"Correct. Preston, your turn. Identify this country." And he moved the stylus east.

"Israel."

"Correct. Wyatt, your turn."

"Yemen." He was right again.

Amari did a fist pump. Zoey grinned.

153

Brain correctly identified Iraq.

Wyatt countered correctly with Kuwait.

Back and forth they went while their team members watched intently. Neither representative made a mistake until Brain stumbled on one of the northernmost countries. "That's, um, Armenia?" he asked.

Mr. James shook his head. "Wyatt?"

"Azerbaijan, sir."

"You're right."

His team cheered.

Wyatt grinned.

Brain's head dropped. "Man!"

"Sorry, Preston," Mr. James offered, "but our winner is Team Wyatt!"

The team erupted. Amari rushed over to give Wyatt an exuberant high five.

Devon turned to Tiff. "How you like him now?"

"Shut up."

And in Zoey's eyes Wyatt's stock soared. Cute *and* smart. Who could ask for more?

The celebration of Wyatt continued outside during lunch break. As he laughed and joked, Zoey noticed that he seemed a lot more comfortable than he had the day before, and she attributed that to everyone being so nice. Eli hadn't said a word to him yesterday, but he and his girlfriend Samantha and her BFF Megan came over and welcomed him to Jefferson Academy. Even Crystal walked to the table and declared,

"Next time, he's on my team. Brain, you're fired."

They all laughed, even Brain.

Brain looked Wyatt in the eye and held out his hand for a shake. "Good job."

Wyatt gave Brain a ritual handshake that caught everyone by surprise.

Eli asked, "You learn that on YouTube?"

Wyatt shook his head. "Grew up on the South Side."

Amari blurted out, "Of Chicago?"

"Yeah. Only White kid in my class."

That dropped jaws.

"Well, you're not the only White kid here," an amused Eli pointed out.

"Doesn't matter. I'm good either way."

Zoey saw wonder pass between Amari and Preston before Amari asked, "Got a little street in you, do you?"

"I'm just me," Wyatt replied.

Brain said, "And we like that. You wouldn't happen to be hooked on physics, would you?"

Wyatt grinned. "No. I want to be a cartographer."

"You want to make maps?" Samantha asked, sounding surprised.

"Yeah."

Zoey had no idea that was a job.

"And what do you want to be, Zoey Raymond Garland?" Wyatt asked her.

Caught off guard again, she cleared her throat,

but before she could answer, Megan said in a mincing voice, "A race car driver like Danica Patrick. How dumb is that?"

Zoey threw back, "Better than actually being so dumb your friends have to do your homework."

"Ouch!" Crystal yelped, and gave Zoey a high five. "Good one, Zo! Guess you'll stay out of other folks' business now, won't you, Megan?"

Megan stormed off angrily.

They watched her hurry back inside, and Amari offered sagely, "And she wonders why nobody likes her. You taking notes, Tiffany?"

"Shut up!"

At the end of the school day, they waved good-bye to Wyatt as he was driven away by the woman they guessed was his grandmother, a short blond lady wearing big sunglasses. They then climbed on their bikes and rode the short distance to the store. It sat across the street from the church and down a ways from the old broken-down Henry Adams hotel. It was a beautiful blue-skied afternoon, but a chill in the air let everyone know that they were experiencing the last days of autumn. Winter often came early to the plains of Kansas, and being from Miami, Zoey wasn't looking forward to the bitter cold.

When they reached the store, the parking lot was packed with the familiar vehicles belonging to the elders like Ms. Marie, Tamar, and Mr. Clay. There were also a bunch of big trucks filled with boxes of goods being unloaded onto dollies by groups of men they didn't know and wheeled toward the back doors.

Inside, "Get Ready" by the Temptations blasted through the building's sound system, while the floor was a beehive of activity, with people stocking shelves and wheeling the dollies they'd seen outside. Preston's pop was on a ladder, putting lights in the ceiling, and Amari's dad, carrying a clipboard, waved but didn't stop as he hurried off to handle whatever mission he was on. Tamar and her crew were over by the big front windows, filling balloons from a helium tank, while Ms. Bernadine and Mr. Clark stood a short distance away, consulting about who knew what. Zoey scanned the chaos for her mom and saw her loading small boxes of gum, candy, and the like in the checkout lanes where the cashiers would be. She hurried over to say hello.

"Hey, Ms. Z. How was the day?"

"Good. How was yours?"

They could barely hear each other over all the noise and the music. "Pretty good. Has Mr. Clark put you all to work yet?"

"No, not yet."

"Well, go check in with him. Lots to do. I'll see you later."

"Okay." Zoey hurried away. It was hard not to get caught up in all the excitement in the air, and although she was still concerned by her mom's phone call and hadn't yet had a chance to talk with Crystal about it, she found herself smiling as she joined the other kids.

Mr. Clark came over. "Thanks for volunteering."

Amari said, "Like we had a choice." But he was smiling.

Mr. Clark nodded understandingly. "I know you guys are probably hungry, so go out back and grab some hot dogs from Clay and Bing, then find me, and I'll put you to work."

Their eyes widened at the prospect of being fed first.

"Thanks!" Preston gushed. And off they went.

Sure enough, outside behind the store, Clay and Bing had the grill going. Zoey and her crew were given hot dogs and drinks, and once the after-school treats were consumed, they went back inside, found Mr. Clark, and were put to work.

A short time later, Crystal and Eli showed up, having driven Megan and Samantha home. Eli went off to handle his assignment in the fruit and veggie section of the store alongside his dad and Rocky, and Crystal joined Zoey putting cans on the shelves. Zoey noted that Crys had changed some since she'd come back home. She seemed more serious and hadn't been verbally smacking the boys around as much as she used to. It occurred to Zoey that maybe Crystal had enough problems of her own without having to help Zoey with hers.

"What's the matter?" Crystal asked.

She shook her head and added another can of creamed corn to her row. "Nothing."

"Quit lying. You've been sad all day."

Zoey tried to play it off with a laugh. "No, I haven't."

"Quit lying," Crystal echoed.

Zoey exhaled a sigh.

"Talk to me."

Zoey grabbed two more cans from the cardboard box and placed them with the others. "Can you be unadopted?"

"Unadopted?"

"Can your parents change their minds?"

Crys shrugged. "I suppose. Why are you asking?"

"I'm the reason my parents aren't getting along."

Crys rolled her eyes as if that was the dumbest thing she'd ever heard. "No, you aren't."

"But I am. I heard my mom say so last night."

"To whom?"

"My dad. They were yelling on the phone. Or at least Mom was, and she told Dad not to put it on me, because it wasn't true or fair."

"Then you're not the reason."

"I am," Zoey insisted. "Me making Mama Roni sing again was when this all started."

Crys shook her head. "If your mom said it's not you, then it's not you. You need to believe her." Crys viewed her closely for a moment. "You think they're going to send you back to foster care?"

She nodded.

"They're not. My mom wouldn't let that happen."

"But suppose they did. What would happen to me? Where would I live?"

"With us. With Ms. Lily. With Brain. Take your pick, but it won't matter, because it won't come to that. Your folks will work it out, and everything will be okay. I promise."

Zoey wanted to believe that, but Crys was a kid like her, even if she was older, and kids didn't know a lot when it came to adults and their thinking on stuff. She looked up to see Amari and Brain coming toward them, pulling a flatbed dolly loaded down with boxes.

"Bringing you more stock," Preston announced. He took a box filled with cans off the dolly and set it on the floor.

Whatever he said next, she didn't hear, because she was too busy staring at Wyatt Dahl and the blond woman she'd seen after school, walking down the aisle in her direction. Amari peered at Zoey's face and then back at the approaching Wyatt. "Zoey? Is there something you want to tell us?"

She turned red and concentrated on stacking cans. "No."

She missed the smile the boys and Crystal passed between themselves.

"Hey, Wyatt," Amari said.

Zoey refused to look up.

"Hey, Amari. Hey, Brain. Hey, Crystal. This is my grandma. Ms. Gemma Dahl. Gram, this is Amari, Brain and Crystal."

"Hi, everybody. Wyatt's been telling me how nice you've been to him. Thanks."

She eyed Zoey and asked, "And who's this little lady?"

Zoey's heart was beating so fast, she just knew it was going to jump out of her chest and land on the floor.

"This is Zoey Raymond Garland," Wyatt announced.

Careful not to look at Wyatt, Zoey glanced up. "Nice to meet you, ma'am."

"Same here. Wyatt said you kids were here helping at the store, and he wanted to help out, too. I'm going to be working here when the place opens."

"Glad to have you, Wyatt," Brain said.

Amari added, "You're going to learn that we get volunteered for a lot of stuff around here."

"That's okay," Wyatt replied. "Gram and I are hoping to move here, just as soon as she meets with Ms. Brown."

Zoey's furiously beating heart stopped. She looked up.

With mischief radiating from his eyes, Amari asked, "That would be real cool, wouldn't it, Zoey?"

She wanted to punch him in his chest. "Yeah."

Crystal asked, "So Wyatt, do you want to work with us, or with the boys?"

"Think I'll hang with Amari and Brain."

Mrs. Dahl said, "Good. I'll go back up front and find Mr. Clark. He said he had some paperwork for me to fill out."

So off they went.

Once she and Crystal were alone again, Crys asked, "So, Zoey. How cute is he?"

"OMG!"

Crystal's laughter echoed through the aisle, and she and the grinning Zoey went back to work.

CHAPTER
11

Bernadine was sitting in Gary Clark's office, looking over some of the store invoices, when a short blonde stuck her head in the door. "Ms. Brown?"

"Yes."

"I'm Gemma Dahl. You got a minute?"

Although Bernadine hadn't a clue as to the woman's identity, she nodded. "Sure."

"I wrote to you a few weeks ago about maybe moving to Henry Adams. My grandson Wyatt and I live in Franklin, but he's enrolled at the academy."

Bernadine placed her then. She was one of the names on the list of newcomers being considered. "Welcome. Nice to meet you."

"Same here. So have you made a decision yet?"

"Truthfully, not yet, but I should be able to tell you something soon."

"Oh, okay."

The woman's disappointment was plain, and Bernadine tried not to let that bother her. "How long have you lived in Franklin?"

"I was born there. Moved back here last year from Chicago."

"How long were you in Chicago?"

"Thirty years. You want to hear the story?"

Bernadine didn't want to be nosy, but if the woman and her grandson were going to be considered, she needed to know as much about them as possible. "Yes, I guess I do. Grab a seat."

She sat, and her story began with her finding herself pregnant at the age of seventeen. "I was young and stupid—headstrong—hardheaded, really. The guy was married, and no way was he going to leave his wife for me. My parents were so embarrassed and angry, they shipped me off to my aunt in Chicago."

She went silent for a moment. Bernadine waited for her to continue.

"After my daughter was born, my aunt let us stay with her for a few months, but she didn't have the money to take on another mouth to feed, so Gabby and I—that was my daughter's name—went on assistance and moved into subsidized housing on the South Side."

The implications of that made Bernadine whisper, "Wow."

"Yeah," she responded with a bittersweet smile. "A little white girl from Kansas living on the South Side. It was okay, though. I made some good friends, lived in a unit where folks looked out for one another, and then at sixteen, Gabby got pregnant." Gemma went quiet and stared off into the distance, as if replaying the memories. "The apple doesn't fall far from the tree, I guess," she said softly. "And I finally understood what my parents must've felt with me."

Bernadine was so grateful she hadn't had to deal with anything of that nature with Crystal—at least so far. "Are your parents still living?"

She shook her head. "Mama died nine years ago. My dad three years later."

"May I ask why you moved back?"

"Wyatt. Not sure how much you know about the gang problem in Chicago, but it's really bad.

Most of the boys he grew up with are either wearing the tats or dead. He was being pressured to join, and when he wouldn't, they started ambushing him going to school and coming home. Last year they beat him so bad he wound up in the ER. Broken arm. Stitches. I'd already lost Gabby in Afghanistan, I wasn't losing my grandson. So I moved us back here."

"How's it been?"

"A bitch."

Bernadine cocked her head.

Gemma colored up a bit. "Sorry. Too much South Side. Most of the people in Franklin knew me growing up, and to them I was just a little whore who got pregnant by a married man. As far as they're concerned, that's who I'll always be. Real sick of the whispering and nasty looks."

"Does your grandson know about any of this?"

"He knows I grew up here, but not the ugly details. I'll tell him when he's a little older. Right now, I just want him to be a kid and not have to worry about maybe catching a bullet or getting a beatdown every time he leaves the house."

Bernadine understood. Most of the Henry Adams kids had had bleak futures before their arrival. No child should have to go through what Gemma's grandson had endured. Because of the story and the sincerity she sensed, Bernadine was ready to take Gemma by the hand, give her the keys to one of the double-wides, and get her moved in in the morning.

"No idea if I can qualify for a mortgage," Gemma confessed, "but if you have a place that I can rent, I can definitely swing that. I'm going to be a cashier here when the store opens this weekend, so I do have a job."

"Good to know. Town has a few double-wides out on Tamar Jefferson's land that are empty and fully furnished. Let me know when you're ready to move in, and I'll get you the keys."

"Just like that?"

"Any warrants?"

"Nope."

"Drug use?"

"No, ma'am."

"I'm going to run a background check, because that's how I roll, but if what you've told me is true, welcome to Henry Adams, Gemma Dahl."

Gemma's lip began quivering, and the tears rolled down her perfectly made-up face. "Bless you. Oh my goodness. You've no idea how happy that makes me. Thank you," she whispered emotionally. "Wyatt really likes the school. I can't wait to tell him."

"Come by the Power Plant in the morning, and we'll get all the paper work signed."

"I will." For a moment she looked into Bernadine's eyes. "God bless you, Ms. Brown."

"Call me Bernadine, and you're welcome."

Alone again, Bernadine didn't angst over whether she'd done the right thing or not. No child should have to stare gangbangers in the face every day. Wyatt would be safe in Henry Adams, and in the end that was all that really mattered. Pleased, she went back to work.

It was well after nine at night when Bernadine finally made it home. Crystal had left the store earlier with Eli and the other kids, and was seated in the kitchen finishing up her homework when Bernadine came in the door.

"Aunt Diane's been crying."

Bernadine put her purse on the counter. "Why?"

Crystal shrugged. "When I came home, she was out on the deck, and her eyes were all red and puffy. I asked her if she was okay, but she started crying and ran to her room."

Bernadine exhaled a heavy sigh. There was no telling what might be going on. "Is she in her room now?"

"Yeah."

"Okay, thanks. Let me go see what's up."

"Good luck."

Bernadine knocked softly on the closed door. "Diane?"

"Go away!"

Because Bernadine wasn't going to beg her to open up she walked away. But before she got halfway down the hallway, she heard the door open, so she stopped and turned back. Diane looked a mess. Her face was splotchy and her eyes were just as Crystal described. Bernadine waited for her to speak.

"I called Harmon a little while ago."

"How is he?"

"That bastard's on his way to Las Vegas to get married!"

The news took Bernadine so totally by surprise, all she could say was, "Wow. Really?"

"How could he do this to me?"

Bernadine longed to answer that question with the truth, but reminded herself that she was striving to be kind, not right. Still, parts of her cheered Harmon. After being so unhappy for so many years, he'd earned the right to a new life. "Did he say who the woman is?"

"Yes. Pat. His hygienist."

Whoa! She shook her head as if in empathy. "I'm so sorry."

"No, you're not! Nobody feels sorry for me. Not you, not my kids, and definitely not Harmon."

"Regardless of our differences, I don't like seeing you in pain, Diane."

"It's Diana, dammit! How many times do I have to tell you?" She began sobbing uncontrollably, went back into her room, and slammed the door.

Bernadine folded her arms and stood there for a moment, thinking that sadly, her sister was correct. No one felt sorry for her, and until she made some changes in her attitude, it would continue to be that way. Deciding she wasn't going to let what was left of the evening be ruined, she walked back to the kitchen and looked in on Crystal before heading up to her room for a shower and a pair of comfy sweats.

She was lying in bed reading when her phone sounded. Picking it up, she was surprised to see her brother-in-law's name on the caller ID. "Hey, Harmon."

"Hey, Dina. How are you?"

"I'm fine. How about you?"

"Okay. Diane tell you?"

"Yes, she said you're getting married?"

"Yeah. Just wanted you to know that I never cheated on her. Pat's been an employee for over twenty years, and although I thought very highly of her, she and I never ever were anything but professional."

"You don't have to justify anything to me, Harmon."

"I know, but I wanted to state my case. I don't want you to think badly of me."

"Never. You put up with my sister with such grace and patience, you're a saint in my eyes. This new marriage is kind of sudden, though."

"I know, but *carpe diem.*"

Bernadine supposed he was right. *Seize the day.*

"So, how's Diana taking it?"

"Crying and playing the victim. She swore the divorce was just you having a midlife crisis and that you'd come crawling back to her with your tail between your legs. Guess not, huh?"

"No. I've had it. Too old for all her drama and craziness."

"Understandable."

"How's she treating you?"

"Badly, but I'm a big girl. I'm making her get a job, though—she needs to be able to take care of herself."

"Good for you."

"We're having an all-family gathering here in town for Thanksgiving, and I'll be inviting the kids. Don't expect you to make an appearance, though."

"No. Pat and I are moving to Florida. We may try and resurrect my practice down there. We'll have to see. I'm sure the kids will be glad to see you, though. They love you a lot."

"I love them too, and I'm wishing you and your bride well. The two of you are always welcome if you feel the need to visit, and I hope you'll stay in touch."

"Will do. Thanks for making this call so easy."

"No problem. She put you through hell, Harmon, so go on with your life and be happy."

"Always did love you, Bernadine. You're the best."

"Talk to you soon."

"Bye."

And the call ended. Was she surprised that he'd married again so quickly? Yes. Was she mad at him? No. As she'd noted earlier, he deserved some happiness, and she hoped his second marriage would give him that and more.

"So, Mom. How do you know when you like a boy?"

Roni was sitting on the edge of Zoey's bed. They were saying their good-nights. "Depends on the girl. Why? Are you liking someone?"

She nodded. "This new kid. His name's Wyatt Dahl."

"Is he nice?"

"Yes."

Roni found the dreamy voice amusing. "You're not really old enough to have gentleman callers right now."

"I know, but can he come over and watch NASCAR?"

"I suppose so, as long as it's downstairs in the living room. Can't have boys in your bedroom. Does he like NASCAR?"

She shrugged. "I don't know. He wants to be a cartographer, though. That's somebody who makes maps."

"Ah. I see."

"And he's really smart."

Roni was then treated to a telling of the

geography competition. She was impressed. "He beat Brain?"

"Yes," she replied with awe in her eyes and voice. "We were like, Whoa!"

"Where's he from?"

"Chicago. Said he was the only white kid in his class. Said he was okay with it, though. Should I be worried about that?"

Roni wasn't sure she knew how to answer what lay beneath the surface of the question. "Does your being of a different race bother you?"

"No," she said easily. "Megan said I was going to be messed up for the rest of my life living in Henry Adams with a bunch of African Americans, but nobody likes Megan."

"I'm not liking her myself. But you need to know that there are some people who'll be upset because you and your parents don't match."

"That's stupid."

"I know, but some people don't like that we don't."

Zoey went quiet for a moment as if mulling that over. "Mr. James and Rocky don't match either."

"No, but there's an old saying: 'Love is blind.' It applies to them, and to me, you, and your dad. We love you to pieces, never doubt that. Okay?"

She nodded. "Are you and Dad going to be happy again?"

Roni paused and viewed the concern in her daughter's eyes. "We will. Don't worry. Sometimes adults are like kids. We have issues, and then we work them out. Sort of like you and Devon right now."

Zoey blew out a breath. "Devon."

Roni smiled. "It'll get better. Just give it some time."

"He's making Amari crazy."

"That's what little brothers do. I wanted to bury both mine in the backyard every day when we were growing up. Made me nuts."

Roni sensed Zoey's mind was elsewhere. It reminded her a bit of what she'd sensed that morning at breakfast. "You okay, honey?"

"Yeah. Just been thinking about a lot of stuff."

"Like what?"

"Kid stuff." She changed the subject. "So you think I can ask Wyatt if he wants to come over and watch NASCAR?"

"If his parents are okay with it, so am I."

"He lives with his grandmother. His mom was a soldier. She died in Afghanistan. He said she stepped on an IED. I didn't know what that was until I looked it up."

"That's very sad. Does he have any brothers or sisters?"

"He didn't say, but I think it's just him and his grandma. Amari told him my mom died too and Devon said something stupid, but Brain smacked him down. I like having big brothers."

"Amari and Brain are great at their job."

173

She went quiet again, then asked, "Do you miss your mom?"

"I do. Very much still. I don't think we ever stop missing them."

"Me either. Your mom was a singer, right?"

"Yep, and Daddy a drummer. They toured all over the world."

"Did you miss them when they were touring?"

"Of course, but my brothers and I stayed with my grandparents when we were real young, and my gram was just so cool. She'd let us stay up late as we wanted on Friday nights. Always had ice cream in the fridge. Then once we got to be about your age, our parents would take us with them when they toured during the summers."

"I liked doing the tour with you."

"And it was awesome having you with me."

"The Eiffel Tower was sick. Especially at night."

Roni laughed. "I thought so too the first time I saw it. I was eleven. We used the word *cool* in those days, not *sick*."

Zoey didn't respond at first, but when she looked up, Roni swore she saw pain. She asked gently, "Do you want to tell me what's going on, Zoey? I can't help if you don't."

"Just wondering. What if Wyatt doesn't like me back?"

Roni knew that wasn't the truth, but she didn't press. "Are you planning on asking him to marry you?"

"No!" She laughed.

"Then how about you concentrate on being his friend? You'll have plenty of time to worry about rocking his world when it's appropriate. Okay?"

"Okay."

"Now get some sleep. School in the morning, and then the big reception for the store tomorrow afternoon."

"Do I have to go to that?"

"Not if you don't want to."

"Good. I'd rather come home instead."

"Okay, but no sneaking TV while I'm gone, because I'll know, trust me. And let's hold off on inviting Wyatt over until after you talk to your dad about the weights."

The head dropped.

"If you can't do the time, don't do the crime," Roni pointed out knowingly.

"Do you think he'll be really mad?"

"Has he ever been really mad at you, ever?"

No response.

"He might get upset like he did the time you jumped on Devon and whipped his butt, but I doubt he'll banish you to the tower."

That brought out a smile.

Roni placed a kiss on Zoey's cheek. "Sleep tight, cupcake."

"Love you, Mom."

"Love you more."

Before leaving the room, Roni looked back at

the child who held her heart. Something was going on. She just wished she knew what.

As Zoey lay in the quiet darkness, she was comforted by the soft glow of her night-lights. Then she asked herself, What ten-year-old sleeps with a stuffed tiger and night-lights? She supposed that made her a baby, but deep inside she knew she wasn't ready to part with either. She turned her mind to something more pleasant. Would Wyatt really move to town? If so, that meant she'd get to see him all the time—at the Dog, the Friday-night movies, maybe even church. She wondered what he'd think when he saw her walking in the procession, proudly holding her torch. She also wondered if he'd like OG and Tamar. Thinking of Tamar brought out the real reason she didn't want to attend the reception. She hadn't been out to check on Mr. Patterson in a few days, and she didn't know if anyone else had either, so while her mom and everyone else was at the reception, she planned to take a quick ride out to his house. She decided that leaving him a couple slices of cake was a good idea, too. He probably never got cake. Getting herself back home without getting caught was also a good idea. She snuggled closer to Tiger Tamar and closed her eyes. As she drifted off to sleep, the last conscious thought was the sound of her mother's voice: If you can't do the time, don't do the crime.

CHAPTER
12

At school the following morning, Zoey and the boys parked their bikes in the racks out front. As they walked toward the doors, Amari called to her, "Hey, Zoey, hold up. Brain and I need to talk to you for a minute."

Uncertain as to what this might be about, she slowed. Devon did too, which made his brother ask, "Is your name Zoey?"

Devon's face soured.

"Just go and let us handle our business, okay?"

It was clear Devon wanted in on whatever was about to transpire, but in the face of their twin glares, he sneered and continued on his way.

Once he was gone, she looked between Amari and Brain and asked, "What's up?"

"Crystal texted us last night about you thinking you're going back to foster care," Amari explained.

She didn't hide her displeasure.

Brain set her straight. "She told us because we're family, not to spread your business."

"Remember the first time we all got together, and the speech Tamar gave about us looking out for one another?" asked Amari.

"Yeah."

"That's what this is about."

She liked that they were concerned, but she didn't like knowing Crystal told.

"So, number one," Amari said, looking concerned. "Whatever is going on with your parents, it's not your fault. Your mom even said that, right?"

She nodded.

Brain added, "And no way is Ms. Bernadine going to let you get sent back to Miami or anyplace else. Not happening, so stop worrying. Let the adults do their thing, and you just lay low until they get it worked out. Everything'll be fine."

"And if you need somebody to talk to you, you got us, Tamar, OG, and Reverend Paula, not to mention your mom and dad. They're all straight and will tell you the same thing. Okay?"

"Okay."

Amari threw his arm around her shoulder and squeezed gently. "We're not letting nothing happen to you, girl. Remember that."

Not wanting them to see the tears of emotion in her eyes, she hastily wiped them away. Flanked by her big brothers, she walked to the doors to begin the school day.

Zoey was still concerned about her parents, however, and being sent back to foster care in Miami weighed heavily on her mind. She was also not happy with Crystal. Big sisters were supposed to hold on to secrets—at least, they did in books and in the movies. After the test, during the free hour Mr. James gave them on Fridays, Zoey went to the art room to speak with Crystal.

"Hey, Zoey."

"Hey."

"How are you?"

Zoey watched Crystal putting paint on a canvas. The image reminded her of the two-faced Roman god Janus they'd studied last spring, only the face was Crystal's. The side facing left looked like the old her, complete with the ugly blond weave. The face profiled on the right wasn't finished but appeared to be the Crystal that Zoey was talking to now, with the nice makeup and the cute haircut. "What's this?"

"The last part of my triptych for the big art show competition in LA next year. I'm calling it *Life*. What do you think?"

"I like it."

"It's not even close to being finished, but I kinda like it, too. How do you think you did on the test?"

"Think I did okay. Talked to Amari and Brain before school. Wish you hadn't told them what I told you yesterday."

The brush paused. "Did they make fun of you? Because I'm going to kill them if they did."

"No," Zoey assured her hastily. "Not at all."

179

She wanted that clear so the boys didn't reap the Wrath of Crystal.

"Good. I told them because you seemed so down, and I wanted them to tell you that we all felt the same way—you're not going back to foster care."

"But I wanted it to be just between us."

Crystal must've seen the distress she felt. "Then I apologize, Zoey. I figured we're all in this together, so we all have to have each other's backs."

"I know, but it's sorta like the night you ran away. You didn't want me to tell, so I didn't—at least not at first."

"But you didn't tell me not to tell."

"Didn't think I had to."

"Oh." Crystal looked embarrassed. "Sorry, but you need to tell me next time, okay?"

"Okay."

"And I'm sorry again. I'll keep my big fat mouth shut from now on. Don't want you to think you can't confide in me. Deal?" She extended her fist.

Zoey bumped hers gently against it. "Deal."

It was a cold day, but rather than eat lunch inside, the kids grabbed their coats, hats, and gloves and braved the weather. As they opened their bags and got set up, Wyatt announced that he and his grandmother were indeed moving to Henry

Adams and would be living in one of the double-wides on Tamar's land. That earned him a series of happy high fives and congratulatory pats on the back. "I'm not sure who Tamar is, though."

"My great-grandmother," Amari said.

"Aka She Who Must Be Obeyed," Brain threw in, grinning. "She's tough, but she's fair."

"And can be a lot of fun, when you take her shotgun away," Leah added.

"Shotgun!"

Zoey sought to reassure Wyatt. "Don't worry, she doesn't shoot kids."

"That we know of," Devon pointed out from his seat next to Zoey.

"You'll meet her at the reception," Leah said. "You are going right?"

He nodded, then asked Zoey, "Are you?"

She looked at him over the sandwich in her gloved hands. "Um, no. I'm going home after school. I'm sorta on punishment."

Every eye turned her way.

"What did you do?" Wyatt asked.

She'd confessed before thinking about the consequences, and now she was on the spot. "I was lifting weights, even though my dad said I shouldn't."

"Why were you lifting weights?" Leah asked.

She really didn't want to admit why, so she said, "It was a misunderstanding."

"Yeah, right," Devon drawled.

"I don't need to lift weights to kick your butt," she tossed back.

A chorus of *ooo*s followed that.

"You sucker-punched me," Devon said accusingly of the incident he was still trying to live down. "And I couldn't hit a girl."

"And you were screaming like a little girl when my daddy pulled me off you."

Laughter.

Seeing the surprise on Wyatt's face, it occurred to her that she might not be making the best impression, so she shut up about that and said, "Have fun at the reception." Avoiding his eyes, she went back to her sandwich.

But Devon, being Devon, wouldn't let things be. He leaned over and whispered in her ear, "You like him, don't you?"

She ignored him.

"I know you do."

"Leave me alone, Devon."

He whispered again in a singsong voice, "Zoey and Wyatt, sitting in a tree. K-I-S-S-I-N-G!"

"Amari. Get your brother."

"First came love. Then came marriage. Then came Zoey with a baby—"

She punched him so hard he fell off the bench, and when he hit the ground, she was already on him, punching and swearing and calling him names. He ducked and screamed and tried to turn himself into a ball to escape her fury, but it was too late. It all happened so fast, the other kids stared frozen, mouths open. Finally, Amari jumped up, grabbed her by the waist, and lifted her free even as her arms continued to flail like the vanes of a windmill.

"Let me go, Amari!"

Hand over his bleeding nose, Devon screamed, "I hate you, Zoey!"

"Let me go!"

Then Mr. James was there. He took in the still-flailing Zoey and Devon, crying on the ground. "What is going on?"

Amari put Zoey on her feet, but held on to her arm.

"She hit me for no reason!"

"Liar! I will kick your country butt back to Mississippi!" Anger brought out her Florida drawl.

"Zoey, quiet!" said Mr. James.

"He's a menace, Mr. James!"

Wyatt was staring her way, but she didn't care.

"Amari, let's get your brother to the bathroom and get this nosebleed stopped. Everyone else, back inside. Zoey, call your mom."

Still heaving with fury, she stormed back to the building and hoped Devon's nose bled until Christmas.

A short while later the still-angry Zoey sat with Mr. James in his office, along with her mom, Ms.

Lily, and Devon—who had toilet paper stuffed in his nose and a cold pack over his swelling eye. Neither of the moms looked pleased.

Mr. James asked, "Who started this?"

"He did!" Zoey snapped. "He was whispering some stupid rhyme about me having a baby."

Ms. Lily turned to Devon. "What?"

He wouldn't meet her eyes.

Zoey said, "He's an idiot, Ms. Lily."

"Zoey . . . ," her mom warned.

"But he is! I should sue you for sexual harassment," she told him.

Her mother said, "You know how he is. Why didn't you just ignore him?"

"I tried, but he wouldn't shut up. Idiot!"

"Stop it," her mom warned again.

Fuming, Zoey sat back against her chair.

Ms. Lily asked Devon, "What did you say to her?"

He didn't reply.

"You were brave enough to say it earlier, so let's hear it, and I do mean now."

He complied, although due to the toilet paper in his nose and the soft pitch of his voice, it was a bit hard to understand the words.

Her mom sighed. "It's just a silly old school rhyme, Zoey, not something to fight your friend over."

"The rhyme's stupid, and so is he!"

Ms. Lily asked with confusion, "Who's Wyatt?"

"A new student," Mr. James explained.

"Oh." She eyed her son and shook her head in what appeared to be disbelief.

Mr. James said, "I'm suspending them both for three days."

Neither mom appeared to have a problem with that.

Zoey didn't either. As long as she didn't have to share air with Devon July, she could be suspended for the rest of her life.

"I'll be sending your assignments home by e-mail and expect them to be turned in on time."

Zoey nodded.

"My head hurts, Mom," Devon whined.

"I'll get you something when we get home. You're going to have to stop picking at people, Devon."

"Nobody likes me."

"You think?" Zoey snapped.

Her mother's eyes flared with disapproval.

"Is there anything else, Mr. James?" Ms. Lily asked.

"No. You can take them home. Zoey, learn to control your temper."

"Yes, sir."

"And Devon?"

"Yes, sir?"

"Grow up."

"Yes, sir."

"I'll see you both after suspension."

And with that, the moms stood and took their kids home.

On the ride back to the house, Roni glanced over at her stone-faced child. "You know you were out of control, right?"

Silence.

"You and Devon used to be best buds."

"Not anymore. Can't stand him. Nobody can."

"But nobody else is punching him out, so what does that tell you?"

Silence.

"Tell you what, I want you to have a sit-down with Reverend Paula. Since you won't talk to me about what's going on with you, maybe she can help. You can't go through life knocking folks out just because they get on your nerves, Zoey. When you're an adult, they put you in jail for that."

Silence.

"So your lockdown is extended until you go back to school. No electronics. Just books. I'll send your dad a text and let him know what's going on."

"Can we just move to Paris so I never have to see Devon again?"

"No."

Zoey went up to her room, and a disappointed Roni sent Reg a text. Zoey gave Devon beat-down. Again. 3 day school suspension. *sigh* Hope you're having a good time.

He came right back at her: Again?! *sigh* Home tomorrow. See you then.

She noted he hadn't mentioned missing her, but then again, she hadn't mentioned missing him either. She ran a hand down her face. Her child was crazy. Her husband was crazy. She was crazy. Good thing she wasn't a drinking woman. She walked to the piano and took a seat on the bench. For whatever reason her fingers began playing "Stormy Weather," so she went with it and sang along.

Up in her room, Zoey was mad at the world: Devon, her mom, Mr. James, Crystal, Amari. After witnessing her actions at lunch, Wyatt probably thought she was some crazy girl, and that made her mad as well. *Why is life so hard?* For the past couple of years life had been awesome. Reverend Paula helped her talk again. She went on tour with her mom. She fell in love with cars—got to work in the garage. Now? Life sucked. She'd had to whip Devon's butt—again. People were all up in her business. Wyatt and her parents had her insides churned up. Life seemed to be raining bricks down on her head, and she felt like Dr. Bruce Banner right before he busted out of his shirt and turned into the Incredible Hulk. Maybe if she went for a ride on her bike, some of the Hulkness would go away.

She grabbed her coat and went downstairs. "Can I go ride my bike? I need air."

Her mom was seated at the piano, scoring a chart. "No."

"But, Mom, I'm going to explode."

"Go out on the deck. Plenty of air out there."

"But, Mom!"

"Or you can go back up to your room."

Zoey recognized that look. "That's not fair!"

"Keep talking, and the next time you see Danica Patrick she'll be driving a walker."

Snapping her mouth closed, she turned and ran out of the room.

"And don't slam your door!"

When Zoey reached her room, she wanted to slam the door so badly. But she was angry, not stupid, so she threw herself on the bed.

A short while later her mom came to her room. "I'm going over to the store now. Do you remember what I told you?"

"Yes," she grumbled. "No electronics. Just books."

"Good. I'll be back in a few hours."

Zoey didn't tell her to have a good time.

Standing in front of her window, she watched her mom drive off, then sat down to wait. When thirty minutes passed, she picked up her outdoor gear and got ready for her mission. She hated wearing her helmet—helmets were for babies—so she left it behind. In the kitchen, she cut a few slices of the chocolate cake she and her mom had had for dessert the day before and put them into a big Ziploc bag. Making sure she had her keys and her phone in her coat pocket, she went to the garage for her bike. Because she was at home, the ride to Mr. Patterson's would be much longer than had she been leaving from the school, but the bad day made her not care about that. She just wanted to ride, do something nice for somebody. Maybe it would make her feel better.

CHAPTER
13

At the reception, Bernadine listened as Trent greeted their guests and thanked them for coming. As always, his remarks were short and sweet, for which everyone was grateful. In attendance were local politicians, business owners, men and women of the cloth, and plain ol' everyday folks. Most were walking around the airy new store, assessing its offerings and checking out the displays of fresh vegetables, bread, and meat. Crystal and Eli were offering face painting, and there was a line of eager children waiting for their turns. Sheila and her committee had done a bang-up job of dressing up the interior with balloons and festive banners, and there was free ice cream, punch, and bite-size samples of meat and cheese from the store's deli for the guests to nibble on. Bernadine was proud to have gotten this project off the ground. With Gary's help, it was a dream come true for both the community and for the Clarks. The residents of Henry Adams now had their very own grocery store, and the recently divorced Gary and his girls had a bright future.

"This is quite a place you have here, Ms. Brown."

She turned to the speaker and plastered on a fake smile. "Hello, Mayor Wiggins. Thanks for coming." The blonde standing with him wasn't someone she'd met. From her artfully tousled hair and deep tan to her peasant-inspired white blouse and tight designer jeans, she could've just blown in from, oh, Palm Springs, but the pricey handbag was a knockoff, as was the gleaming black leather jacket lying so casually over her arm.

"Let me introduce my wife, Astrid Franklin Wiggins."

"Pleased to meet you."

"Same here." The eyes told the lie as she looked Bernadine up and down like a boxer sizing up an opponent.

Having had no idea that Wiggins was married or what his wife was about, Bernadine did her best to maintain a pleasant demeanor.

The wife glanced around critically at the goings-on, then turned back. "All the hoopla you've been causing since you came to town is making Franklin's residents somewhat jealous." There was acid hidden beneath the mild tone.

Bernadine shrugged. "Just doing what I feel is best for Henry Adams."

"My family founded Franklin, and we've always been the center of things. We built the first library and the school. Had the first gaslit house and the first telephone. Franklin money built the first municipal pool."

Bernadine wondered if she was supposed to be intimidated. "That's a lot of firsts, but where's this going, Ms. Wiggins?"

"Because of you, our people are demanding the same level of services. They want a new senior center, movies on Friday nights, a new school. New roads downtown. If Henry Adams has something, they want it to. I need you to stop throwing your money around."

Wiggins's eyes went big. "Um, honey . . ."

"Shush!" his wife snarled softly. Red-faced, he complied.

Bernadine found this very interesting. "Mrs. Wiggins, I will tell you what I told your husband last summer during the Big Box incident. This is *my* money. No one can make me spend it on what I don't want, or stop me from spending it on what I do want."

That apparently made Astrid so angry that she lost her mind. "My ancestors were founding this country when you people were shoeless and picking cotton. I will not play second fiddle to a bunch of—"

The wide-eyed Mayor Wiggins sucked in a shocked breath and grabbed his wife's arm. Bernadine gave her a crocodile's smile. "I can't believe you went there, but because you did, this is what's going to happen. The kids here want a pool, so in the spring I'm going to build the biggest, baddest swimming pool you've ever seen. It'll have diving boards and slides and all the stuff kids like—and on the day it opens, the Franklin kids will get a personal invite, so they can enjoy it, too. And every time you drive by and see it, you'll know that you and your nasty mouth are the reason it was built. Nice meeting you."

Bernadine threaded her way through the crowd to look for Mal. She was so hot she wanted to go back and sock Astrid Wiggins in her nose, but the swimming pool would put her nose out of joint in a far more powerful way, and that would have to do. What a bitch. She wanted the skinny on Astrid Franklin Wiggins and knew Mal could probably fill her in, but she hadn't seen him since the reception began. She spotted Reverend Paula and Roni by the cookie aisle. Hoping they might have seen him, she made her way over.

"He was by the meat counter when I last saw

him," Roni offered. The aftermath of the encounter with the Wigginses must have still been on her face, because Roni asked, "Are you okay, Bernadine?"

"I am. Just a little drama."

"It's not your sister, is it? How is she?"

"The drama had nothing to do with her. She's at home, doing her best impression of Blanche Dubois because her personal life is unraveling like an old sweater, and she's clinging to denial rather than dealing with it."

"I can talk to her if she wants," Paula said.

"I doubt she'll agree, but I'll let her know. Okay. Let me go find Mal. See you later."

The store would officially open in the morning, and to help make sure people returned, door prizes of gift cards were being given away. In a little while, one lucky person would receive a hundred-dollar shopping spree. Bernadine had been tapped to draw the winning entry. Until then there was Mal to find, more folks to say hello to, and little kids with ice cream cones to lighten her mood and make her smile.

Barrett stopped her. "I just escorted two under-age teens off the property."

"Shoplifting?"

"Yes, watched them slip a six-pack of beer into a backpack on the monitors. Told them next time it happens, I call the sheriff."

Bernadine approved of his largesse. "Good

to know the cameras have proven themselves already."

"Yes, it is. The fact that they're camouflaged makes people think we don't have security, and that's to our advantage."

Henry Adams was testing a new high-tech camera system that was cleverly embedded into the ceiling tiles. The company's owner was one of Barrett's marine buddies. Once again Bernadine was pleased that Barrett had discovered his niche. "Carry on, Mr. Homeland Security."

He saluted and melted back into the crowd.

She finally found Mal helping Bing and Clay stock the meat cases. He greeted her with a kiss on the cheek. "Quite a crowd you have here, Ms. Brown." He was stacking packaged hot dogs into one of the cold bins.

"This is wonderful, isn't it?" Streams of people flowed by. The store was one more item she could scratch off her Henry Adams wish list. "Tell me about Astrid Wiggins."

He studied her silently for a moment, and like Roni, he must've seen something. "What happened?"

So she told him. When she'd finished, he nodded. "Sounds like her. Family had lots of money at one time, but now, not so much. She still thinks she's queen though, and no one in Franklin blows his nose without her permission. Heads up the historical society, library board, school board. Her daddy was a vet back in the day. He handled the white farmers, and I handled our side. Pretty decent guy, died ten years ago, but his daddy—Astrid's grandfather Walter—was a real bastard. Led the Klan here. He's dead now, too. You've let folks around here know just what a tiny fish she is, and she's not liking it."

"How long have she and the mayor been married?"

"Probably fifteen years. Rumor at the time was that granddaddy paid Austin to marry her."

Her jaw dropped.

"You met her. Between her hoity-toity attitude and that horse face, not even her money could get her a man."

With her wide jaw and large teeth, Astrid did resemble a horse.

Mal stacked more hotdogs and added, "Growing up, the girls over in Franklin called her Seabiscuit behind her back."

"Wow."

"So you go ahead and build that pool. It'll make her choke half to death every time she sees it, and that'll be a good thing."

"Thanks for the history lesson."

"Always here for you."

"What are you doing after this is over?" she asked him. "Can I treat you to the movies tonight?"

"Sure. What's Tamar showing?"

"*The Princess Bride* and *The Green Pastures*."

"Okay. And after it's over, we can take the truck down to the creek and catch up on our smooching."

She laughed. "You are a mess." Her fingers went to his promise necklace hanging from its delicate chain around her neck. Since he'd presented her with it, she'd been wearing it twenty-four/seven to remind herself that she was loved by an awesome and, yes, crazy man.

Over the speaker system Gary announced more gift card winners. A squeal of delight sounded nearby. Bernadine turned to see an obviously giddy woman running toward the front of the store. Onlookers smiled.

Gary's voice came over the sound system again. "It's now time to draw for the big $100 shopping spree. If Ms. Brown would please make her way to the front of the store, we'll have her pick the winning ticket."

"Guess that's me."

"It is indeed. I'll see you in a bit."

"Love you, Mal."

"Love you too, Ms. Brown."

Everyone in the store was crowded around the area at the front of the store. Gary was standing on a large wooden crate. On the floor beside him stood Gemma Dahl, decked out in her snazzy indigo-toned employee vest. She was holding the large cardboard box that people had been putting their entries into. She gave Bernadine a smile of greeting.

"Ms. Brown, would you do the honors?" said Gary.

Gemma removed the top. Bernadine reached in, stirred the slips around, and, one hand over her eyes, drew out the winner. "Pete Bantam!"

A yell of "Yes!" shot up from the back of the crowd, and he came forward as the onlookers applauded wildly. She knew Pete. He was a pipefitter from Franklin. A big bear of a man who sported a graying waist-long ponytail, he'd worked on the Henry Adams construction crew her first summer in town. When he reached Bernadine, he gave her a huge hug and everyone cheered.

Gary said, "Mr. Bantam, you can take advantage of your prize any time in the next thirty days."

"Got three growing boys. I'll be here first thing in the morning!" he declared, to much laughter.

He moved back into the crowd, and Bernadine watched him receive a happy welcome from his wife, Maria.

Gary then announced, "Tomorrow the first one hundred people to arrive will get a chance at one of the three $50 and two $25 sprees up for grabs, so make sure you come on back."

The buzzing crowd began to disperse. Some people headed for the exits, while others who'd just arrived drifted away to check out the store.

"This was great," said Gemma. "Can't wait to start work in the morning."

Before Bernadine could respond, she saw Gemma stiffen and her eyes widen, then narrow ominously. Curious, Bernadine turned to find the root of the reaction. There stood the Wigginses. Austin was speaking with someone, but Astrid was staring daggers. "You know her?"

"Oh yeah," Gemma said in a voice tinged with bitterness.

"You sound as if there's history there."

"There is. Remember the nasty remarks and whispers I told you I was getting? Astrid is the head witch in charge. She and I have been beefing since high school. My shift's done, so I'm going to grab my coat. I'll see you in the morning."

"Okay." Gemma walked away, and Bernadine turned to Astrid, who stared back with eyes as cold as January on the plains.

Zoey finally made it to Mr. Patterson's place. Only in hindsight did she realize this had been a really bad idea. Her thighs were burning from all the pedaling, and it had taken her such a long time to get there, she just knew her mom would get back to the house first. She hopped off her bike and ran to the fence to leave the bag, then heard, "Stop right there!"

It was Mr. Patterson. He didn't have his gun, but he was walking toward her like he was really mad. Zoey straightened slowly.

"What're you doing here again, Raymond!"

Zoey was shaking so badly, it took a moment for her to form speech. "I—wanted to bring you some cake."

"Why?"

"I thought you might like some," she whispered.

"Scared of me, are you?"

She wanted to lie but couldn't. "Yes, sir."

"Good. You should be scared of people you don't know!" he barked, leaning in and yelling the last three words.

She jumped with fright.

He stuck out his hand.

Shaking, Zoey passed the bag holding the cake to him over the broken-down fence.

"Come back here, again, Raymond and I'll shoot you! Now git!"

Her tears flowed as she ran back to her bike. Jumping on, she pedaled like her life was in danger. Maybe it was. She didn't know. She'd tried to be nice to an old man, and all she'd gotten out of it was being yelled at and scared half to death. Her mom was going to be so angry when she got home and found her not there. Why was her life so awful?

Pedaling over open land now, the tears clouding

her eyes kept her from seeing well, and instead of steering around a large hole ahead, she pedaled right into it. The abrupt stop sent her flying over the bars. When she landed, her head hit the ground, and everything went black.

Roni was pulling in to her garage when her phone sounded. Seeing Tamar's name on the caller ID, she wondered what she wanted.

"Hey, Tamar."

"I'm on the way to the Hays hospital with Zoey."

Roni's heart stopped. "What! What happened?"

Tamar told her of finding the unconscious Zoey in the field near Genevieve's old place.

"Oh my god!"

"The EMTs just loaded her into the ambulance."

"Did they say it was life-threatening?"

"Looks like her arm's broken, and she's still out. That's all I know for sure."

Roni began praying. "Okay. I'm on my way!" Roaring down the driveway, she fought for calm because she'd need that to make the drive. Common sense told her to call Lily or Bernadine and have them drive, but she didn't want to waste the time it might take for them to arrive.

Praying nonstop, she blew down the street and took off toward the highway. Using the sync on her car, she put in a call to Reg and got his voice mail. Irritated, she said, "Zoey's had a bike accident and is on her way to the Hays hospital. All I know for sure is that she's unconscious and has a broken arm. Call me back ASAP."

She'd just reached the ramp to the highway when he called back. "What happened?"

"No idea. On my way to the hospital now. Tamar found her."

"Where was she?"

"Out by Genevieve's old place, for some reason."

"You didn't know she was there?"

"No, Reg, I didn't. She was supposed to be home."

"Where the hell were you—at the damn studio?"

She cut the link and ended the call. She had no time for stupidity.

CHAPTER
14

Roni rushed into the hospital's ER and was quickly escorted to one of the trauma rooms. Tamar stood when she entered, but Roni's attention went straight to her child, lying still as death against the stark white sheets on the bed. Her eyes were closed, and an IV was hooked into her left arm. She fought back tears as she approached. "Oh, baby."

Tamar said gently, "She's going to be okay. She woke up on the ride, and they gave her something for the pain. They took her straight to x-ray. Her arm's broken in a couple of places. Doc's on her way back in a few minutes to put the cast on."

Roni stroked her brow. In spite of the beefing she and Reg were doing, Roni desperately wanted him at her side. He'd know what needed to be done and if it was being done correctly.

The doctor returned and introduced herself as Malinda Tomas. "We needed your permission to go forward, so I'm glad you were able to get here so quickly, Ms. Garland."

A nurse entered and handed Roni a clipboard. After quickly reading and filling out all the forms, she signed them and handed them back to the nurse.

Her phone buzzed. It was a text message from Reg: On my way!

She was grateful.

Zoey's eyes fluttered open.

Roni whispered, "Hey, cupcake."

"I'm so sleepy."

"I know, sweetie."

"Where am I?"

"Hospital. You crashed on your bike. Tamar found you."

Tamar smiled down.

"I'm sorry," Zoey whispered.

"Go on back to sleep. We just want you to get better. Don't worry about anything else."

A lone tear slid down Zoey's cheek, and she drifted away.

Roni watched as the cast was applied.

Dr. Tomas said, "It won't hurt as much if she's asleep, so it's a good thing."

"What kind of tests have you done?"

"We've x-rayed both arms, her legs, and her spine, just to make sure nothing else is broken. We'll be monitoring her vitals for the next twenty-four hours."

"Will she be okay?"

"The next twenty-four will tell. We'll give her an MRI in the morning to check for swelling on the brain and to rule out any skull fractures. Does she have a bike helmet?"

"Yes—but she didn't have it on, I take it?"

"No," Tamar said testily.

Roni sighed in frustration.

Once the cast was complete, Dr. Tomas said, "I'm on the evening shift, so I'll be back to check on her in a bit."

"Thanks, Dr. Tomas."

"You're welcome."

Tamar held out her arms, and Roni let herself be enfolded. "It'll be okay," Tamar whispered. "It'll take more than a bike spill to take Zoey out. She's tough."

Roni agreed, but it was killing her to see her baby lying so motionless, but for the quiet rise and fall of her breath.

Tamar stepped out of the embrace. "Of course, she's earned herself some pretty serious talking-to once she's healed up."

"You got that right."

"But until then, you hang tough. Have you talked to Reg?"

"He's on his way."

"Good. I'll stay with you until he comes."

"No, it's getting late. You go on home." She'd trailed the ambulance in Olivia.

"Are you sure?"

"Yes, and thanks so much for finding her."

"You're welcome. I had the ambulance folks put her busted bike in the truck. I'll drop it off at Trent's, if you want."

"No. Hold on to it. I'll come pick it up once we get her home. She's not going to be riding it for a while."

Tamar nodded understandingly. "Okay. I'll head home. Text me in the morning and let me know how she is, and if you need anything."

"Will do. I promise."

Once alone, Roni sat next to Zoey's bed and prayed.

It was midnight when a frantic Reggie reached the hospital. A nurse took him up to Zoey's room on the third floor. Entering, he saw his wife sitting on a chair, and the pain and weariness in her eyes put a tightness in his chest.

"Hey," he said softly.

"Hey," she replied.

He walked over to the sleeping Zoey. "How's she doing?" He placed his hand on her forehead and glanced at the cast. He then checked the read-out of the machine monitoring her vitals. As a doctor he'd learned to distance himself from his patients to get the job done, but this was different. The girl lying in the bed was the daughter of his heart.

"She seems to be okay. The tests they ran don't show any other breaks or fractures. They did a preliminary scan of her skull, and it looks good, too. For once, I'm glad she's so hardheaded. They also did a scan of her spine. Dr. Tomas said they'll do some more tests in the morning, including an MRI."

"Good." He walked over to Roni so he could address the elephant in the room. "I'm sorry for the crack about the studio."

"Apology accepted." Her voice was chilly, but in truth he knew he was lucky she was speaking to him at all.

"So what was she doing out by Genevieve's when she was supposed to be at home?"

"Tamar thinks she was out checking on Mr. Patterson."

"Who's that?"

Roni told him the story and how it related to the old man Zoey and Bonnie had looked after in Miami.

He shook his head with disbelief. "First the weights, then the fight, and now this."

"I understand her wanting to check on him. We know she has a big heart, but she doesn't know him, and it's not her job. In fact, Tamar was on her way to see him when she spotted Zoey lying in the grass. Had it been an hour later, it would've been dark, and she might not have been seen until the next day." She fought back tears. "I'm torn between waking her up and telling her she's on lockdown for the rest of her life, and holding her tight and never letting her out of my sight ever again."

Reggie felt the same, and seeing Roni in pain hurt as well. "Do you want to drive home to get some sleep and come back in the morning? I can stay with her tonight."

She shook her head. "I'll be here until the doctor says she can go home."

"Then we'll stay together."

"Glad you're here."

He didn't know if she was telling the truth, but he took it on face value and settled into a chair at her side.

Zoey was released on Sunday morning. When they got her home, she was weak and still groggy from the pain meds. "Do you want me to carry you up to your room?" Reggie asked her.

"No. I can walk."

"Are you sure?"

"Yeah."

But it was a slow climb. He and Roni trailed behind to make sure she didn't pitch back down the stairs.

Once in her room, she sat down heavily on the bed. Her breathing was labored. "I think I want to go to sleep."

"Do you want help getting out of your clothes?" Roni asked.

She viewed her cast and nodded. "Daddy, can you wait outside until Mom's done helping me?"

"Absolutely." Reggie didn't balk. She was growing up. He closed the door behind him and waited until he was called.

When he returned, she was in her NASCAR pajamas and tucked in. He viewed the cast on her arm. It would take her a while to become accustomed to it, and at the moment she probably found it pretty awkward.

"How long do I have to wear this thing?"

"About six weeks."

She looked put out. "Can we wait a few days before I get yelled at?"

Both parents smiled.

"Sure can," Roni said. "You just rest up for now. There'll be plenty of yelling at the appropriate time. We're just glad you're home."

"Me, too."

It was plain that she was having difficulty keeping her eyes open, but she had one last request. "Can I have blueberry waffles when I wake up?"

"No problem," Roni said.

After receiving a kiss on the forehead from first Roni and then Reg, she was asleep before they tiptoed from the room.

Roni didn't have much of anything to say to Reggie for the rest of the day. He tried to tell himself it was okay, but truthfully it wasn't. That evening, after they shared a silent dinner, he found her seated at the piano, working on some charts. That she would be going back into the studio weighed on his mind also.

"Dads Inc. meeting tonight at Trent's. Should be back in a few hours." Reggie enjoyed the camaraderie of the men of Henry Adams and was looking forward to some chill time, if only to take his mind off the situation at home.

"Okay. Enjoy yourself. I'll keep an eye on the patient."

The eyes he looked into were distant. The doctor in him wanted to remind her to make sure Zoey received her pain meds on time and to call him if anything came up, but he knew it wasn't necessary. Saddened by the place they were in, he left her to her music.

• • •

As he descended the stairs into Trent's spacious basement, the first thing everyone wanted to know was Zoey's condition.

"She's home and resting."

"Glad Tamar found her," Mal said.

"So are we. Her arm's in a cast for the next six weeks, so fence painting is out as her punishment, but we'll come up with something. She asked if we'd put off yelling at her for a couple days. How's Devon, by the way? Roni let me know about the fight."

"Patched up, but okay," Trent replied. "I think his pride's hurt more than anything. We keep telling him to stop being such a pain in the ass. Maybe now he'll listen."

Before taking a seat, Reggie grabbed a soda and put some chips and pretzels on his plate. The meetings were usually informal, and this one was no exception. Opening remarks centered on the new store. The colonel talked about the shoplifters he'd sent packing. "I'm starting a wall of shame. It'll have all the faces of everyone caught shoplifting. Nice deterrent, I think."

Mal chuckled. "Cold, but on point."

Everyone agreed.

Gary brought Reggie up to speed on the grand opening. "It went really well. Looked like half the county showed up."

"And Amari won one of the twenty-five-dollar gift cards," Trent added.

Reggie thought that was great. "What'd he buy?"

"Chips, nachos, frozen pizzas. All the basic food groups necessary for a teenager's existence."

Jack James raised his beer. "Hear, hear!"

Reg smiled.

Trent asked, "So how was the conference?"

He shrugged. "It was okay. Didn't enjoy it like I could've, though."

"Why not?" Mal asked.

Reg sighed. "Issues with me and Roni. Is it so bad for me to admit that I want my wife to be at home and not in the studio or off gallivanting around the world?"

The men went still. Reg saw them pass looks before Mal replied, "Nothing wrong with admitting it. In fact, that's probably a good thing, but since you know that's not who she is, how are you going to deal with it?"

The colonel cracked, "Weren't you the one all up in my grill about how I was dealing with Sheila?"

Chuckles followed that, and Reg dropped his head in mock shame, then raised his soda. "Touché, Barrett."

"Just wanted clarification. Not so easy being a man of the twenty-first century, is it?"

"Not for those of us who've evolved," Jack boasted.

"Not talking to you, James."

The two men grinned at each other.

Gary got up for more munchies. "So, Reg, what're you going to do? Have you talked to her about how you feel?"

"Every time I open my mouth, something stupid comes out, so basically she's dealing with me like I'm a piece of the furniture."

"Example," said Mal.

Reg sighed. "When she called me about Zoey's accident, I asked her why she didn't know Zoey was out on her bike, and if it was because she'd been in the damn studio."

Trent shook his head. "Ouch."

Jack concurred. "Yep. Definitely stupid."

Mal asked, "What did she say?"

"Nothing. She hung up on me."

Gary winced. "Double ouch."

"Not sure how to make things better, because I was raised in a traditional household. Dad worked. Mom stayed home."

"Sorta like June Cleaver, right?" said Trent.

Reggie's face soured. He remembered the conversation they'd had on the ride to the airport.

Mal leaned over. "As I said, there's nothing wrong with admitting it. And if I remember correctly, didn't she build the studio in town as a compromise?"

211

"Yeah."

"So why are you still beefing?"

"Because I'm a man, dammit. I want it to be my way or the highway."

They laughed.

Jack said, "You're going to mess around and be on that highway, if you're not careful."

Trent asked, "Since you're being truthful, and there's only us Neanderthals here—"

Jack said, "Hey. Speak for yourself."

"Shut up, Jack," said Barrett.

Jack smiled and took a draw on his beer.

"—is that your only issue?" Trent finished.

"No."

They waited.

"She also makes a good hundred times more than what I'm pulling down in my practice."

Mal shook his head. "And Bernadine makes a million times what I'm pulling down. So what?"

"I'm the man."

Mal replied, "You keep saying that, but is that getting you any closer to resolving the problem?"

Gary said, "You'd make a mean Dr. Phil, Mal."

Jack interrupted them. "Saw an article online the other day. It said that forty percent of women in this country are the primary breadwinners, and that many men feel exactly the same way you do, Reg. But most of the comments posted in response were just the opposite. A lot of the men said they were proud of their ladies. One guy said he not only loved staying home and being with his kids, but the fact that his wife made enough money to take the family to Hawaii every year was awesome, too. All depends on how you look at it, I suppose."

"So what do I do?"

"Grow up," Mal said pointedly.

"Dad . . . ," Trent warned.

"Hey. We started this group to hang out and help one another. I'm not going to tell him to club Roni over the head until she does what he wants. Not going to happen."

"So I'm just supposed to suck it up?"

Barrett asked, "What's your alternative? You want out of your marriage?"

"Thinking about a trial separation."

Jack rolled his eyes. "I see why she's treating you like a piece of the furniture. You have a beautiful, talented woman who adores you, and you want out because she won't be June Cleaver? That's crazy, Reg."

"You asked, I answered."

"Understood and appreciated, but really? To me, that makes no sense."

"I'm not you, man."

The atmosphere in the room turned tense. Reg could tell by their faces that no one approved, and that was their choice. He stood. "Look, I need to get back and make sure Zoey's okay."

"You just got here," Trent pointed out.

"I know, but I'd only planned to stay for a few."

They all mumbled what passed for understanding, but everyone knew the deal. His abrupt departure was just an excuse to get out from under the gun.

"Talk to you all later."

On the short walk home, Reg looked up at the stars and wondered what had happened to his idyllic life. Now that he'd publicly admitted what was going on inside, he needed to find a way to get Roni to understand, though he doubted she would. All in all, he felt like a spoiled brat, pouting because he wasn't getting his way . . . and, truthfully, it wasn't who he wanted to be.

CHAPTER
15

While the residents of Henry Adams filed into the Dog for the monthly town meeting, Bernadine looked over the agenda. She had no idea how things would go when she presented her proposal for adding new residents, but she was hopeful that her neighbors would embrace her vision for the town's future.

As always folks spent the first few moments greeting one another and finding their seats. Marie Jefferson, sporting her cat-eyed glasses, stood talking with Genevieve, Clay Dobbs, and Bing Shepard, who was still getting around on a cane. The kids, led by Crystal and Eli, came in and took a booth in the back. Reverend Paula and the Paynes sat with Jack, Tamar, and Mal, while Lily and the eye-patch-wearing Devon sat at a table by themselves. Bernadine noted that the Garlands weren't in attendance. She assumed they were home, taking care of Zoey.

Once everyone was settled in with their beverages and the nibbles provided by Rocky and her assistant chef, Siz—who was sporting a new kelly-green Mohawk—Trent stood and brought the meeting to order.

"Okay. Let's get started." He turned to the first person on the agenda, Sheila Payne, who let people in on the idea of a townwide Thanksgiving celebration.

"I know that some of you may have plans to visit family elsewhere that day, but those who will be here, please join us."

"Who's cooking?" Bing asked.

"I thought maybe everyone could contribute a dish, just to keep Siz and Rocky from being too tired to enjoy themselves."

Everyone seemed to find that agreeable.

Preston stood and asked, "Can we invite our biological parents?"

The surprised-looking Sheila turned to Bernadine for an answer.

She shrugged and replied, "I've no problem with that, as long as your parents here don't mind."

Sheila said, "Preston, I think that's a marvelous idea."

Bernadine knew he'd been longing to meet his NASA scientist mom in person and that recently they'd been communicating via e-mail. She wasn't so sure about extending an invitation to his crazy grandmother, but that would be his decision to make. The kids had their heads together, and she guessed they were discussing the possible attendance of their bio parents.

Mal asked, "Are we inviting uncle Thad and the Oklahoma crew?"

Tamar replied with one word: "No." And the look on her face made it plain she had no plans to debate the issue, so Mal chuckled and didn't press. The visit by the Oklahoma clan for Trent and Lily's wedding last year had been quite memorable. Bernadine was okay with not seeing them anytime soon.

Sheila's voice brought her back to the meeting, "The Ladies Auxiliary will be handling the logistics, so please let us know by November fifteenth how many people in your family will be attending so we can plan for seating and that kind of thing. We'd like to hold the gathering here at the Dog, but if we have to move to the rec, that'll work too." She took her seat.

Next up was Gary, and he gave a quick report on the store. "Business was booming this weekend, as everyone knows, but I need to beef up the night crew janitorial staff, so if you know of anyone in need of work, have them drop by the store."

Bernadine instantly thought of her sister, who'd refused to attend the meeting. It was a good thing she'd be interviewing with Reg Garland for the assistant's position. Although janitorial work was a good and honest way to make a living, Diane would probably rather be boiled in oil than push a broom or clean toilets.

The colonel stood up next and announced the establishment of his Hall of Shame for shoplifters. Since this was the first Bernadine had heard of it, she asked, "Is that legal?"

"No idea—but if stores can post bounced checks on their walls, which I've seen, I don't see why it wouldn't be."

She thought he had a point. It would definitely make any potential thieves think twice, or at least it should. She'd have to consult with her legal people, but admittedly she liked the idea.

Barrett sat down again, and Trent asked if anyone had a concern or issue they wanted to talk about. Devon raised his hand.

"Yeah, Dev?"

"Zoey's got a broken arm. Big deal. When's she going to paint the fence?"

Boos and catcalls followed that. Trent looked as if he couldn't believe his ears. Apparently Lily had had enough. Next they knew, she had Devon by the collar and was quick-stepping him to the exit. Chuckles followed that.

"What are we going to do with him?" Trent asked no one in particular.

"Cage match," Genevieve called out, laughing. "Him and Zoey. Two out of three. My money's on Miss Miami."

Howls followed that.

Trent used his gavel to restore order. Once it was restored, there were smiles on faces all over the room. "Okay. If no else has a *legitimate* issue, I'll turn this over to Bernadine."

She stood and told them about her plans to open the town to new residents. "In order to keep this town alive, we need new residents. I know this isn't something we've discussed before, but it's vital that we do. Your thoughts?"

Marie was first. "I think it's a great idea, if only to fill up that big, beautiful school we've built. Be a sin to waste the potential there."

Bernadine saw Jack nod his head in agreement.

Clay asked, "Who's going to decide who gets in and who doesn't?"

"I figured we could form a small committee."

"Are you going to, like, advertise?" Siz asked.

"Maybe, but I already have a list of people who've written to me in the past two years, wanting in. In fact, one of them is a clerk at Gary's store. Her name's Gemma Dahl. Her grandson, Wyatt, is already enrolled at the academy. She was born in Franklin. She came back here recently to get Wyatt away from the gangs. They beat him to the point where he was hospitalized."

Wow, she saw Eli mouth.

"And I don't expect you kids to say anything about that to him, okay?"

They nodded. She could tell by their shocked faces that they hadn't known this about their new classmate. "I think she and her grandson could use a safe haven."

"Does she need help moving her stuff?" Trent asked. "The Dads can certainly help."

His offer made her heart swell with emotion and pride. "I'll ask her."

"Do you have anyone else in mind?" asked Tamar.

"I do. Crystal, will you tell us about your friends in Dallas?"

"Really?" Crys asked excitedly.

She nodded. "Go ahead."

Crys stood. "Kiki—her real name's Kelly—and her husband, Bobby, are super nice. Bobby's working two jobs and is getting his GED. They have twin babies—"

"I love babies!" Genevieve interrupted in an excited voice.

Laughter followed.

Crystal continued, "Kiki and Bobby drive this wack van that you can hear a mile away, and they live in a little bitty place with a broken window. They're on aid and food stamps. I've known them since middle school. When I told them how great Henry Adams is, they told me I was stupid for running away—which I was."

That drew smiles.

"Kelly does hair, and Bobby wants to open a business pimping cars, so he'd be perfect at the garage." She turned to Trent, who gave her an encouraging nod. "Can they please live here with us? Please?" she asked genuinely. "Oh, and Bobby has a lot of tats because he used to be a banger, but he quit all that the day Tiara and Bobby Jr. were born. That's the twins." She looked around expectantly.

Reverend Paula asked, "He's left the gangs behind?"

"Yes. He's working so hard, trying to give the twins a better life than he had. He grew up in foster care, too."

Tamar asked, "Are you sure they'd be okay moving all this way, Crystal?"

"Yes, ma'am. Positive."

"Do we want to take a vote?" said Bernadine.

Bing seemed to speak for the group. "Let's just get them up here. If they don't fit, we'll figure out what to do when the time comes, but from what

220

Crystal is saying, sounds like these young people could use a hand."

"I agree," Tamar said. And who was going to argue with the resident matriarch?

So it was decided that Henry Adams would open its arms to Crystal's friends, and that they and the Dahls would become the town's first new residents.

Crystal had tears in her eyes. "Thank you."

"Anything else, Bernadine?" said Trent.

"Only, if anyone wants to be on the committee to help me evaluate the other requests, just let me know."

And with that, Trent's gavel brought the meeting to a close.

The Garlands were indeed at home. Zoey's pain was still sharp enough that she needed her pain meds, so she'd slept away most of the day. Her injury presented a dilemma for her parents—what should they do about her punishment? As a doctor, Reggie knew happy patients healed more quickly, so he and Roni talked of rescinding her lockdown and allowing her to watch some television until she was well enough to resume serving time in the hole for the issue with the weights and visiting Mr. Patterson.

"I think that's a good idea, Reg," Roni said. "No sense punishing her at this point. She's already laid up as it is, and life's given her hard head its own special kind of smackdown."

"I agree."

"You think she's learned anything from this?"

"Who knows. We'll have to see what the future holds."

They were seated in the living room. *Monday Night Football* was on, but they weren't really paying it much attention. His use of the word *future* made her ask, "So, what about us? I can't be the girl you want me to be, Reggie," she said softly. "I'm from a family of musicians, it's in my blood. I've compromised with the studio, and it still hasn't made you happy." Her tone was statement, and not accusatory. "What else can I do?"

"Can I tell you that I liked our life better when you needed me more?"

"Yes."

"How can I say this? After the shooting, you were like this fragile little bird who needed me to hold and shelter and take care of you."

"And you helped me heal, baby. I wouldn't be whole without you, but people do heal. As a doctor, aren't you happy when your patients get well and go on with their lives?"

He looked away for a long moment, as if seeing something visible only to him. "I do, but this is different."

"How so?"

"I don't know. It is. Inside is this fear that one

day you're going to wake up, look at this short, funny-looking guy with the glasses you married, and wonder what you were thinking."

"You don't think I love you? Is that what this is about?" She found this hard to believe, but she was relieved that he'd finally opened up.

He shrugged. "I think you clung to me because you were that broken little bird, and marrying me was a comfortable choice at the time."

"Oh, Reggie, baby. No."

He held up a hand. "Hear me out, please."

She waited.

"I keep asking myself why, at the end of the day, you'd choose me. Roni, you're a beautiful, magnificent woman. You're rich, you're famous, and you could have any man in the world."

"But I chose, and continue to choose, you, Reginald Jackson Garland. You."

"I understand that, but I'm so lost right now, and yes, resentful too about your career. I have so many issues pulling at me, I think I'm losing my mind."

"So, do you want out?" she asked quietly.

He nodded. "I think so. At least for a little while."

The wind went out of her for a few moments, and her love for him keened with sorrow, but she buried that for the present and drew on the strength that was at her core so she could say without faltering, "Then go and do whatever it is

223

you need to, to realize that I love you madly and want no other man but you. Zoey and I will be here." She wondered how he could doubt how much she loved him, cared for him, needed him in her world.

He stood. She stood. He opened his arms. She went to him and let herself be held against his heart, and she held him against hers. "I love you," she whispered.

"I love you, too. I just need to sort some things out, okay?"

"No, it isn't okay, but that's how much I love you. Go to the wizard and get a brain and come back to me. You hear?"

He smiled bittersweetly. Both had tears in their eyes.

"I'm closing down my practice. I want to spend some time with my parents. I'll leave in the morning."

She wiped her tears. "Whatever you need to do."

He placed a kiss on her brow. "Thank you for being so understanding."

"It's either that or start cussing and rocking my neck, and that wouldn't help."

He chuckled softly. "No."

They studied each other for a long moment. "I do love you, Reg."

"And I do love you. I'll go up and try to explain to Zoey why I'm leaving, and say good-bye. Going to be hard." He left the room.

Roni stood in the echoing silence and prayed he'd come back to her soon.

Upstairs, Reggie tapped softly on his daughter's door.

"Come in."

"How are you, shorty?"

"I feel a thousand times better. My cast itches, though."

He walked over and took a look at it. "Your arm's healing. The itch is normal."

Zoey looked into his face and must have seen the remnants of his tears. "You're leaving, aren't you?"

Reg didn't lie. "For just a little while."

"This is all my fault! All my fault," she cried. "Please don't leave. I'll be good. I promise. I'll do everything you and Mom say."

He sat down on the bed and pulled her onto his lap. She threw her uninjured arm around his neck, and her broken sobs shattered what was left of his aching heart. "This isn't your fault, sweetheart."

"Yes, it is. I was the one who got Mama to sing again. I was the one who broke my arm because I didn't listen. I'm sorry. Please."

He rocked her while tears ran down his face. "Oh, Zoey, don't cry."

"I'll be good. I will. I promise. Please!"

Reggie looked over and saw Roni standing in the doorway, her face wet with tears. He turned back to his child. "Zoey, this is something I have to do so that we can be a family again. Please don't cry. I'm coming back. I promise."

"No, you aren't. You're going to be gone forever, just like Leah's mom."

"No, I won't."

"Yes, you will. Mom, please make him stay!"

"I wish I could, cupcake, but I can't."

"Then send me back to foster care so you can be happy again," she pleaded. "I'll be okay."

He saw Roni's hand fly to her mouth in horror. He felt the same. Was this the price he had to pay? Would the end result be worth—this? "Zoey, listen. No one's sending you anywhere. I love you, and I love your mom. I just need a time-out to clear my head, that's all."

She snapped fiercely, "You're never coming back. Never." Freeing herself from his arms, she scrambled off the bed and ran to Roni, pressed her face against her, and wept inconsolably. The look in his wife's eyes seemed to mirror the question he'd asked himself: Is it worth—this?

And in his heart he knew it was. If he didn't figure things out, he would be gone forever, and their world would never be the same. Rising from the bed, he walked out.

The following morning, he called Nathan for a ride to the airport. Neither Roni nor Zoey came downstairs to see him off, and he supposed that was as it should be. He felt bad about closing the clinic, but it couldn't be helped. The kids in the area could go back to the clinic in Hays for treatment like before. The reality of leaving felt no better than it had last night. If anything, he felt worse, and he supposed that was as it should be, too.

When Nathan pulled the town car into the drive, Reg took one last look around the house that had come to be home. Standing there, he listened, hoping to hear Roni or Zoey moving around upstairs, but only silence returned. Drawing in a deep breath, he rolled his suitcase to the door.

Nathan put the case in the trunk. Reg looked up to the bedroom windows and saw Zoey framed by her drapes. She resembled a little ghost. He waved. She didn't respond. Filled with the pain of her rejection, he looked away. When he raised his eyes to her window again, she was gone. Feeling like hell, he got in the car, and Nathan drove him away.

Upstairs, Roni answered the soft knock on her door.

"Come on in, baby."

"Dad's gone."

Roni was sitting up in bed. "I know." She patted the bed, and Zoey walked over and sat beside her. Roni drew her close.

"He waved but I was too sad, so I didn't wave back. Was that bad?"

"I didn't want to get up and see him go either, so we're in the same boat, I suppose."

"Is he really coming back?"

"He says he is."

"Do you believe him?"

"Until he tells me something different, I have to, but you and I are going to be okay."

"I'm going to be sad the whole time he's gone."

"Me, too."

"I wanted him to stay."

"So do I, but if he says he needs time away, we have to love him enough to allow him to do that."

"Are you going to go back into the studio?"

"Yes, but not until you get the okay to go back to school. One of us has to pay the bills around here, and the state of Kansas says you're too young to work."

She smiled, and that made Roni feel better. "And honey, it's okay to be mad and sad and feel a little lost. This has rocked our world, and we're in unchartered territory."

"Sorta like *Star Trek*."

Roni laughed. "I guess you can look at it that way. What would Captain Kirk say?"

"Shields!"

"Then we'll put up our shields and keep it moving."

"Aye, Captain."

"And Zoey. You are never going back into foster care—ever, okay?"

She nodded. "Can we have blueberry waffles?"

"Sure can."

CHAPTER
16

Henry Adams was both rocked and saddened by the news of the Garland separation. Everyone knew Reg had been brooding for quite some time, but no one believed he'd actually leave. The day after his departure, Bernadine spent the morning on the phone trying to find a doctor to replace him, if only temporarily. She was admittedly irritated that he'd left town without making arrangements. Then again, he probably had other things on his mind, like the fractured state of his marriage, she told herself, so she cut him some slack.

When she spoke with Roni the day he left, she seemed to have reconciled herself to the situation and was determined to make life as normal for Zoey as possible. Zoey would also be visiting Paula for counseling on a regular basis for the next little while, in the hope that their talks would aid her in coping with the abrupt change in her life, and managing her anger.

Another problem for Bernadine was that Reg's leaving also snatched the rug from beneath Diane's chance of securing a job. Since learning of Harmon's plans to remarry, Diane had spent the majority of her time sequestered in her room. The few times she had let herself be seen, she wore the look of a woman devastated by the hand she'd been dealt by life. Bernadine could sympathize. When she'd walked in on Leo and his secretary that day in his office, she'd been knocked to her knees, but she'd gotten up and laced on her boxing gloves. Granted, Harmon hadn't committed adultery, but it had to be hard for her sister, knowing he'd remarried before the ink on the divorce decree had a chance to dry. However, she couldn't wallow forever, at least not on Bernadine's dime. She needed a job.

"So what's up, baby girl? Why so glum?" Mal asked as he slipped into the booth she was sitting in.

Bernadine had come down to the Dog to get some time away from the office and to think. As always, no matter the situation, circumstances, or time of day, Mal lifted her spirits.

"Trying to imagine how much of a fit Diane's going to throw when I tell her the only jobs in town are on the janitorial staff at the store."

"It's an honest living. Folks have put their

230

kids through school with mops and brooms."

"Agreed, but she thinks of herself as way too special for that."

"Hard to call yourself special when you're flat broke."

She raised her cup to her lips. "I know. She was supposed to be talking to Reg Garland about an assistant's position at the clinic, but now?"

"Any luck with finding a replacement for him?"

"Not so far. For the time being, the kids will have to use the clinic in Hays. I really wish he'd made some arrangements, but it probably wasn't a priority at the time."

"Probably not. Hope they work it out. I like them both."

She agreed.

"So what are you going to do about your sister?"

"Lay it out for her and see what she decides to do. Letting her just sit around watching the judge shows all day is not going to happen. She can either go see Gary or move elsewhere. My name is not Bernadine Enabler Brown."

His mustache lifted with his smile.

She drained the last of her coffee and set the cup down. "Well, no sense in delaying this any longer. I'm going to swing by home and let her know her appointment is at two today."

"Good luck."

"Thanks."

When she arrived, she found Diane lounging on the living room couch in sweats and slippers, watching *Judge Judy*. Upon seeing Bernadine, she jumped. Guilt filled her face. "What're you doing home so early?"

"Came to drive you to your job interview."

"The one with the doctor?"

"No. He's had to close down his practice temporarily. The interview is with Gary Clark over at the grocery store."

She cocked her head. "Grocery store?"

"Yes. It's the only job available at the moment, so you need to apply."

She shook her head. "No, I don't think I'd like doing something like that," she said, and went back to watching *Judge Judy*.

Holding on to her temper, Bernadine very calmly walked over to the remote, picked it up, and pressed POWER.

"Hey!"

"Either you speak with Gary, or you move out. Those are your choices."

"Some choice," she grumbled. "What job am I applying for?"

"Janitorial. Night shift."

She laughed. "Oh, you got me that time, Bernie. Janitorial. Good one."

"Do you see me laughing?"

In the silence Diane searched her stony features. "You. Are. Kidding."

"No. I'm. Not."

She sprang to her feet. "You can't possibly expect me to work as a janitor!"

"Do you have another option?"

"Of course not. There are no jobs in this depressing little place."

"Then you interview this afternoon, or move on."

"You hate me that much," Diane replied knowingly, shaking her head with disgust. "Mama's probably spinning in her grave knowing—"

"Don't you dare say a word to me about Mama!" Bernadine stormed. "Ms. I'm Too Busy to See Her on Her Death Bed!"

Diane folded her arms and stared off into the distance.

Bernadine took in a few calming breaths to counteract the seething canyon fire burning inside. "So, what are you going to do?"

"You love my being in this position, don't you?"

"Cut the crap. Decide."

"I'll do the interview. Happy?"

Bernadine wanted to shake her.

"Of course there's no guarantee he'll actually hire me," Diane pointed out smugly.

"Then you'd better give him the best damn interview he's ever seen, because if you don't get the job, I will personally pack your stuff and put it out on the street."

Diane's eyes widened, but Bernadine had nothing else to relay. She left her staring and speechless sister standing in the living room.

Shortly before two, Diane made her appearance. Decked out in leather and full makeup she was way overdressed. Apparently seeing that in Bernadine's face, she explained, "I'm wearing this because I want him to know that if he has a job available in his office I can dress the part."

"There aren't any other jobs."

"We'll see."

Bernadine sighed tiredly. "Let's go."

Like most kids, Zoey always dreamed of not having to go to school, but the reality left a lot to be desired. First of all, due to the injuries from the bike wreck, she was supposed to be taking things easy, so between that and the pain meds, which kept putting her to sleep, she'd spent most of the time in bed, which meant she had all day to think about her dad, and where he might be, what he might be doing, and whether he missed her and her mom. Were she in school, she'd be too busy doing work to be so worried and sad.

Crystal had come to see her after dinner yesterday, and the boys had, too. They knew about her parents getting separated and told her everything would be okay, but having her business in the street and wanting to scream that nothing would be okay again left her embarrassed and angry. At least Devon had the sense to stay away. When she went back to school, if he had one smart thing to say about what was happening in her family, she'd knock him into next week. Guaranteed. She didn't care if Mr. James suspended her for the rest of her life. In fact, she owed him another pounding anyway. Amari told her what he'd said at the town meeting about her painting the fence. She supposed he'd conveniently forgotten who stood up to the adults last year to help him paint it when he was busted for stealing money.

The pain meds she'd been given with some juice a short while ago were making her woozy, so she snuggled beneath the covers and let them carry her into sleep.

In her dream she was walking down Main Street. She knew she was in Henry Adams, but some of the places looked like Miami. She saw Reverend Paula's old church and the place beneath the highway where she and her mother Bonnie used to live. Up ahead by the Power Plant, she spotted her dad. He waved at her to join him, but then for reasons unknown he started running away. She ran after him, calling for him to stop and wait for her, but he kept getting farther and farther away. Soon she was in the open field near Ms. Genevieve's place. She could see her dad running toward the horizon, and then the dream shifted. She was back under the highway.

The place looked just as it had on her last day there. The old bare mattress where she slept was in its spot, and beside it the big brown shopping bags that held her and her mom's stuff. Cars sped by overhead, and there in the shadows lay something that made her scared. Newspapers, just like the ones she'd placed over Bonnie's corpse, were covering something. She didn't want to look at whatever they were shrouding, but she couldn't make herself stop walking toward it. Kneeling down, her hand shook as she moved the paper aside, and there lay Mr. Patterson. He was dead. His shotgun was across his chest. Then the rats came. Thousands of them. They were big and made of gold and had sharp gold teeth. They jumped on him and began feeding. She grabbed the gun and tried to beat them back, but there were too many. When they turned on her and knocked her down, she woke up screaming.

Then her mom was there. "Zoey! What's wrong? Are you okay? I could hear you screaming from downstairs."

Still shaking with fear, Zoey said, "The rats! They came back!" Another part of the dream floated to the surface, and she went still. "Mr. Patterson's dead!"

Her mom's soft hand brushed the sweaty hair away from her face. "Sweetie, you just had a bad dream. Remember the doctor said the meds could have that effect?"

"No, Mom, he's dead! The rats were eating him, then they jumped on me. Please call Tamar. Please!"

"Okay. Calm down, honey."

"No, no. She needs to go to his house."

"Okay, okay. I'll call her. Take a deep breath."

"Hurry, Mom!"

"Let me get you some water—"

"No! Call Tamar!" Zoey felt hot tears running down her cheeks.

Her mom pulled out her phone and went out into the hallway to make the call. Shaking, Zoey fell back against the pillows.

Her mom came back into the bedroom. "Tamar's at the rec, but she's on her way there."

"Thank you."

"So, do you want to tell me about the dream?"

"Dad was in it. He was running, and I was trying to catch up, but he kept running faster. Then he disappeared, and I was back in Miami in the place where my mom and I used to sleep at night. And Mr. Patterson was laying beneath a bunch of newspaper, then these rats showed up, and they were made out of gold."

"Gold rats?"

"Yeah."

"No idea what that means."

"Me neither, but I was so scared."

She was pulled close by her mom, who also placed a kiss on her forehead. "You're safe now."

But she wasn't safe from the awful memories. "They had big, sharp teeth, and they were huge. I don't want to take that medicine anymore if it makes me have dreams like that." Zoey hated that she was so scared, but she couldn't help it.

"I'll talk to the doctor and see what she says. Maybe she can prescribe something different."

Zoey hoped so. "Did Tamar say she'd call you back?"

"She did. While we wait, are you hungry? You want something to eat?"

"No. I just want to wait for Tamar to call back. You can go back to doing what you were doing. I'm okay now."

"You sure?"

She nodded.

"Okay. I'll let you know what Tamar says when she calls."

Her mom left the room, and Zoey took in a deep breath in an effort to rid herself of the terrifying dream before settling back to wait.

Bernadine dropped her overdressed sister off at the store for her interview and was on her way back to the Power Plant when Tamar's voice came over her sync. "Bernadine, are you in the office?"

"Nope, but on the way there. What's up?"

"I need you to swing by Roni's first."

"Something happen? She okay?"

"She and Zoey are fine. Cephus Patterson passed away at some point in the past twelve hours."

She wondered what this had to do with dropping by Roni's place. "Sorry to hear about his passing, but what's this got to do with Roni?"

"Just stop by Roni's. Something here you need to see."

"What is it?"

But Tamar was gone.

Sighing because this was Henry Adams, and lord knew what this was about, Bernadine turned Baby toward the subdivision.

Roni answered the door. "Hey. Thanks for coming. You're not going to believe this. Come with me."

Roni led her upstairs to Zoey's bedroom. She expected to see Zoey in bed, but not with her lap covered by a pile of gold coins.

Zoey's eyes flashed excitedly. "How sick is this, Ms. Bernadine? There's two hundred and fifty of them. I counted them. Aren't they beautiful? I think this is why all the rats were made out of gold."

Having no idea what that meant, she asked, "Where'd they come from?"

"Mr. Patterson."

Bernadine walked over to the bed and picked

one up. On one side of the coin there was a woman wearing a coronet. On the verso side was a fancy eagle. "They aren't real, are they?"

Tamar said, "I think they are."

Bernadine was so confused, her head was beginning to spin.

"They're double eagles," Tamar added. "I was going through Cephas's things to see if he had a suit to be buried in, and this saddlebag was on his kitchen table." She handed Bernadine a bag similar to the ones used by the cowboys in the Hollywood westerns her daddy always enjoyed. It was old, though—from the crisp feel of the dried-out black leather, very old.

"This was inside." Tamar held up a cellophane bag yellowed with age. "And in the cellophane was this—"

Bernadine took the folded newspaper from Tamar's hand. The banner read "Nicodemus Cyclone." That she was holding an original Exoduster newspaper was enough to add to her swoon, and the date beneath the banner almost made her faint. "Eighteen eighty-five!"

Roni chuckled. "And as they say on the television game shows, There's more! Take a look at the story at the top of the page, and at the drawing with it."

Bernadine read aloud: "Colorful outlaw Griffin Blake"—she glanced down at the ink drawing of a man wearing a weathered cowboy hat, then resumed reading—"also known as Kansas Red, Oklahoma Red, and a slew of other aliases too numerous for this journalist to recount—has struck again. His latest victim, the Kansas Pacific Railroad."

The article went on to say that Blake made off with a mine company's payroll worth $5,000 in gold. Speechless, she looked at the gold again.

Zoey smiled. "Awesome, right? Tamar said the Henry Adams gold was just an old myth. Guess not." Using her good hand, she threw a handful of coins in the air. "Ms. Bernadine, do you know anyone selling a go-kart track? Because I want to buy one, if this is enough money."

The request drew Bernadine up straight. Staring at Zoey and then the gold, she put one and one together and almost had a heart attack for real. "He left all this gold to you?"

"Yep," she replied proudly.

Bernadine's eyes widened.

Zoey continued, "Tamar said there was a note taped to that saddlebag. It had 'For Raymond' written on it."

"Raymond?"

"He thought that was my name."

"Okay, I need to sit down."

Roni dragged over a chair. Bernadine sat, set her purse down, and peered quizzically at Zoey's beaming face. She had so many questions she wasn't sure where to begin, so she started with the obvious. "Why'd he leave the gold to you?"

She shrugged her thin shoulders beneath her NASCAR pajamas. "Maybe because I took him some cake."

"Cake?"

She nodded. "The first time I left him an apple."

Roni suddenly interrupted, "Wait. Hold up. Are you saying that last Friday, when you had the accident, wasn't the first time you'd been out there?"

Zoey's eyes dropped to her lap.

"How many times?" her mother asked.

"Twice," she confessed softly.

"And this first time was?"

"Early last week."

Tamar asked, "What did I tell you about visiting him?"

That garnered a whispery, "Not to."

"Was I speaking German or French or Ibo?"

"No, ma'am," she said, smiling, but the censure in Tamar's eyes erased that immediately.

"Just checking," Tamar replied.

Bernadine now had a clearer explanation of Zoey's role, but not Patterson's. "Where'd he get the gold?"

"No idea," Tamar admitted. "Maybe he dug it up while putting in fence posts—who knows? But he's been ranting for decades about keeping folks away from it. We've all heard the rumors

242

about Griffin Blake supposedly burying the gold here somewhere, but I never believed it."

"Can I keep it?" Zoey asked.

Bernadine responded honestly, "I don't know. I'll have to make some calls, but in the meantime it needs to be in a safe place. Was anyone with you when you found the bag, Tamar?"

"Just Trent and Mal."

"Roni, do you have a safe?"

"No."

"I have one at the Power Plant, but if word gets out about the gold, everyone and their mama is going to storm the place."

"I can put it in my safe," Tamar offered. "Shotguns tend to discourage everyone and their mamas."

Bernadine thought that was a good idea. "Zoey, let's get your coins in a box or something so Tamar can take it with her."

Zoey looked disappointed.

Roni produced a small tablecloth and a box. The coins were placed in the cloth, the cloth in the box, and then the box was given to Tamar.

Bernadine took in Zoey's despondent face and promised, "I'll let you and your mom know as soon as possible about whether you can keep it."

"Okay," she said gloomily.

"Cheer up. You have a fifty-fifty chance."

"I guess."

Roni walked them back down the stairs. "This is nuts," she said. "I can't imagine how much it's worth."

"I can't either, but I'm sure my friend Tina will know." Tina Craig was the financial adviser for the Bottom Women's Society.

"I'll take this and lock it up good and tight," Tamar said.

"Thanks."

As Bernadine got into her truck and drove back to see if Diane had finished her interview, she thought about some of the jaw-dropping things that had happened in Henry Adams during her reign: Crystal's kidnapping; the visit by the outrageous Oklahoma Julys; Riley Curry and his hog Cletus going on the lam after the death of Morton Prell and subsequent court trial that past summer. She decided that Zoey being presented with Griffin Blake's gold had to be near the top of the list.

When she reached the grocery store, Diane was standing out front. Bernadine hoped the interview had gone well. "So?" she asked once her sister was in the passenger seat.

"I got the job. Happy?"

"Doesn't matter. When do you start?"

"Tonight at ten. I get off at six a.m. Any idea how I'm supposed to get there and back?"

"We can go look at some cars tomorrow if you

244

want, but I'll drive you tonight and pick you up in the morning."

"And how am I supposed to buy this car?"

"I'll make the purchase. You pay me back."

"Oh."

"And once you get a couple of paychecks under your belt, you can find a place to stay."

Silence.

Bernadine said into the breach, "You can't stay with me for the rest of your life, and I'd think you wouldn't want to."

"Believe me, I don't."

"Then good. We agree."

"Isn't that house across the street from you empty?"

"For now, yes, but someone will be moving in in a few days. You may be able to take one of the trailers out by Tamar." She wanted that house to go to Gemma and Wyatt, so he could bond with the kids.

"I'm not living in a trailer."

Bernadine glanced over, saw the mutinous face, and wanted to remind Diane that she didn't have a pot to piss in nor a window to throw it out of, as the old folks used to say, but she kept it to herself. Silence reigned for the rest of the drive home.

CHAPTER 17

Reggie flew to Charleston, South Carolina. His parents lived on the outskirts of the city, but he checked into a hotel to give himself a few days of time alone. He needed to think.

With his room secured, he drove his rental car down to the Battery, famous for its restored antebellum mansions overlooking Charleston's bay. He found a place to park and took a slow walk along the promenade that ran along the seawall. On weekends the area teemed with tourists and locals jogging, pushing strollers, and walking dogs, but at midafternoon on a workday he had the area pretty much to himself. The chilly gray day mirrored his mood. A strong breeze ruffled his jacket and stirred up white caps of foam on the waves. He found it somewhat ironic that he was standing in the spot where the Civil War began. South Carolinians had been willing to fracture the Union to preserve their way of life, and in some ways his leaving Henry Adams mimicked that notion. In truth, his quest was proving just as futile as the Confederacy's had been.

Looking up, he tracked the flight of two gulls

soaring high overhead, and as he stood there, with the sounds and sights of the crashing waves, myriad voices played in his head: Mal, bluntly suggesting he grow up; Roni, telling him to see the wizard for a brain; but mostly it was Zoey's pain-filled cries, begging him to stay. Hearing her pleading to be sent back to foster care for the sake of her parents' love was horrifying. He drew a weary hand down his face and wished he could prescribe himself something to help him get over himself and be content. But he wasn't, and that was the problem. He wasn't content with his response to Roni's career any more than he was content with what his stance on the matter had wrought. He mulled over his dilemma for quite a while, then walked back to the car.

The next morning his mother answered the doorbell.

"Reggie!" Enveloping him in an exuberant hug, she placed a kiss on his cheek. "What a surprise. So good to see you! Come on in. Your father's at the hardware store and should be back in a few minutes. I'm baking cookies for the reverend. His reward for giving a short sermon on Sunday."

Laughing, he followed her into the kitchen and, yes, fresh-baked Toll House cookies were cooling atop racks on the countertop, their mouth-watering fragrance filling the air. She was wearing jeans and a T-shirt sporting the name of her church. To him she'd only aged maybe one minute since he'd seen her this past summer. Her coffee-brown face bore the soft lines of a woman approaching seventy, but the eyes were still as sharp as they'd always been. "How're my girls?" she asked. "And how dare you visit without them."

He stopped.

She must've have seen something in his face. "Please tell me you aren't divorcing."

"No. I just need some time away to think."

She didn't hide her skepticism. "About what?"

He sat. "I don't know, Ma. I thought I was happy with her going back into the business, but truthfully, I'm not."

They took seats at the kitchen table.

"That makes me an unenlightened man, I guess, but a part of me wants her at home—not criss-crossing the globe or spending all her time in the studio."

"You're not proud of all the strides she's made since the shooting?"

"I am, but—"

Her voice turned soft. "But what? You really want to deny the world the gift she's been given?"

"No, but what about her responsibilities at home and to Zoey?"

"If my granddaughter were a newborn or a toddler, I'd have to agree, but Zoey's ten, and lord knows she isn't helpless. She can help make dinner when Roni's away, and she's old enough to clean up after herself and do her own laundry, if it comes down to that. Is she upset about Roni's career, too?"

He shook his head.

"So this is just you."

"Yeah."

"Then let me be honest. I'm so proud of Roni I can't stand it. After witnessing all that violence, if it had been me, I'm not sure I'd've ever found the strength to go back out on a stage again. But she has. She did. That's something to celebrate. Nothing about her says Suzy Homemaker, Reggie."

"I know, but is it wrong for me to want her to be that?"

"Of course not, but you need to come down from Planet Ideal and live here with the rest of us on Planet Real Life. Roni is who she is. Just like I am who I am. I love being June Cleaver and Donna Reed. In fact, the reason I went to college was to get my MRS."

"What?"

She nodded. "I had no desire at all to enter the workplace. Your grandmother worked her fingers until they bled raising four girls alone, and her goal was to send me and my sisters to college so we could marry well and not have to work from dawn to dark, or as the old folks used to call it, from no light to no light, the way she did."

"Mom, I don't believe that."

"Why not?" she asked, sounding amused. "All I ever wanted was to marry a man who adored me, keep his house, and have his sons. And your daddy was nice enough to play along."

Reggie didn't know what to say.

"God gave Roni work to do, and as her biggest fan, I need you to chill. She'd never be happy being me, Reg. You know who Dear Abby was, right?"

He nodded, not sure how this tied in to the conversation, and waited for her to explain.

"I read her every day while growing up, and when people wrote to her to ask if they should get divorced, she told them to ask themselves this: Are you better off with them or without them? So you, my eldest son, need to ask yourself the same. Are you better with Roni or without her?"

"With."

"Exactly."

The timer went off on the oven, and she left the table to grab a potholder and take out the last baking sheet holding the reverend's now done cookies. Reggie watched her use the spatula to lift each one off the sheet and place it gently on the rack to cool. "Can I ask you a personal question?" he said to her.

"Sure."

"Did you love Dad when you two got married?"

"Honestly? No, not at first. In fact, when we

first hooked up, I barely knew him, but what I did know, I liked."

"What do you mean?"

"While the rest of us were raising our fists and taking over campus buildings, your father was in class. When everyone was partying on weekends, he was at the library. He stood out for that. That and the fact that he was on the dean's list. I thought he'd make a good husband and a good provider, so I checked him out. He was funny, smart, and charming. The love came much later, but it didn't stop us from having fun or pulling together as we made our way. Now he's my world, and I know I'm his." She glanced his way and said sincerely, "That you and Roni love each other and always have is something special, Reggie. Don't screw it up by trying to fit her into a box. *Carpe diem*, because not many couples have what you have with that beautiful wife of yours."

He sighed audibly.

"Not what you thought you'd hear?"

"No."

"It's a mama's job to tell you the truth, even when you don't want to hear it."

He chuckled. "I guess." He looked over at the amazing woman who'd raised him, and realized he'd learned more about her in the past few minutes than he had his entire life growing up. Every kid he knew wanted her to be their mom because no matter what he or his brothers were into, she was there: field trips, science projects, making costumes for Halloween, den mother, after-school chauffeur . . . and no one could bless out an umpire better or more colorfully than Jasmine Rochelle Garland.

"Remember the time you were kicked out of Drew's high school baseball game?" he said. Drew, named for the Dallas Cowboys star receiver Drew Pearson, was Reggie's middle brother.

"Yes, and I still say that ump went to the Ray Charles School of Umpiring. I was right behind the plate, and your brother threw a strike."

Drew was on the mound with the bases loaded, thanks to an error by his left fielder. There were two outs. The count on the batter in the box was three and two. Drew threw the pitch. The ump called a ball, walking in the man on third, and their mom, who lived and breathed sports, went ballistic. You'd've thought she was the coach, the way she jumped down from the stands and got in the ump's face. The crowd went nuts. The ump threw her out. Reggie's dad very calmly picked her up and carried her off the field while she kicked and yelled the entire way. She was banned from games for the rest of the year.

Hearing the front door close, Reggie looked up and smiled as his dad entered the kitchen. Charlie Garland was approaching seventy, but like his wife, he wore his age well. When he saw Reggie, his face lit up with surprise. "What are you doing here, Doc?"

They shared an embrace. "Thought I'd pay you a visit. Make sure you weren't causing trouble."

"Now, you know your mama's the only trouble-maker in this family. Speaking of family, where's my songbird and my baby bird?"

"They're at home."

"She hasn't kicked you out, has she?" he asked, laughing.

When Reg went quiet, his dad said, "Aw hell. What happened?"

His mother interrupted them. "I'm due at the library for a board meeting." She kissed her husband on the cheek. "You two visit. I'll be back later—and Charlie, remember what the doctor said about you and sweets. One cookie, okay?"

He chuckled. "Yeah, right. I won't eat a dozen. That's all I'll promise. You go on so me and the doc can have our man time."

She rolled her eyes. "Reg, are you staying for dinner?"

"If you'll have me."

"Good. See you later."

Once she was gone, his dad grabbed three cookies. "Come on out to the garage. You talk and I can load up the truck."

On the way, Reg asked, "What're you working on?" His father had been building houses for as long as Reg was alive. Drew was also an architect and builder. Baby brother Isaac, named by their mom for All-Pro running back Isaac Curtis, was a hotshot landscaper.

"Driving down to Pin Point in the morning to help your brother with some Habitat houses he and his crew are putting up. Ike promised to fly in, but when he checked with Candi, she told him he had a wedding to attend and couldn't come."

Ike was married to a witch of a woman no one in the family could abide, not even Ike, to be truthful, but they'd been man and wife for five years. "Why doesn't he just divorce her?"

"Because she's the most beautiful woman this side of the Mississippi—outside of your mother, of course."

The garage, although orderly and neat, was filled with the tools of his father's trade. Table saws, levels, hammers, lengths of stacked wood —if a carpenter or builder used it, his father owned at least two.

His father leaned against his well-used and well-loved truck and munched on his second cookie. "Your mother and I have bets on how long it'll take Ike to wake up and kick Candi to the curb. Now, Drew and his dynamic Darlene will probably be married till an asteroid takes out the earth."

Reg laughed softly.

"Not sure why, but we Garland men seem to attract gorgeous women, and in your brother's case that initially blinded him to that girl's obvious faults. I mean, look at us. None of us would qualify to be heroes in those romance novels your mother's always reading—we're short, squat, and if you take away our glasses we'd be lost for the rest of our lives. We're not handsome men."

Reggie had to agree.

"But you married Roni, who is as fine as that voice of hers, and your mother? Goodness. The day she walked up to me on campus and asked if I'd marry her, I thought I was going to have a heart attack and drop dead right there at her feet."

"She asked you?"

"Yeah. Craziest damn thing that ever happened to me. I thought I was being—what do the kids call it today?"

"Punked?"

"Yeah, punked. I just knew the frat boys had put her up to it, or that I was on *Candid Camera*."

"But you weren't."

"No. She was sincere, and what was a boy like me supposed to do? Say no? She was a tall, leggy sorority goddess. A campus beauty. Even her name was beautiful. Jasmine." He chuckled as he appeared to think back. "My mother—your grandmother—wanted to know if something was wrong with Jas. 'Why would a girl like that want to marry into our family?' she asked. I had no idea, but we got married the day I graduated, and I've been thanking the gods and worshipping at her feet since. She's my princess, and I'm her very happy frog."

Reggie wondered why he'd known none of this.

"So," his father said, "let's cut to the chase. Do you think that because your songbird has left the nest, she's going to fly away?"

Reggie didn't want to answer.

"I'll take that as a 'Yes, Dad' and tell you there's no shame in that, son. Took me years to realize that when Jas said, 'Till death do us part,' she meant it. Worrying whether my beauty was going to wake up one morning and wonder what the hell she'd been thinking kept me awake many a night in the beginning. Roni loves you. I've seen the way she looks at you when you two are together. If she wanted someone else, she'd have no problem finding him, and we both know it."

Reggie agreed. That his father had suffered with the same issue helped him immensely.

"I named it the Garland Panic. It will pass. I promise."

"When did you become so wise?"

"Your old man's always been Yoda. You and the rest of the grasshoppers just never listened."

"Then this grasshopper says thank you."

"No problem. Feel better?"

"I do." And truthfully he did.

"Good. Now, how's the clinic? Busy?"

"No. In fact, I closed it down when I left."

"You need to keep busy. Having time on your hands and nothing to occupy the mind can give you what the Buddhists call Monkey Brain."

"Monkey Brain?"

"Look it up. In the meantime, I'm going to sign you up to work with me for the next thirty days."

Reggie's eyes widened. "Dad, I can't be gone thirty days."

"Why not? Didn't you come down here to work this stuff out?"

"I did."

"Then thirty days will give you time to think, miss your wife, and for her to miss you. Absence does make the heart fonder. Years ago I spent thirty days on a build in Texas, and nine months to the day after I got back, Ike was born."

"Dad!"

"What—you think you and your brothers got here by immaculate conception?"

Reggie dropped his head.

"Come on. I know building houses isn't your forte, but if somebody gets hurt, you'll be good to have around. Let's get this stuff loaded. We'll leave first thing in the morning."

That evening, after checking out of the hotel

and bringing his luggage to his parents' home, Reggie made himself comfortable in the bed in their guest room and listened to the quietness of the night through the open window. His conversations with them seemed to have lifted the shadows covering his heart and soul, and he felt more like himself again. He knew his issues wouldn't be cured overnight; life rarely waved a magic wand to make problems instantly disappear. But the sense of renewal that filled him made him want to hop on a plane, fly home to beg Roni's forgiveness, and make love to her until the cows came home. He checked the time on the illuminated clock on the nightstand. He was pretty sure she was still up, so he dug his phone from beneath his pillow and called. "Hey, baby."

"Hey," she said softly.

"I'm sorry."

Silence.

Feeling awkward, he plunged ahead. "I had a talk with Mom and Dad, and they set me straight on some things."

"Such as?"

So he told her. Everything. Especially the parts about his dad having the same anxieties and fears when he married Reg's beautiful mom.

Roni responded with, "So this Garland Panic, as Charlie calls this craziness, is hereditary? Is that what you're telling me?"

He couldn't help it. He laughed.

"It's good to hear you laughing again, Reg."

"It's good to be laughing together."

For the next two hours they talked about big things like Zoey's gold and how she was healing, and even bigger things such as how much their lives together meant. "I do love you, Roni."

"Ditto. I'm just glad you figured it out. So when are you coming home?"

He explained how he'd been drafted for thirty days. "That okay?"

"Tell your daddy, don't make me come down there and sing, 'Let My People Go.' "

They laughed, and she said sincerely, "No, it's okay. Habitat is doing real good work. As long as I know you're heading home eventually, I can handle you being gone for a month. Zoey's been cleared to go back to school, so Jason's flying in tomorrow. Told him I'll only be working while she's in school."

"That's a good plan."

"You sure?"

"I'll probably never be happy sharing you, but I'll deal with it. I need to get on Team Roni."

"Yes, you do."

He glanced at the clock. "God, look at the time." It was nearly one in the morning.

"It is kinda late for me to be talking to a boy on the phone."

"Then go to bed. I'll call Zoey in the morning,

early, and let her know I'm coming home."

"She'll like that. And I told her no matter the circumstances, her going back into foster care wasn't happening."

"That broke my heart."

"Mine, too. To offer herself up that way . . . She has a heart of gold. And a head hard as concrete."

He chuckled. "Good night."

" 'Night, Reg. Glad you're better."

"Me, too."

Silence.

"Are you going to hang up?" he asked. In truth he could talk to her until sunrise.

"You're supposed to hang up first. You're the boy."

"Is that some kind of rule?"

"Yeah. You never talked to a girl on the phone at night?"

"Not really."

"Well, the boy should hang up first."

"How about we do it together. On the count of three."

He counted down, but they didn't follow through. Laughing, they wound up talking for another hour. Finally he said, " 'Night, baby. I love you."

"I love you, too."

A content Reg turned over, and for the first time in what felt like months drifted off and slept like a baby.

• • •

Back in Henry Adams, a thoughtful Roni put her phone down and lay back against the pillows. Talking with him had been a good thing, but had he really put his demons to rest? She dearly hoped so, but time would tell. Time would also tell how long it would take her to forget all the pain she'd shouldered over this. It wasn't realistic to believe his saying sorry magically negated everything—life wasn't like the movies. Yes, she loved him and she wanted him home with every breath she took because the forgiving part was easy. It was the forgetting part that was the fly in the ointment. Certain it would fade eventually, she hoped it would be sooner than later—but it was there, and she'd be lying to herself to deny it. Content with that inner honesty, she burrowed into the bedding and let sleep take her away.

CHAPTER
18

At six a.m., Bernadine drove to the store to pick up her sister. She hoped the girl hadn't managed to get herself fired, because with her crappy attitude, it was a definite possibility. There were three people waiting outside when she pulled up, two women and a man. They were talking—one smoking—and she wondered if they were waiting for their rides home as well. Diane was standing a short distance away, and she looked miserable. The carefully applied makeup was now streaky and faded. Her high-gloss lipstick was gone. The eyes she turned Bernadine's way appeared defeated and old. She got in the truck, strapped herself into the belt, and leaned back against the seat.

"How'd it go?" Bernadine asked quietly.

"Hard. Awful. Humiliating. Since I'm low man on the totem pole, I had to clean the toilets." The last word came out as a whisper, and there were tears in her eyes. "A public toilet."

In spite of their battling, Bernadine felt her pain.

"How did I get here, Bernadine?" she asked, sounding genuine for the very first time.

"Life, sis. It's called life, and we can either cry and wallow, or lace on the gloves and start punching back."

"This is so not where I'd expected to be at my age." She wiped at her eyes.

"We plan, and God laughs."

"Then He's probably in hysterics."

"Was the crew kind to you?"

"Not really. They seemed to get a big kick out of the look on my face when the supervisor told me what I'd be doing."

Bernadine wondered if Diane's attitude had

anything to do with that. *More than likely,* said the voice in her head.

"How am I going to do this day after day?" she asked. "One of the women said she'd been mopping floors for ten years. Ten years! Is that my future?"

"It depends on you." Bernadine was pleased to hear her starting to give some serious thought to her future. "And only you."

"This is all Harmon's fault."

Back to denial. "Is it?"

"Yes! If he hadn't left me . . ."

"But he did leave. You can't change that, and blaming him and being angry isn't going to put clothes on your back or food on your table. Other women have gone on alone, and so can you. You don't have a choice." Bernadine looked her way and said as kindly as she could manage, "Di, the part of your life with Harmon is over, the end. It's time to start writing a new chapter."

"But I don't know how."

"Then look around, see how other women have done it. Some used a crappy job as a stepping stone to a better one. Some went back to school. You have options, but yes, you will be still cleaning toilets in ten years if you just throw in the towel. Every day is a gift—start unwrapping them."

Diane didn't respond, but she didn't throw back a nasty retort either, which made Bernadine think the advice had hit home. That gave her hope. "When we get home, get some rest and we'll go look for a car later on this afternoon."

"Okay," Diane said in a tiny voice. "Thanks."

"You're welcome."

When she got to her office, she poured her coffee and booted up the laptop, but her sister was still on her mind. The job seemed to be having a sobering effect on all the craziness, and she wondered if it might be time to put in a call to Harmon Jr. and let him know how his mom was faring. If having to clean toilets and wield a mop could instill a measure of growth maybe it could also serve to bring her closer to her children. As it stood now, Diane would be facing her golden years estranged from them, alone. Not a good thing, but she decided to hold off on calling him for now. She'd wait and see how her first week on the job played out and then make her decision.

In the meantime there was work to do, so she sat with her cup and opened up the file that contained the architect's mock-up of the strip mall that could be built on the site of the old Henry Adams Hotel. Although the building was a complete wreck, she hated the idea of tearing down the only original building still standing in town.

She beeped Lily on the intercom. "Hey, can you

come in a minute and let me run something by you?"

"Sure."

When she entered, Lily asked, "What's up?"

"Is there any way we can restore the old hotel?"

"Restore, as in how?"

"Rebuild it so it can be viable again?" She had Lily come over and take a look at the architect's drawings.

Lily frowned. "A strip mall. I'm not a big fan of those."

"Neither am I. But I like the idea of the businesses, so I'm thinking we put them inside the hotel."

"Like a loft kind of place?"

"Yeah, maybe. I just hate to demolish the only original Henry Adams building that we have."

"That is kind of a shame, but it's little more than rubble now, sis."

"Can we maybe restore the outside facade? Don't we have pictures somewhere of what it looked like?"

"I'm sure Tamar has some in the archives."

"Good morning," came a curt voice.

In the doorway stood Astrid Wiggins. Bernadine had told Lily about their grocery store encounter, so neither of them were pleased by her presence. An annoyed Bernadine asked, "What can I do for you, Ms. Wiggins?"

"I need to speak with you. Privately."

Lily backed away from the desk. "I'll leave you two alone."

Once Lily was gone, Bernadine asked, "What's this about?"

"I'm here to let you know I'll be running for mayor in the next election. My husband has been ineffective. I've asked him not to run again."

Bernadine didn't see what this had to do with her, but . . . "Okay, thanks for the information. Is there anything else?"

"Yes. When I'm elected, I'm going to do everything I can to make your life miserable. Every time you want to build something, I'm going to challenge you in court. I'm going to demand soil tests, throw roadblocks in front of your permits—whatever it takes."

Bernadine looked her up and down. "Does Franklin have the money for that?"

Astrid went still.

"I'm only asking because hiring lawyers for what you have in mind is very expensive, especially firms with enough clout to take on the Class A ones I have on retainer. And how will your residents react when they learn you're using their hard-earned tax dollars to fund your petty little vendetta?"

Astrid's lips tightened, and she looked away.

Bernadine gentled her voice. "You can't win this. It would be better for both towns if we worked together."

"I'm not working with you."

"Fine. Bring it on, but don't be surprised when I bury you."

Astrid scoffed. "You wish. I'm already looking into ways to keep you from building that pool."

"The one I'm naming for you?"

Her eyes widened. "Don't you dare!"

Bernadine chuckled softly. "Oh, I dare, honey. And then maybe I'll get one of your residents to start a petition drive to have us annex Franklin. You want to play hardball, I have a very large bat."

Astrid's face went red with fury.

"There's an old saying that a tigress doesn't flinch when scratched by a kitten. Guess which one I am? Now go home. I have work to do."

For a moment Astrid stood there, silently spitting fire and brimstone from every cell in her body, but they both knew her only recourse was to comply.

"This isn't over."

"If you say so."

Astrid stormed out. Bernadine rolled her eyes and wondered how much it might cost to install a moat around the Power Plant and stock it with alligators that dined only on people named Wiggins.

Lily stuck her head in the door. "What did Secretariat want?"

Bernadine laughed. "I thought it was Seabiscuit."

"That too, along with a whole lot of other inappropriate names."

Bernadine filled her in.

"Really?" Lily replied in a tone filled with sarcasm. "She came here to throw down a gauntlet—she'd better hope it doesn't bounce back up and put her eye out. Wonder how Squirrel Head reacted to being told he wouldn't be running for reelection?"

"Don't know. Don't care." Well maybe she did, just a little. Had he meekly said, "Yes, dear," or pitched a fit?

"Anyway, I talked with Tamar. I'm going to make a run out to her place to get some photos of the hotel. Should be back shortly."

"Okay. Thanks, Lil."

On the heels of Lily's departure, Tina Craig called to answer the questions surrounding Zoey's gold. "Are you sure?" Bernadine asked.

"Positive. Checked with the IRS. When Mr. Patterson came into possession of that gold, it became his property. With no Patterson relatives around to step in front of Zoey's claim, the gold's hers. And I checked the value. The coins are worth anywhere from a bit over eight hundred to fifteen hundred bucks—apiece. Miss Zoey is a very wealthy girl."

"Wow."

"Exactly. She and her mom can decide what they want to do with them, but they will owe taxes no matter what. Let me know if they want to put them up for auction. Collectors will lose their minds if those coins come up for sale."

"Okay, Tina. Thanks."

"You're welcome. Give Zoey my best."

"Will do."

With the call ended, Bernadine sat back amazed. She'd hoped Zoey would be able to keep the stash, and now she had confirmation. She sent Roni a text to let her know.

Over at the studio an elated Roni turned to her manager, Jason West. "She's going to be able to keep the gold!"

"Wow. How much do you think it's worth?"

"Zoey looked on the Net and said coins like hers were going for as high as a grand."

"She's going to be one rich little mama."

Ronnie chuckled. "This day can't get any better. Between this and talking to Reggie last night, I think I'm in heaven."

"How is he?"

"Better. He's worked out his issues and will be home after he helps his dad and brother with some houses they're building for Habit for Humanity."

"Oh."

His tone made her ask, "Why'd you say it like that?"

"No reason. Let's get to work. Look at this list

of musicians and tell me who you want to use."

"Wait, Jason. If you have something you want to say, you should. We've been together a long time—you owe me that."

"Okay. I was hoping he'd stay gone."

She forced herself to remain calm. "Why?"

"You can do so much better."

"Better than a man who loves me as much as he does?"

"Does he? A week ago he walked out on you. What kind of love is that? In my mind, he took advantage of you when you were at your lowest."

"What are you talking about?"

"The shooting. Had you not been in the mental state you were in, you wouldn't've given him the time of day, let alone married him."

Roni found this whole conversation bizarre. "Jason, where's this coming from?"

"From a guy who knows you, cares about you, and worries about you."

"And this is how you show that? You really believe he manipulated me into marrying him? How long have you known me again?"

"I should've kept my mouth shut."

"No. It's obvious that we needed to have this conversation. Who am I supposed to be with? You, who never met a woman he didn't want to sleep with?"

"Oh, now you're getting personal."

"And you weren't? Reggie is my husband. I

may have been in a bad place when we met, but I was in my right mind, Jason. Yes, he's had some issues dealing with me and the music, but couples have issues about stuff all the time. At least he manned up and tried to figure it out."

Jason's face turned stony.

"Look, I appreciate you wanting to have my back, but if my husband being in my life is going to be a problem for you, then we need to part ways."

"You're firing me?"

"No. I'm telling you how I feel."

"And I feel like he's screwing up your career. You should be on the road right now. How many gigs have you turned down in the past year? And who builds a recording studio in the middle of damn Kansas?"

"A woman who loves her family, Jason. Are you going to start in on my adopting Zoey, too?"

His jaw hardened.

"I'm trying to balance house and home the best way I know how. Until you find someone you love as much as you love the business, you'll never understand that."

"I guess I won't."

The sarcasm in his voice sealed the deal. "Send me a bill for whatever I owe you. I'll be looking for a new manager."

"You're kidding, right?"

"No. Give me my keys."

Eyes blazing, he fished his ring out of his pocket and slapped the key to the studio onto her outstretched palm. "You'll regret this."

"Maybe. We'll see."

He punctuated his exit by slamming the door.

As the sound faded, she stood in the silence. It never occurred to her that he felt the way did about Reggie. Was he just jealous? She tended to think not; he'd never tried to hit on her or push their relationship past professional boundaries. More than likely it was about the business, and in his mind the business should always be paramount. He was a genius at his job, and he'd helped put her career into orbit, but this? How dare he pretend to know what was best for her life? He was her manager, not her daddy. They'd made some beautiful award-winning music together, but she wasn't going to put up with someone who belittled the choices she'd made with her heart and mind. Replacing him was going to be tough, but their conversation proved it was time to move on, and she had no intentions of looking back.

Roni picked her daughter up after school, and as soon as Zoey entered the truck, she asked excitedly, "Did Ms. Bernadine find out whether I can keep my gold?"

"She did, and you can!"

Zoey screamed with joy. She was so elated Roni thought she'd bounce free of the seat belt and clear out the window of the truck. "How about we stop by and see her and talk to her about what happens next."

"OMG! This is so awesome!"

Zoey was still bouncing off the walls when they reached the Power Plant, and she ran right to Bernadine and gave her a big hug. "Thank you! Thank you! Thank you!"

Bernadine laughed. "You're welcome, but thank Mr. Patterson."

Zoey broke the embrace and danced. "I am so happy!"

Laughing, Roni asked, "You think you could sit a moment so we can talk?"

"Yes!" She sat, but happiness kept her from sitting still. "I know exactly what I want to do with some of it."

"What?" Roni asked as she took a seat, too.

"I'm going to give everybody I know one coin."

"Really?"

She nodded proudly. "Even if I give out thirty, I'll still have big bank—right, Ms. Bernadine?"

"Yes, you will."

"Do you think I can call a town meeting?"

"I don't see why not," Bernadine replied.

"But don't tell anyone why I want to talk to them. I want it to be a surprise."

"Got it."

"And after that, I want to go to Toledo and see my aunt Yvette."

The out-of-the-blue request caught both women by surprise. Roni saw her own concern mirrored in Bernadine's eyes. "Can I ask why?" Roni inquired.

"My mom owed her money, and I don't think she paid her back."

"Oh."

"Are you sure?" Bernadine asked gently.

"Yes."

Roni knew that Bernadine had visited Bonnie's sister Yvette the first summer the kids came to town. Although she'd been decent enough to send along the picture of Bonnie Zoey now held so close to her heart, the aunt hadn't been very kind. "You know, we can probably send your aunt a check instead."

"No. I want to give it to her in person. I think my mom would like that."

Roni didn't push, but the mother in her wanted to protect her child from what could be a disastrous encounter.

"Maybe she'll even come for the family Thanksgiving the town is having," Zoey speculated, looking to Roni for approval.

"Maybe."

"That would be awesome. I have some cousins, too. Maybe they'd want to come here for the summer sometime."

Roni prayed. "They'd certainly be welcome. So when do you want to go?"

"You think we could go this weekend?" She directed her next question at Bernadine. "Can Ms. Katie fly us down there?"

"Most certainly."

"Great. I'm the happiest kid on Planet Earth."

Roni hoped she'd still hold that title when they returned from Toledo.

That evening, because Roni didn't want to show up on the aunt's doorstep unannounced, she got Yvette's phone number from Bernadine. And after dinner, while Zoey worked on her homework up in her room, Roni placed the call. It didn't go well. The aunt expressed no interest in seeing her niece. Roni tried to change her mind. "Zoey's ten years old, Mrs. Caseman, and you're her only family. Certainly you can understand her desire to meet you, if only one time. I promise we won't bother you again, if that's what you choose."

"I don't want to see her."

Roni forced herself to remain calm. "She really has her heart set on this. I'd hate to have to tell her you prefer not to be contacted."

"I don't care what you tell her, frankly. My sister was a drug addict. I don't want my children exposed to that lifestyle."

"Zoey isn't an addict, Mrs. Caseman, and neither are my husband and I. She'd really like to meet her cousins, too."

"Absolutely not."

Roni wanted to reach through the phone and strangle the woman for being so mean-spirited. "Again, she's ten years old. She's no threat to you or to your family whatsoever." Roni hated having to beg, but this meant so much to Zoey. "Look, see her for a few seconds. You don't even have to let us in your house. We'll stand on the porch. Please, Mrs. Caseman."

The other end of the phone was silent for so long, Roni thought they'd been disconnected.

Finally she replied tersely. "Okay, fine. I'll see her this one time only."

"We'll be there next weekend."

"And, Mrs. Garland—after this, lose my number."

"Understood."

Roni put down the phone. How could a person be so uncharitable? According to Bernadine, Yvette Raymond Caseman had been jealous of her sister Bonnie's musical talents and the attention they earned her from their parents. But none of that had anything to do with Zoey. Roni hoped the woman would change her mind, or at least pretend to be happy about seeing her niece, but there was no guarantee. The only thing guaranteed was that she didn't have the heart to tell Zoey the truth.

CHAPTER
19

At school the next day, the weather was too cold to eat lunch outside, so Zoey and her classmates sat in the conference room instead. Wyatt announced that he and his gram were moving into their house tomorrow, and he sounded really excited.

Amari nodded. "It's a great house, man. My dad and I lived there before he and my mom got married. You'll like the place."

Zoey was as elated about his news as she was about having her own stash of gold. Now she could see him nearly twenty-four/seven. Of course, after witnessing her confrontation with Devon, she wasn't sure what he thought of her now.

"So, Zoey," Leah asked. "What's this town meeting about, my dad said you want everybody to come to?"

"Yeah," said Preston. "I was wondering that, too."

She took a sip from the straw in her juice pouch. "It's a secret."

"What kind of secret?" Amari asked.

"A secret secret."

Wyatt watched with quizzical eyes.

"Give us a hint."

"No."

"Come on," Amari pleaded.

"Nope. You'll have to wait until the meet."

"Maybe she's going to announce she's leaving town," Devon tossed out sarcastically.

"Maybe I'll announce I'll kick your behind for the third time if you ever talk to me again."

That drew snickers and some sage advice from Amari. "You really need to let this go, Devon. She's giving you beatdowns right and left."

"Left and right," Preston added.

"East and west. North and south," Leah threw in.

Devon snapped, "All of you can kiss my butt."

"No thanks," Amari replied and made a point of turning his attention back to Zoey. "Now about this secret—"

But no matter how much he and the rest of the kids pushed and prodded, Zoey's lips remained sealed. And when it came time to return to the classroom, her friends were still in the dark.

From her bedroom window, Zoey watched Dads Inc. move Wyatt and his gram's stuff into Amari's old place. She thought it was nice that they were moving in, not only because Wyatt was so awesome but because there'd be someone else to hang out with who was closer to her age. In the past that had been Devon's role, but he was being such a butthead, she didn't want to do anything with him anymore.

"So the cutie-pie is moving in, huh?"

Zoey turned to see her smiling mom walking in. "Yep."

"I went over to welcome them to the neighborhood. Both he and his grandmother seem to be nice people."

"They don't have a lot of stuff." She'd seen some beds go in, a couch, and a couple of chairs.

"Stuff isn't important."

"I know, but are they poor?"

"I don't know, honey."

"I'm going to give his gram two coins."

Her mom stroked her hair softly. "You have a good heart."

They both stood silently and watched Trent and the colonel carry in some boxes. Her mom asked, "Did you enjoy talking to Dad this morning?"

Zoey nodded. "I'm glad he's coming home. I really miss him. He said he was helping Papa Charlie and Uncle Drew build some houses for poor people."

"Yes. Papa Charlie and Gigi Jas helped him figure some stuff out so he could come back."

"I'm glad."

"So am I."

"Are they coming for Thanksgiving?"

"I hope so." Her mom gave her shoulders a loving squeeze. "Is there anything you want to talk to me about regarding Dad coming back? Anything bugging you—worrying you?"

"Nope. Just glad he's coming back."

"You sure?"

"I'm fine, Mom."

Roni chuckled "Okay. Understood. We'll leave for the Dog in about an hour."

"Okay."

After she left, Zoey watched the move-in for a short while longer, then changed clothes for her town meeting.

As everyone filed into the Dog, Zoey tried to hold on to her excitement. She felt real important, sitting at the big center table with her mom, Ms. Bernadine, and Tamar. She wondered if this was how her mom felt right before a big press conference. All the people she cared about and who cared about her had come—even Wyatt and his gram. When he smiled her way, she smiled back, and her heart took off like the engine on Ms. Rocky's Silver Shadow.

Mr. Bing stopped at the table to ask, "What's all this secrecy about, Miss Miami?"

"Secrecy," she whispered back, and gave him an exaggerated wink that made him laugh very loud.

"Okay. Gotcha." He was still chuckling as

he and his cane walked over to sit with Mr. Clay.

She'd asked Tamar to bring thirty of the coins, and they were in an old cigar box on the table in front of her.

After everyone found their seats, Ms. Bernadine leaned close. "Are you ready?"

"Yes, ma'am." She glanced at her mom and then at Tamar and received approving nods from both. Why she was so nervous she didn't know, but she drew in a deep breath in an effort to calm herself down.

Ms. Bernadine stood. "Okay, folks, let's get this show on the road. Zoey?"

Zoey stood and picked up the box. "I got a really big surprise yesterday, and I want to share it, so when I come over to you, just open your hand."

Because OG was seated in the first booth, he was her first. When she placed the coin on his palm, he viewed it with puzzled eyes that suddenly widened, and his jaw dropped. Next, Mr. James, Rocky, and Siz. They too studied the coin, and when she moved on, they were staring at one another in confusion. She gave coins to Crystal and Eli, Amari and Preston, Leah and Tiffany and their dad. By then everyone was staring her way, but she kept moving: Mr. Bing and Mr. Clay. Ms. Marie and Ms. Genevieve. Reverend Paula. Then on to the Paynes and Amari's parents. When she stopped before

Devon, he sheepishly dropped his gaze. "Hold out your hand," she demanded.

He looked up, and she placed the coin in his hand. Although he didn't deserve one, he did. She saw that Wyatt and his gram had taken seats in the very back and off to the side, as if they weren't certain of their standing in their new community, but she marched right over and gave one to him and two to his grandmother, as she'd told her mom she would.

Every eye in the place followed her when she walked back to her seat, and you could hear a pin drop.

Tamar stood. "Well?"

Finally Preston asked, "What is this?"

"Is it real?" Clay asked.

"They're 1885 uncirculated Double Eagles. Very real, and very, very valuable. The *s* signifies they were minted in San Francisco. And from what little we know, they were originally intended for a miners' payroll, but were stolen en route by outlaw Griffin Blake."

"Wow!" the colonel said, and a buzz filled the room.

Marie asked excitedly, "This is the gold the old people always talked about being buried somewhere close by?"

Trent added. "And every kid who grew up here spent summer after summer trying to find."

"Yes. Cephas had it."

Louder buzz.

"So how'd Cephas get his hands on it?" Bing wanted to know.

"No idea, but after he died I found an old saddlebag that had the gold inside, along with a newspaper account of the robbery. I'm assuming Blake buried the gold somewhere on the property back in 1885."

Genevieve asked, "Zoey, why'd he leave it to you?"

She shrugged. "I don't know. Maybe because I took him some cake."

That drew laughs, and heads shook in amazement.

"How much are they worth?" Rocky asked.

Jack was already on his phone doing a search. "Says here, they can go as high as fourteen hundred dollars?" he exclaimed in a stunned voice.

Eli did a fist pump. "Yes!"

Everyone began talking at once after that revelation. Zoey glanced over at Wyatt and saw tears standing in his grandmother's eyes. They looked like happy tears, so she hoped the gold would help them not be poor.

Amari, ever the realist, asked, "So, how do we turn this into cash?"

Tamar gestured for Ms. Bernadine to answer. "My friend Tina has offered to help. Collectors will pay top dollar for those coins at auction, so if you want to cash them in, she can set something up. I assume you want as much for them as possible."

"Oh, yeah, " Crystal called out.

For the next little while questions were asked, and Ms. Bernadine did her best to answer. In the midst of that, Rocky and Siz came out of the kitchen carrying a tray holding sliced pieces of chocolate cake, and the sight drew a round of applause. She said, "I figure if cake brought Zoey this gold, we all need to eat some. Who knows what it may bring next?"

Laughter.

"And the first piece goes to our very own golden girl."

A thunderous standing ovation followed, and everyone began shouting her name. "Zoey! Zoey! Zoey!"

Emotion made her heart so full, Zoey started crying. Her mom was crying too, and even Tamar, who no one had ever seen cry before, wiped at her tears.

All in all it was a pretty memorable evening at the Henry Adams Dog and Cow.

That night, as a happy Zoey lay in bed, she looked up at her mom and said, "I think everybody really liked their gold."

"I think so, too. You did a good thing this evening, cupcake."

"Did you see Wyatt's gram? She was crying."

"Everybody was crying. Even Tamar."

"I saw that. That was so awesome."

"I was proud of you for giving one to Devon, too."

"He's a dummy, but he's sorta my brother too, just like Amari and Preston. Amari said he's buying every video game Amazon sells."

Her mom laughed, leaned over, and gave her a kiss on the cheek "You rock, girlfriend."

"Thanks, Mom."

"Now get some sleep."

Her mom left, and as the night-light lifted the darkness, she hugged Tiger Tamar, smiled, and burrowed deep to sleep.

Friday after school, Roni and Zoey flew down to Toledo. The visit with the aunt was scheduled for the next morning, so they checked into a hotel. Roni continued to give Yvette Caseman the benefit of the doubt, hoping she'd change her mind and embrace Zoey as her niece.

On Saturday morning, Roni drove the rental car to the neighborhood where the Casemans lived and stopped in front of the house. "Here we are," she said, keeping her voice light.

"I like their house," Zoey said.

They got out, and Roni braced herself, praying this wouldn't go sideways.

As they walked up, a woman of average height wearing blue sweats stepped out onto the porch. According to Bernadine, Yvette's hair had been brown, but it was now blond. She must've just stepped out of the shower, because it was wet and hung in strands close to her face. Even from a distance her resemblance to Bonnie and Zoey was plain.

"That's her," Zoey cried excitedly, and before Roni could stop her, she took off running, calling, "Aunt Yvette! It's me, Zoey!"

The woman instantly drew back, and her reaction stopped Zoey in her tracks. Roni's heart broke.

The aunt tried to fake a smile, but it didn't work. The silent Zoey checked her out and glanced back at Roni, as if seeking an explanation.

When Roni came abreast of her, she took Zoey's hand. "Come on," she said softly. "It'll be okay."

Mrs. Caseman stood silently as they approached the porch. Roni took the lead. "Hi, Mrs. Caseman. I'm Roni Garland, and this is your niece, Zoey."

Yvette stared at Roni with surprised eyes. "You didn't tell me you were—" She waved away whatever else she was about to say. Roni assumed she was referencing her race, but didn't allow herself to be offended.

Looking out from inside the screen door were

a girl and boy who appeared to be near Zoey's age. The girl sneered, "We don't like crackheads."

Zoey stiffened.

The boy added nastily, "Mom said we're not letting you in the house because you'll try and steal something."

Yvette turned beet red. "Get away from the door!" she snapped.

But the damage was done.

Zoey's chin rose, and she met her aunt's eyes.

The woman appeared embarrassed and stammered, "So, Zoey. How are you?"

"Fine." She reached into the pocket of her Danica jacket and pulled out a gold coin. "My mom Bonnie owed you some money, and I wanted to pay you back." She handed over the coin and turned to Roni. "I'm going to sit in the car."

Roni watched her daughter walk stiffly away before she turned on Zoe's aunt, who was staring with awe at the coin in her hand. Her first instinct was to curse her up one side of her house and down the other, but she held her tongue.

"What is this, something out of a candy machine?"

"No. It's an 1885 double eagle. It's gold and worth about fifteen hundred dollars."

"Where'd she get this?"

"She didn't steal it, if that's what you're

worried about. Your niece is a very wealthy young woman, but that doesn't matter because you'll never see her again, just like you asked. Thanks for taking the time to see us. Have a good day." Roni started toward the car.

"Wait! Why don't you come in?"

Roni shook her head in disgust at the sudden change in tune but didn't slow. Furious, she got in the car and drove away. She glanced over at her sad, silent child. "I'm sorry, baby." Roni didn't ask if Zoe was okay; the answer was obvious. "Do you want to get something to eat before we meet Katie at the airport?"

"She didn't want to see me, did she?"

"No, honey, she didn't. She told me that on the phone, but I was hoping she'd find it in her heart to change her mind."

"I hate those kids."

"They weren't very nice."

When Roni looked her way, Zoey was staring out the window. "So, do you want to get something to eat?"

"No, Mom. I just want to go home."

"Then that's what we'll do."

CHAPTER
20

In her office on Monday morning, Bernadine was saddened to learn that the visit with Yvette Caseman hadn't gone well. Like Roni, she'd really hoped Zoey would be welcomed by the family. What would her sister Diane have done had Bernadine treated her with similar disdain? Instead, she'd been taken in, and as promised Bernadine purchased a car for her; a small sparrow-brown economy sedan that had lots of mileage on the odometer but was in relatively decent shape. She sensed Diane wasn't ecstatic about the vehicle's age and looks, but she had the good sense to keep her complaints to herself. She didn't seem any happier about her job than she'd been the first day, but there'd been no further complaints or tears. Bernadine dared to hope she was growing up, but knew only time would tell.

"Ms. Brown?"

"Hi there, Gemma."

"Do you have a minute?"

"For you, I have all the time in the world."

She took a seat. "I just wanted to swing by and say thanks for everything, again. The house is fabulous. Never lived in anything so nice before.

I signed all the paperwork Lily gave me, and knowing that my rent is actually going toward buying it—there are no words."

"Just trying to give you a helping hand."

"You've given me way more than that. And the gold! Oh my goodness. Do folks here do that kind of thing all the time? I was so excited I couldn't sleep."

"That was pretty special, wasn't it?"

"Yes, it was, but Zoey gave me two coins. She probably didn't notice, with all that was going on, so I just wanted to return the extra one."

Bernadine found herself adoring this woman. "There was no mistake. Her mom told me she intentionally gave you two because she thought you and Wyatt might need a little extra help."

Tears glistened in Gemma's eyes. "What a sweetheart."

"Gemma, girl. You and those waterworks have to stop."

They both laughed, and Gemma wiped at her eyes. "I've just never been blessed this way before."

"Hopefully it will be the first of many. Henry Adams is a very special place. You and Wyatt will thrive here."

"I'm thinking of going back to school once we get settled in. Not sure what kind of classes, but I want Wyatt to go to college, so I need to set an example."

"That's great, and you can always talk to Jack about which classes would be right."

"That's a great idea. One sour note, though. Astrid Wiggins stopped by my place last night."

"What did she want?"

"To know about the gold. Where it came from. Was it really all Zoey's. How many people got coins."

Bernadine tensed. "What did you tell her?"

"That it was none of her damn business."

"Did she say how she found out about it?"

"She said from her niece, Megan Tripp. Since Megan goes to the academy, I'm assuming one of the kids must've told her."

"Megan Tripp is a Franklin?"

"Yes. Her mother is Astrid's younger sister, Becca, but Becca and her husband are good people, not crazy like Astrid."

Bernadine blew out a breath. In hindsight maybe she should've told the kids to keep the coins on the down-low.

Gemma reinforced her concerns. "If Astrid can figure out a way to turn this into drama, she will. She made it real clear she doesn't like you."

"I know—she's made that clear to me, too."

"Didn't mean to mess up your day but I thought you should know."

"You did the right thing. Thanks."

"You're welcome." Gemma stood. "I need to get to work."

"Thanks again, Gemma."

Bernadine wasn't happy knowing Astrid was nosing around, especially hearing that she'd specifically asked about Zoey. If even a drop of drama touched Zoey's life as a result, Bernadine would blow the woman straight to hell.

Lily came on the intercom. "Walk to your window and look out."

"What?"

"Just go. I'll be right there, soon as I make a few quick calls."

Confused, Bernadine went to the window. The stream of trucks and cars and jeeps slowly making their way down Main dropped her jaw.

Her phone rang. It was Astrid. "Good morning, Ms. Brown. Just so you'll know, I've alerted all the newspapers and TV stations around about Zoey's good fortune. With any luck every piece of riffraff that can spell the word *gold* will descend on your little town, hoping to dig up more. Not bad for a kitten, huh? Have a nice day."

Furious, Bernadine immediately began making calls.

After Bernadine's call to her, Roni took a look out her front window and saw her lawn swarming with reporters and camera people. "Dammit!" She was going to have to run a gauntlet to get to the school, and she wasn't looking forward to it. One her way to the garage, she put in a call to

Reggie down in South Carolina. She got his voice mail, so she told him to call her as soon as possible. She started the truck and hoped the press had sense enough to get out of her driveway, because she'd be backing out at full speed and she didn't have time to let them know.

She managed to drive away from the house without too much of an issue, although a lady reporter wearing stilettos wound up diving into the rosebushes next to the garage to keep from being flattened when her truck came barreling out of the raised door. Roni's mirror treated her to a view of the reporters futilely running after her, but she swung onto the street that led to Main and kept going.

Her biggest fear was kidnapping. The world was filled with crazies, and when one put crazies in the same equation with a little girl worth as much money as that gold added up to, there was no telling what they might be capable of plotting. A few years ago, Crystal had been kidnapped and held for ransom. Roni didn't want Zoey to have to go through that, too.

As she turned the truck onto Main, all the traffic choking the road brought her to a dead stop. It was gridlock. Cars were lined up bumper-to-bumper and crammed into the parking lot of the Power Plant, the rec, the school, and the church. She couldn't see the Dog, but she assumed its lot was packed as well. In the vehicles nearby sat grizzled bearded men who looked like they hadn't seen a shower since the Bush administration; tired-faced women driving pickups filled with kids; two guys decked out in camouflage gear, driving a huge blue monster truck with a bunch of baying hounds in the bed; and all manner of strange characters, running the gamut from the ordinary to the weird. It was if someone had filled sleepy little Henry Adams with the cast and vehicles of the next version of *Mad Max*. It was both bizarre and surreal.

The sound of knocking startled her back to reality and she turned to see a woman standing by her passenger window who looked like she'd gone through life ridden hard and put up wet. She motioned for Roni to roll down the glass. Roni obliged but only lowered it enough to ask, "Can I help you?"

"Yeah." The grin showed missing teeth. "You know where the little girl found the gold?"

"No." Roni immediately raised the window. Good lord! Looking down the street, she weighed her options. She could leave the truck and walk to the school, or bully her way into the flow of traffic. Neither were good. If she left the truck, there was no guarantee it would be there when she returned, considering how dubious many of the people appeared, and bullying her way into standstill traffic would get her nowhere.

Bernadine's voice came over the sync. "Roni. How close are you to the school?"

"I'm stuck in traffic at the corner of Main."

"Okay. The kids are at Tamar's, so go there when you can. Sheriff Dalton and his people are trying to get these fools out of our hair, but it may take a while. Watch your back while you're driving. Mr. Patterson's place was broken into and trashed. Trent and some deputies are on their way to our subdivision to make sure there are no break-ins there."

"Good grief."

"I know. Also, calls are coming in from the network morning shows, wanting Zoey to come on and be interviewed."

"Tell them no. Maybe when she's eighteen."

"My feelings exactly. Text me when you get to Tamar's."

"Will do." When the sync ended, Roni whispered, "Wow."

Reggie's voice came over the sync. She clicked in and told him what was going on.

Bernadine watched the circus below her window and wondered how long this madness would continue. The voice of Sheriff Dalton on the bullhorn floated up to where she stood. "Please leave the area. This town is private property. No digging or camping will be allowed. Turn your vehicles around."

The county police were out in force, as were men and women of the highway patrol. There were even uniformed national guardsmen on the scene, but law enforcement was probably out-numbered fifty to one. She couldn't tell how many people there were. At the sheriff's urging every building in town had been closed and locked up tight, not only for safety reasons but so the unwanted visitors would have no place to go or reasons to hang around. The large crowds were reminiscent of the ones that descended on the area last summer for the trial of Riley's hog Cletus. These people weren't wearing pig masks, though, and instead of silliness in the air, there was tension. In spite of the sheriff's warning, some people were refusing to leave. There were pockets of people arguing with the deputies, and across the street a belligerent man was hand-cuffed and escorted to a gray police van that had "County Jail" stenciled in red letters on its side.

"You have five minutes to leave the area," Sheriff Dalton announced. "If you do not, you will be arrested!"

A wave of catcalls and boos greeted that.

"This is a mess," she said in the silent office. And she had Astrid Franklin Wiggins to thank.

The jarring sound of glass breaking somewhere on the street sent her rushing to her computer to pull up the surveillance cameras. It was the recreation center. People began pouring from their cars, and as the numbers swelled, the riot was on.

In the aftermath, Bernadine toured the damage with Trent, Barrett, and Dalton. She felt much the same way she had the night of the Stillwell fire—angry, disgusted, and heartbroken. Fortunately, this time around no lives were lost, but the rec sustained considerable damage. Every window was broken, and areas inside the building and out were covered with shattered glass. Due to the gridlock, the police couldn't get enough officers to the building to put on a show of force when the disturbance began, so the looters helped themselves to DVDs, the sound system, the computers from the senior center, and all the town's emergency supplies—bedding, cots, cases of water, cases of soup, hot plates, small generators. As the thieves loaded their booty into their trucks and others not involved in looting did their best to get out of Dodge, utter chaos ensued, resulting in car accidents and fistfights between angry drivers. To the officers' credit, they did manage to retrieve some of the stolen goods, but the vast majority left town with their new owners.

"Sorry my people couldn't stop this before it got out of hand," Dalton said.

She waved it off. "You did your best. Imagine what would've happened had you not been here at all? Besides, insurance should replace most of it."

They moved into the auditorium. The place was littered with empty boxes, plastic bottles of water, and cans of soup, apparently dropped and left behind. Kernels of unpopped corn crunched beneath their feet.

Trent bent to pick up a mangled DVD case. He opened it. It was empty. He tossed it back on the floor in disgust. "At least the rest of the town was spared."

Bernadine was thankful for that as well.

Trent said, "I think they took one look at that weapon Barrett was armed with outside Gary's store and decided to shop elsewhere."

Dalton chuckled. "Did you borrow that thing from the Terminator?"

Barrett gave him a small smile. "I'm just glad I didn't have to use it. Unlike Ms. Dancer."

A couple of men trying to break into the Dog were greeted by Rocky and her shotgun.

"Will she be charged?" Bernadine asked.

Dalton shook his head. "She was protecting her business. My men took them to the hospital. The docs will pry the slugs out of their legs and send them over to the jail—which is pretty full, by the way."

"How many people were arrested?"

"Eighty."

"Good."

That night, while the police sat in cars outside the homes in the subdivision, Bernadine checked her e-mail before going to bed. There was only one—from Astrid Wiggins. Heard you had a busy day. Enjoy the cleanup. LOL.

In the days that followed, everybody pitched in to help with the cleanup. A steady stream of prospectors continued to arrive, but deputies had cars blocking the road into town and that was enough to make the unwanted visitors turn around. Bernadine also began receiving calls and e-mails from people claiming to be (a) related to Cephas and (b) Zoey's distant relatives. She forwarded all the bogus inquiries to Sheriff Dalton's office.

A week later, over at the Garlands' house, Roni was on the phone, talking with her baby brother and fellow musician Randy about Zoey's gold, the riot, and hooking up with a new producer. Her old one, who happened to be a good friend of Jason's, was suddenly too busy to help with her newest project, and she was sure Jason had poisoned the water.

"You should get in touch with Cassidy Sullivan," Randy offered. He was in San Francisco.

"Never heard of her."

"She rolls on the down-low, but she's fabulous

in the studio." He ran off the names of some of the people she'd worked with, and Roni was admittedly impressed.

"How old, and where's she from?"

"Late thirties, I'd say, and from Ireland."

"Ireland?"

"Yeah. Not your average stateside producer, but I've worked with her in the past. Knows her stuff."

He gave Roni her e-mail address and said, "I'll let her know you'll be getting in touch."

Roni had her doubts. "I don't know about this, Randy."

"Have I ever steered you wrong?"

"No."

"Then trust me, okay? And just so you'll know, she's an über Roni Moore fan."

That made Roni smile. They spent a few more minutes talking about her and Reggie, and then his time frame for flying in for the town's Thanksgiving dinner. When they were done, she bit down on her doubts and sent the Sullivan woman an e-mail.

Roni got a response later that day. Cassidy was honored to be considered and wanted to fly in later in the week. She sent along her phone number so they could talk in the meantime. Roni was also looking for a manager to replace Jason, but she decided that could wait for the time being.

300

The producer was more of an immediate need, because she really wanted to get going on the tribute CD.

When she looked up, it was time to pick up Zoey from school, so she hurried to get her jacket and left the house. Life had seemingly gone back to normal. Bernadine hadn't received any more claims from people posing as Zoey's relatives, so Roni hoped the insanity had run its course.

"How'd the day go?" she asked once Zoey got in and did up her seat belt.

"Good, but I keep bumping this stupid cast on stuff. How much longer do I have to wear it?"

"Going to be a while."

Zoey blew out an exasperated breath. "Can we eat dinner at the Dog?"

"Yes. I've been on the phone most of the day, so not having to cook would be awesome."

"Did Uncle Randy help you find a new producer?"

"He did. Her name's Cassidy Sullivan. She's Irish."

"Never met anybody from there before."

"Neither have I."

"Is she nice?"

"Randy says she is."

"Then I think I'll like her."

On the afternoon Ms. Sullivan was set to arrive, Roni and Zoey drove up to the Hays airport to meet her flight from Miami. Roni still wasn't sure they'd mesh—after all, what did an Irish woman know about jazz? But because of Randy's recommendation, she was willing to give her a chance.

When Cassidy Sullivan walked into baggage claim, everyone stopped and stared. She was thin, of average height, and decked out in black leather pants, a black vest over a green silk blouse, and knee-high black leather boots accented with silver buckles. Her jet black hair was short and cut close to her pretty face, with emerald green highlights that matched her eyes.

Zoey whispered, "Wow!"

"Wow is right," Roni echoed.

Cassidy had a confident, breezy stride, and when she spotted Roni, her smile lit up the room. "Ms. Moore?"

"Call me Roni."

"Thanks. Call me Cass." Her voice was pure Ireland.

"Welcome to Kansas."

"I'm so honored to meet you." She glanced down at the staring Zoey and asked, "And who might you be, a fairy princess?"

Looking dazzled, Zoey blinked. "Um, no. I'm Zoey Raymond Garland."

"Pleased to meet you, Lady Zoey. I'm Cassidy Grace Sullivan. All that dark hair and dark eyes, you could be one of my nieces. You wouldn't happen to be Irish, now, would you?"

"Um, no. I don't think so. I love the way you talk. You're so awesome."

"No, I'm just Cass. How'd you hurt your arm?"

"Crashed my bike."

"Can I sign the cast later?"

"Yeah!"

Roni chuckled. "Cass, do you have luggage?"

"A lot, I'm afraid. When your brother's a rocker and your mum's an old-school rocker too, you travel with a ton of stuff, even if it's only for a few days. Genetic, I think."

"Your mom's a rocker?" Zoey asked.

"Yep. Way before your time, though. She was lead guitarist for a group called Emerald Isle."

Roni said, "I know that name. They were a force back in the day."

Cassidy smiled. "Mum's a huge fan of yours too, and she sends her regards."

"I'm flattered. Be nice if I could thank her in person sometime soon. Let's get your bags."

Zoey continued to stare as if frozen in place.

"Zoey, you coming?" Roni asked.

She shook herself loose. "Yeah."

On the drive away from the airport, Zoey was glad to be riding in the back seat because she couldn't stop staring at Cassidy Sullivan. She loved her clothes and her hair, the black paint on her short manicured nails, and especially the Irish accent. She wondered how long it would take her to learn to speak that way. She knew she was being a geek but couldn't help herself. She'd never met anyone like her before, and in that moment, Danica Patrick dropped down a notch on Zoey's fan-girl crush poll because Cassidy Sullivan ruled.

Cassidy turned in her seat and asked, "So what do you like to do, Lady Zoey?"

"Work on cars and play music."

"Work on cars, really?"

"Yes."

"And you're a musician, too. That's pretty fabulous. Do you play an instrument, or do you sing?"

"Both. I play piano."

"I play piano, too, but I can't sing a note. I play guitar, though—bass, not lead like me brother and mum."

Zoey asked, "What's your brother's name?"

"Conor. His stage name is Conor Dublin. His band's called Balor."

Her mom piped up. "I know that name, too. They've won all types of Grammys."

"Almost as many as you," Cassidy countered.

"Can you teach me to play guitar?" Zoey asked.

"Zoey," her mom warned. "We don't want to impose."

Cass said, "No, it's quite all right. As long as it's okay with your mum, sure."

"No problem here then."

"Great!"

Cass's next question was for Roni. "So what hotel do you recommend?"

"There aren't any. While you're here, you'll be our guest at Chez Garland."

"I can't stay at your home. That wouldn't be right."

"Your only other option is outside in a field somewhere, maybe." Roni laughed. "Henry Adams is a really tiny place. Wonderful, but tiny."

"You sure you I won't be putting you out?"

"Positive."

"Then thank you."

For the rest of the ride, while her mom and Cassidy talked and laughed, Zoey sat in the back and fantasized about wearing black leather, playing bass guitar, and speaking with an Irish accent.

After they got home, Cassidy was shown into the guest room, and then they went to have dinner at the Dog. Like all new visitors, Cassidy was struck by the diner's odd name.

Roni replied, "Alcohol was involved."

"Ahh. No other explanation needed."

The place was rocking, as always. "Lady Marmalade" by Labelle was blasting on the box, but when Roni and Zoey stepped in with their guest, everything came to a halt. Well, except Siz, who was so overcome by Cassidy that he walked into the wall beside the kitchen doors. While Mal hurried over to check on him, someone turned the music down, and Roni made the introductions. "Everybody, this is Cassidy Sullivan. She's my new producer."

She was given a rousing welcome, and Amari called out, "Will you marry me?"

Laughter.

Cassidy told Roni, "I like your tiny town."

"Come on, let's find a seat."

The volume on the music was turned back up, and Rocky came over to the table to take their orders.

"Ms. Sullivan, you have no idea how glad I am to have you here," Rocky said.

Cass looked puzzled.

"It's been lonely being the only woman with the power to make men walk into walls." Cassidy roared.

After returning from the Dog, Zoey went up to her room to do her homework, and Roni and Cassidy relaxed at the kitchen table to talk about the CD. The role of a producer encompasses many things, from picking the songs and musicians, to controlling the sessions, to coaching the artist to be all she can be. Producers also serve as visionaries, and the best of the best know almost intuitively how a project will sound even before it comes together.

"None of these songs work for me, Roni," Cass

declared after checking out the songs Jason had lined up before his firing.

Roni was instantly wary. "Why not?"

"Because yes, these are all standards, but I don't think they showcase your pipes very well. They're all also the same tempo, pretty much. You need more sass in this list."

"Sass?"

She nodded. "Tell you what. Give me a day or so to do some searching around and come up with some songs that will not only be best for that award-winning voice of yours but will also sell a CD. You do want this to sell, right? This isn't just a vanity-type project?"

Roni hadn't thought about it in quite those terms. "Jason said it probably wouldn't go platinum, but I wanted to do the songs anyway."

"Honoring the matriarchs is a wonderful idea, but making money while doing so is better."

Roni liked her. "I agree. Welcome aboard, Ms. Sullivan."

She bowed. "Glad to be here.

CHAPTER
21

At lunch the next day, Cassidy was all Zoey could talk about, and the kids who'd seen her at the Dog were right with her.

"Loved her hair," Leah said.

"And the leather. Especially the boots," Crystal added.

"She's the hottest thing in town," Amari said. "Right, Brain?"

With his girlfriend Leah giving him the eye, Brain shrugged. "She was okay."

Amari looked from Leah to his best bud and winced. "Sorry. Wasn't trying to get you in trouble."

"No problem."

Wyatt asked, "I didn't get to see her. When do you think I can meet her, Zoey?"

"Come by after school, and I'll introduce you."

"Okay."

Devon rolled his eyes and for the first time in a long time didn't offer his opinion—which everyone appreciated.

As they were walking back to the classroom, Zoey suddenly remembered something, so she caught up with Wyatt. "I forgot. I'm going to see Reverend Paula right after school, so I'll text you when I get back so you can come meet Cassidy."

"Okay."

As they retook their seats, she was glad he hadn't asked why she had to see the reverend. She didn't want him knowing why.

Due to her broken arm, Zoey hadn't been on her bike since the crash—not that it was in any condition to be ridden—so her mom had been driving her to school. The church was only a short walk away, so once they were dismissed for the day, she headed there, but not without Amari as an escort. Because of the craziness with the gold seekers, the adults didn't want any of the kids to walk anywhere alone. She supposed they were afraid some nut would jump out and grab them —especially her, because everybody knew she owned the coins.

When they reached the church, he waited until she went inside, then went on his way.

Reverend Paula was in her office. "Hey, Zoey. Come on in."

Zoey did so, taking a seat on the nice sofa.

"You want anything? Juice? A snack?"

She shook her head. Being alone with the reverend always made Zoey think about Miami and her mom Bonnie, because that's where they'd first met.

"I enjoyed meeting Ms. Sullivan last night."

"Isn't she the stuff?" She knew better than to say "the shitz" around the priest.

Paula smiled. "She is the shizzle."

Zoey grinned.

"So, tell me what's been going on with you and Devon. Why're you beefing?"

Zoey's face soured. "We're not. He's just an idiot."

"But you got suspended, right?"

"Yeah. Because he won't leave me alone."

"Tell me what happened."

So she did.

The reverend nodded in sympathy. "It's embarrassing to be teased when you like somebody, and even more so when the teasing mentions someone having a baby."

"Yes, it is!" Zoey was glad somebody finally understood her side.

"However—"

Zoey's happiness deflated.

"—is that justification to pound him?"

Zoey didn't respond.

"Let's look at it this way. Is Devon the boss of you?"

"No!"

"Who's the boss of you?"

"Me. And my parents and the other adults," she added as an afterthought.

"Okay, so Devon is not in charge."

"No."

"Then why are you letting Devon be the boss of you, if he isn't?"

"But he's not."

"Ah, but he is. Otherwise, when he pushes your buttons, you wouldn't go into Angry Girl Knucklehead mode."

Her kind and wise eyes held Zoey's.

"You can't control Devon, but you can control Zoey. And just think about how mad he'll be when you don't react the next time he's being a pain in the rear. Sometimes silence is better than a punch."

"Never thought about it like that."

"Now you can."

And Zoey did, long and hard. "But he makes me so mad."

"*You* are the boss of you. You. If you have to count to ten or sing 'Amazing Grace' or 'Mary Had a Little Lamb' to yourself, find something that helps you remember that *you* control your response. We can't have you breaking into Angry Girl Knucklehead mode every time something happens. The court frowns on that when you get older."

"That's sorta what my mom said."

"Wise lady, your mom." She silently studied Zoey for a few moments. "Will you do yourself a favor, and try and remember who's in control?"

She nodded.

"Good, because the more you try something, the better it works."

"Okay."

"Now, anything else you want to talk about? I heard about your aunt."

"Her kids called me a crackhead."

"Not very nice. Probably made you mad."

"It did. They said their mom wasn't going to let me in the house because I was going to steal something. I don't steal."

"No, you don't, so this is another instance of being in charge of yourself. You know you're an honest and loving person, but you can't control what they think. If they knew you better, they'd figure out how wrong they are, so in this instance we have to be like Christ and forgive them."

"That's kind of hard."

"I know, but when you say your prayers at night, ask God to watch over them and put love in their hearts. Who knows, the next time you meet them, maybe things will be different."

"I don't want to see them again."

"Understandable, but you can still pray for them."

Zoey wasn't sure she agreed with the reverend on that one, but said, "Okay, I'll try it."

"That's all God asks, honey," Reverend Paula replied. "So did us talking help any?"

"It did. A lot. Thank you."

"You're welcome. Anytime you need to think

something through, you have me and your mom and dad—the whole town, really."

Zoey smiled. "I know."

"How about I drive you home?"

"Great."

When Zoey got home, Cassidy was at the piano. "Hey there, Lady Zoey. How'd the day go?"

"Pretty good. Where's Mom?"

"On the phone upstairs, talking to your dad."

"What're you doing?"

"Going over some songs I think might be good for your mum's CD."

Zoey joined her on the bench and looked at the music on the stand. " 'A-Tisket, A-Tasket'?"

"Yes, it's an old song by the great Ella Fitzgerald."

Zoey'd never heard the song before, but using the chart she began picking out the notes.

"You can sight-read."

"Yes."

"Did your mum teach you?"

"No. I always knew how. Same as my bio mom."

"That's amazing."

Zoey continued picking out notes.

"Can you sing it while you play?"

So Zoey did, and in the middle of it asked, "This is a song about a basket?"

313

Cassidy laughed. "I'm afraid so, but Ms. Fitzgerald made it a very famous basket. So your biological mum played piano, too."

Zoey nodded. "She went to a school called Juilliard in New York."

"My brother went there, too. I wonder if they knew each other."

"Your rocker brother?"

"Yeah. What was your mum's name?"

"Bonnie. Bonnie Raymond."

Cassidy had such a strange look on her face that Zoey asked, "What's the matter?"

"Nothing, sweetheart. You know how sometimes you forget something, and when you suddenly remember, it sorta freezes you for a sec?"

Zoey didn't really, but she said "Yes."

"I think I forgot to give my neighbor the key to get in and feed my dog. Excuse me a minute. I need to go call her."

"Okay."

Upstairs, Roni had just ended her call with Reggie when Cass stuck her head in the doorway. "Roni, may I ask you something personal?"

Roni stilled. "Sure. What is it?"

"This may sound crazy, but do you believe that God puts people in your life for a reason?"

"I do. Why?"

"Here comes the real personal part. Do you know anything about Zoey's father?"

"No. Not a thing. And as far as we know, she doesn't either. Why?"

"I think it might be my brother, Conor."

Down the street at Bernadine's house, Crystal was trying to convince her mom that she really needed a pair of black leather boots like the ones she'd seen Cassidy wearing.

"How much are they?" Bernadine asked as they sat eating dinner.

"The cheapest pair I found online was like two hundred and seventy-five dollars."

Bernadine choked on her water, and it took her a second to recover. "And you're going to pay for them how?"

"If you order them for me, I can pay you back thirty dollars a month."

"Do you make that much in tips?"

Crystal toyed with the food on her plate and admitted, "Not really. How about ten bucks a month?"

"How about you save up half, and we'll see what Santa says about the balance."

"Okay." It was obviously not the answer she'd been seeking, but she let it go.

Diane was at the table as well, but said nothing. Crystal said, "I talked to Kiki today."

"How's she doing?"

"She and Bobby are real excited about moving up here, but they want to wait until after

315

Thanksgiving. He finishes school the second week of November."

"Okay, that's fine. Glad they have their priorities straight."

"You're really going to like them. Everybody will. Thanks for letting them come."

"No problem."

Done with her dinner, she stood. "I'm going to finish up my homework. I'll do the dishes later, so just put your stuff in the sink."

"Will do," Bernadine said.

After she was gone, Diane said, "You have a good relationship with her."

"I do, but it hasn't been easy. She's grown up a lot being here, and as long as we keep making progress, it's all good."

Seeing Diane staring off, she asked quietly, "What's up?"

"Just thinking. The women at work have their lockers covered with pictures of their kids and grandkids. Marlene, the one I told you about who's been a janitor for ten years, brags big-time about how good her kids are doing, about the grandkids' birthday parties, and how they all get together at her place on Sundays for dinner." The eyes she lifted to Bernadine's were sad. "I don't have that. In fact, I've a three-year-old grand-daughter I've never even met. How pitiful is that?"

Bernadine stayed silent.

"You told me to look around at how other women are making it, and I've noticed that some of them don't have a lot going on financially, but they're okay with that because what they have outside work means so much to them. Last night, Marlene told us about her two-year-old grandson. Her daughter went out to get the mail, and when she came back, he'd locked the door. She had to climb in a window to get back into the house. We laughed and laughed, but I have no stories to tell, Bernadine. Not a one."

"So what do you do to change that?"

"Eat crow, I suppose."

Bernadine nodded solemnly.

"I don't want to die old and alone," Diane whispered.

"Your kids are only a phone call away, Di."

"I know, but what if they reject me?"

"What if they don't?"

Diane wiped at the water glistening in her eyes. "This is so hard."

"Change is never easy."

"I need to ask the wizard for some courage."

They laughed at that.

Diane said, "You've been a godsend. I know I haven't been very appreciative, but . . . I am. Thank you so much for everything."

And the hug they shared held such genuine love, Bernadine had tears in her eyes. "You can do this," she whispered to her sister. "Just keep pushing."

"Keep on me, please."

Bernadine pulled back. "I will. Promise. And call your kids. They may surprise you, but you have to be honest with them, Di."

"I know."

They broke the embrace, and Diane said, "I'll let you know what happens."

"Okay."

As she left the kitchen, Bernadine wiped her tears and for the first time in decades felt as if she truly had a sister.

Mal stopped by a short time later. "Hey, beautiful."

"Hey, handsome."

They shared a kiss and walked into the living room, where they took seats side by side on the sofa. He draped an arm across the sofa's back, and she snuggled close.

"How'd the day go?" he asked.

"I think my sister's made a breakthrough," she said, and explained.

"Sounds like progress to me."

"Me, too. Keeping my fingers crossed. She might finally find the happiness she's been looking for. And in other news, Crystal wants me to buy her some boots like Cassidy Sullivan's for two hundred and seventy-five dollars."

"Whoa, that's a chunk of cash."

"Yes, it is. Wants to me to pay for them, and she'll pay me back at ten dollars a month."

He chuckled. "And you said?"

She told him, adding, "She could always use some of the money from her coin, but I'll let her figure that out."

"Good for you. How's her painting for the competition coming?"

"She's almost done, and it looks wonderful. If she doesn't win, I'll be really disappointed. How was your day?"

"Same old stuff. Missed seeing you, though."

"I missed you, too. Spent the day on lockdown, working on the auction with Tina and talking to a thousand and one stonemasons about rebuilding the hotel. Might actually have found a firm that can redo the facade. Old guy in California owns a business with his grandson. He's going to send me some samples to look at in a few days."

He placed a kiss on her forehead. "That's just a reminder to rest."

"I'm trying. In fact, I want you to look at something." She got up and brought back the travel brochure she'd received in the mail.

"River cruises?" he asked, leafing through the brochure's glossy pages.

"Yes, I've always wanted to see Angkor Wat. Thought maybe we could go next year some-time."

"No," he said, and placed the brochure on the coffee table.

His abrupt refusal was surprising. "No?"

He shook his head. "If you want to go somewhere else, fine, but I'm never going back to Southeast Asia."

She understood. After doing his tours in Vietnam, he'd returned to the States broken inside. "We'll choose another spot."

"No, babe—if you really want to go, take Lily or one of your girlfriends. I just have no desire to revisit my nightmares. Don't want to risk messing up my life by drinking again, and if I go to Cambodia, that might happen."

His army experiences were something they'd never gone into in depth because he seemed content not to talk about them, and she loved him enough not to stir up his pain. She placed a hand against his cheek and kissed him. "I love you, so how about a safari in South Africa?"

The shadows fell away from his face. "Now that sounds like a winner."

"Then let's plan on that."

As Bernadine lay in bed that night, her thoughts drifted back to Mal. She supposed when presented with his issues, someone else might have encouraged him to face his fears and visit Cambodia anyway, but she wasn't that person. Finding peace in one's life was often a fragile gift, and she had no desire to send the strides he'd made crashing into the abyss by making unreasonable demands. He knew his strengths and he knew his weaknesses, and if he felt endangered, she loved him enough to respect that.

CHAPTER
22

Reggie was so happy to be home that when Nathan pulled up to the curb in front of the house, he wanted to jump out and run to the door like a kid at Grandma's house. But he waited for Nathan to remove his luggage from the trunk, pocket his tip, and drive away. Then he ran to the door.

Entering the foyer, he shouted à la Fred Flintstone, "Wilma, I'm home!"

The strange leather-clad woman standing in his kitchen, holding a coffee mug, stared. He stared right back and asked warily, "And you are?"

"Cassidy Sullivan. And you?"

"Reggie Garland."

"Oh, you're Roni's husband. Come on in, she's upstairs."

He blinked. Between the leather outfit and the Irish accent, he wasn't quite sure what to make of her, let alone figure out why she was standing in their kitchen. And then it didn't matter, because

Roni walked in and screamed, "Reggie!" and he pulled her into his arms and held her so tight, he never wanted to let her go. As they kissed, a smiling Cass said, "I'll leave you two lovebirds alone."

Roni slowly broke the kiss. "No. Stay. Did you introduce yourselves?"

Reggie was still taking in the loveliness that was his wife. "Yes, but I don't know who she is."

"My new producer, and maybe Zoey's aunt."

"Wait. What?" He glanced over at Cass, and back at Roni. "Aunt?" He knew she'd fired Jason and was looking for a replacement, but Zoey's aunt? "Okay. Let me sit down, because I think I need to."

He took a seat. "Now, start at the beginning."

Cassidy began, "My brother Conor was enrolled at Juilliard eleven years ago, and while there, fell head over heels for a young woman named Bonnie Raymond. Every letter he sent home was filled with Bonnie this and Bonnie that. I was surprised because he'd had quite a few flirtations back at home, but he'd never proclaimed himself in love, as he did with this girl from America. Then my dad got sick, and Conor had to leave Juilliard and return home to Ireland. He hated to leave his Bonnie behind, but he's the only son, and we Irish take our family responsibilities very seriously. Conor wrote to Bonnie nearly every day, sent poor Mum's phone bill through the roof making overseas calls to her. Dad died three months later, and after the funeral Conor wanted to return to the States, but no true son leaves a grieving mother, so he stayed. Then his letters began returning unopened. In a panic he called the school, and was told she was no longer enrolled and they didn't know where she'd gone."

Reggie waited.

"Conor had the phone numbers of a few of their shared friends, and finally got the real story. Bonnie was pregnant. She'd withdrawn from Juilliard, and because she was too ashamed to go home to her parents, she moved to Atlanta with another student she knew instead. But she and the student friend had a falling-out over something, and she left. It was the last time any of their shared friends had any contact with her."

"Wow," Reggie said quietly. He glanced Roni's way and saw her sadness.

"Conor was beside himself, not knowing what had happened, because he knew the baby was his. We'd never seen him so devastated. With our mum's blessing, he flew to Atlanta to try and find her. He searched for weeks. Nothing. He finally gave up, and right after that he formed the band."

"Is he married now?"

"Twice married, twice divorced, and both my ex-sisters-in-law are dark-haired and green-eyed like Bonnie. And, Roni, thanks for showing me the picture of her."

Roni said, "You're welcome, but if it turns out he is Zoey's father and he wants custody, Reg and I will fight him to the grave."

"Don't worry, he won't. He has four girls now, and he loves them almost as much as he does his music, but he's not the full-time-parent type of guy. He spoils the girls rotten, takes them on holiday in the summer to places like Nice and Rio, skiing in Zurich in the winter, sends them outrageous gifts for Christmas and birthdays, and sends monthly checks for their support. He doesn't want them full-time because he knows he's not cut out for that. He's a rocker, after all, and that's the lifestyle he leads. He's more like a favorite uncle than a dad, but his exes are okay with it, and his girls absolutely adore him. I know Zoey will, too."

Reggie said sagely, "*If* he's the dad."

"We can do the DNA testing, but I'm going to tell you now, Conor is her father." She looked between the two of them. "If you want to talk privately, I'll head up to the guest room."

"Thanks, Cass—but before you go, have you spoken to him about any of this yet?" Reg asked.

"No. That wouldn't be fair to you, and I won't say anything to Zoey either. You're her parents. Whatever is decided, it should come from you. My brother's had a darkness in his heart since losing Bonnie, so maybe knowing she's alive in Zoey will help him back into the light again."

"Okay. Let me and Roni talk for a few, so we can figure out how to handle this."

"No problem."

Once she was gone, he asked, "Do you believe this? Sounds pretty out there, if you ask me."

"It does—but why would she claim to be related, when a false DNA test would shoot the theory to hell and back?"

"True. Do you want to do the test?"

"Yes. It wouldn't be right not to. The only other family she has outside us is that nasty Caseman woman and her wretched kids. Even though I've known Cassidy less than a day, I like her a lot, and Zoey worships at her feet. Be nice if they are related."

"I agree, but do we tell her the truth about why we need to do the test?"

"No. On the odd chance that he isn't the dad, she'd be heartbroken. We'll have to make up something."

"Okay, let's tell her we want to test her just in case those wretched cousins need a transfusion or a transplant."

"Oh, she'll love that, but she'll go along with it because her heart's always in the right place."

"Helluva thing to come home to."

"You ain't seen nothing yet. Wait until tonight." And she gave him a big wink.

"I love you."

"Yes, you do."

It was decided that Cass would call her brother and let him know what was going on. Reggie and Roni let her talk to him privately, and when she was done, she came down with tears in her eyes. "He bawled like a baby," she told them. "At first he didn't believe me, told me he'd catch the next flight here and kick my tail if I was pulling his leg, but I finally convinced him I was telling the truth. He's had a couple of women sue him for paternity in the past—falsely—so he knows the drill on the testing, but he wants to see Zoey on Skype, if that would be okay."

Reggie looked to Roni, who said, "As long as he doesn't mention anything about their connection. We want to wait for the test results, so she isn't hurt if it comes back negative."

"I understand. Suppose I get him on Skype and tell her I just want her to meet my brother?"

"That would work. That okay with you, Reg?"

"Yes."

When Zoey came home from school, seeing her dad in the kitchen made her grin and run to him. "Daddy!"

He hugged her tight and kissed her cheek. "Hi! How are you?"

"I'm good! How are you? I'm so glad you're back."

"So am I. You've been taking care of Mom?"

"Yeah, but she's been taking care of me, too."

"How's the arm?"

"Itching like crazy. Do you think I can take it off early?"

"Probably not, but we can have the docs x-ray it and see how it's healing."

"Okay."

"Did you meet Cass?" she asked.

"I did. Very nice lady."

"She is the shizzle. Crystal wants her boots. Where's Mom?"

"Upstairs with Cass. I think they're talking to her brother on Skype."

"The rocker? Can I say hello?"

"I don't see why not. Let's go."

Zoey ran up the steps, and Reg hurried to keep up. He was anxious to see how this would turn out. When he and Zoey entered, Roni and Cass were looking at the screen on the laptop. "Hey, cupcake," her mom said. "How was your day?"

"It was school. Hi, Cass."

"Hi, Lady Zoey. I'm Skyping with my brother. Want to say hello?"

"Sure."

Zoey took the seat Cass vacated, and Reg saw a man on the screen who looked a lot like Cass. He was wearing a leather jacket decorated with a lot of zippers.

He smiled, "Hi. Are you Zoey?"

"Yes."

"I'm Cass's baby brother, Conor. How are you, little one?"

"I'm fine. How are you?"

"Truly honored to meet you."

"Same here. You look like you're crying. Are you okay?"

"I am. Something in the air's got me going, I think, but I'm pretty happy."

Reg was moved by the man's emotional response.

"Where are you?" Zoey asked.

"In Dublin with me mum."

"Can I say hi to her, too?" Zoey looked to Roni and Reg for approval and got nods. "My mom and dad said it's okay."

Conor said, "Hey, Dad."

Reg laughed. "Hey, Conor. Pleased to meet you."

"Same here. Hold on, Zoey, let me get her."

While they waited, Zoey said to Cass, "Your brother's nice."

"He's a big brat, is what he is."

Then an older lady's face filled the screen. She had Cass's face, but her black hair was long, striped with gray, and pulled back in a ponytail. "Hi, Zoey. I'm Fiona Sullivan, Cass and Conor's mom. How are you?"

"I'm fine, Ms. Sullivan. Maybe you and Mr. Conor should open some windows or something. He was crying, too."

Mrs. Sullivan wiped her eyes. "I know. We'll do that. It's wonderful to meet you."

"It's nice meeting you, too. I never met a lady rocker before. Cass is going to teach me to play the bass."

"Good for her," she whispered through her tears.

Zoey turned to her mom and Cass. "Is she okay?"

Cass nodded. "She is. Just allergies, I think."

"Oh. Okay."

"Zoey, I want you to keep my Cassie out of trouble while she's there."

Zoey grinned. "Yes, ma'am. I will."

Roni said softly, "Okay, hon. Tell Ms. Fiona 'bye so that Cass can finish visiting."

She nodded. "Okay, Ms. Fiona, I have to go. Say good-bye to Mr. Conor for me."

"I will, sweetheart. Take care."

"You, too."

Cass slid back into the seat. "I'll call you later. Give my brother a big hug. Love you."

"Love you back."

And she was gone.

Zoey said, "I like your brother and mom. Maybe Dad can give them a prescription to help with their allergies."

"Sounds like a good idea."

Amused, Reggie smiled. "I think so too."

"Okay, go get you a snack and then home-work," Roni said to Zoey. "Dinner later."

"Okay. Thank you again, Cass."

"You're welcome."

Once she was gone, both Roni and Cass let go of the tears they'd been holding back.

"Wow," Cass said, wiping her eyes.

"Ditto."

Reggie said, "If you are Zoey's family, she couldn't ask for better folks. I could see the love in your mother's eyes."

Roni added, "And your brother—oh my goodness. It took all I had no to break into what Oprah calls the ugly cry."

"You have no idea how hard it was to convince them not to hop on a plane and fly straight here," Cass said. "Mom loves her granddaughters, and to have one more—she's over the moon."

"I lost my mom when I was growing up, so Zoey only has Reg's mom, but maybe now she'll have two."

"And four little sisters," Cass pointed out. "Zoey's Conor's eldest."

Reg laughed. "She's going to love that. The big sister."

Roni agreed. "Yes, she will."

"So let's get this test done," Reg said. He felt much better now that the initial meet-and-greet had gone so well. "Usually the labs wants both samples sent in together. With him in Dublin, that won't work, but I can make a few calls and see what we need to do so we can get the results back as quickly as possible."

"On behalf of my family, thank you," Cass whispered through another round of tears. "You have no idea how happy your open hearts have made us."

"Maybe if everything goes well, your mom and brother can join us for Thanksgiving," Roni offered.

"You really mean that?"

"No, Cass. I'm really lying."

Cass laughed. "I can see you and I are going to get along famously."

"Looking forward to it."

That night, after having his world rocked—his father was right, absence does make the heart fonder—Reg lay in bed with his wife cuddled against his side. He placed a kiss on her forehead. "What do you think of this whole Sullivan thing?"

"Feels like I'm on a runaway train, but it's a good feeling."

"Yeah?"

She raised up. "Are you having Garland Panic?"

"Just a little bit. Not sure how I feel about sharing our daughter."

"Nothing wrong with that. I sort of feel the same way, but then I tell myself this isn't about me. It's about Zoey, and as her parents, we need to do our best to do what's right for her."

"Going to be real hard for me to compete against a rocker who wears leather."

She laughed. "I don't think that'll be a problem. Miss Miami's pretty grounded, and she loves her Daddy Reg—always has, always will."

"I know. He seemed like an okay guy, though."

"Yes, he did. And just think, when he takes Zoey to Rio or Nice for the summer, you and I can do the do in every room in the house."

He laughed. "Never thought about it like that."

"That's why you have me."

He kissed her. "I love you, Wilma."

She laughed. "Go to sleep, crazy man."

CHAPTER
23

The month of October seemed to fly by. Zoey and the kids groaned under the mountain of work assigned at school. She did protest having to donate the buccal cells in her cheek to benefit her wretched cousins, but as Roni predicted, she went along with it because it was the right thing to do. Reg reopened the clinic, and after witnessing the extreme poverty in South Carolina while working with his dad and brother, he decided he needed to make health-care services more available to the children in the county. With Roni's help he purchased a van, outfitted it with all the medical bells and whistles, and took it on the road. Zoey named it Dr. Reggie's Health-Mobile.

The auction for the coins went well, and by midmonth those who'd participated saw a nice bump in the balances of their checking accounts. Lily and Trent didn't allow Amari to buy as many video games as he wanted, but he purchased enough to get him through the long winter ahead, and the rest went into his college fund. Speaking of winter, Henry Adams was on the cusp. The warm reds and golds of early fall gave way to frost and temperatures that made everyone wear heavier outerwear to keep the shivers at bay. Snow shovels and window scrapers came out of hibernation, along with rock salt for walks and driveways. Folks no longer lingered in the parking lot of the Dog to chat; once their bills were paid, they hustled to their vehicles and turned on the heat. Daylight became scarce too, making it dark when people left for work and nearly as dark when they returned home.

After the townwide Halloween party at the rec, everyone began looking forward to the big Thanksgiving dinner. Rocky ordered all the turkeys and stored them in a big freezer over at Gary's store. Folks were calling relatives to make certain they were still coming, and Sheila sat in the Dog and took down the names of those expected so she'd know how many to plan for. Diane finally made peace with her children, and she was ecstatic that they were coming to town for the holiday.

And then, just as the rec reopened and the bitter taste of the riot faded, life in Bernadine's town went off the rails again.

It began with two visitors to Bernadine's office. One was a scruffy and decidedly smelly young man with badly done tats up and down his arms named Tommy Stewart. She'd never met him before. The man accompanying him was dressed for business—lawyer business, as it turned out.

He stepped to her and stuck out his hand. "Name's Steve Tuller. Pleased to meet you, Ms. Brown."

"Same here. What can I do for you, Mr. Tuller?"

"May I sit?"

"Of course."

She didn't like the catbird gleam in Stewart's eyes at all.

"My client was in your grocery store yesterday, and he purchased one of the prewrapped sandwiches from the deli."

Her eye swung to the man in question. Putting two and two together, she already knew what was coming. "And he found—what?"

Tuller seemed a bit taken aback, but she didn't

say anything more, so he cleared his throat and continued. "He found a cockroach in the sandwich."

Stewart leaned in. "And I'm sure you don't want this news to get out—not this close to Thanksgiving. Who's going to patronize a store that uses cockroaches as deli meat?"

Tuller cleared his throat. "My client is asking for twenty-five thousand dollars."

"Oh, is that all?" she asked sarcastically.

"She told me you wouldn't blink," Stewart crowed. "Said you probably carry that much around in your purse." Then, as if having heard himself, he blanched and shut up.

Tuller stared, shocked. "What? Who said that?"

Stewart hastily shook his head. "Nobody told me nothing. I made it up." He began taking furtive looks at the door, as if contemplating bolting.

"Who put you up to this, Mr. Stewart?" Bernadine asked calmly. She had a pretty good idea, but she needed it confirmed.

"I want to talk to my lawyer."

Tuller snapped, "You have a lawyer. Me!"

He slumped in his seat and mumbled something that sounded like "She said this would be easy."

"Mr. Stewart, do you know Astrid Wiggins?" Bernadine asked.

His eyes went wide. He started to twitch, then

forced himself to sit still. "No. Never heard of nobody with that name."

She sat back, crossed her arms, and met the narrowed eyes of Tuller, who asked her, "You think Mrs. Wiggins put him up to this?"

"You're his lawyer. Ask him."

"Well, Mr. Stewart?"

"I found a roach in my sandwich from her store," he declared, pointing at Bernadine. "And I want to be compensated for my pain and suffering."

"And if I find out this is all a scam," she countered, "I'm going to sue *you*."

His eyes went big, and he stood. "I gotta go. My boss at the gas station said if I'm late one more time, he'd fire me." That said, he ran out of the office.

Tuller looked embarrassed and angry. "I hope you'll accept my apology for taking up your time with this nonsense. I had no idea. We're a top-flight firm, and we'd never be associated with something this rancid."

"Apology accepted. Did he contact you directly, or did someone call on his behalf?"

"I can't divulge that, but rest assured no one from my firm will bother you again." He handed her his card. The firm's name—Tully, Green, and Kent—was printed tastefully across the top.

"Thanks for your time, Ms. Brown, again. My apologies."

"No problem. Have a good day."

• • •

Furious over the extortion attempt and convinced this was more of Astrid's antics, Bernadine picked up the phone to call Gary, but a call came in before she could hit him up on her speed dial, his name on the caller ID. Before she could say hello, he said in a rush, "You need to get over here. Health Department's shut us down. The store's infested with cockroaches!"

She bit back an expletive and exhaled an angry sigh. "Okay. Be right there." She hit the intercom, told Lily to grab her coat, and they left for the store.

Inside, Gary had all the employees gathered around him. He was saying, "I'll let you know when we can reopen. Sorry this had to happen so close to the holiday."

"Will we get paid while during the shutdown?" Gemma Dahl asked.

Seeing Bernadine, Gary looked to her for the answer. She nodded affirmatively.

Everyone seemed to relax after that. He offered a few last words and sent his staff home.

The first thing he said to Bernadine was, "Health Department guy is still here. Roaches are everywhere. Once we get rid of the infestation, then we have to get the place professionally cleaned from top to bottom and dump all the food—including the canned goods."

Lily asked, "Why the canned stuff, too?"

"Roaches lay eggs that could be on the tops of the cans. People open the cans—"

Bernadine waved away the rest of the disgusting image. "Okay. How much longer will the Health Department be here?"

A male voice behind her said, "We're done."

He introduced himself and then gave them the bad news. "You have a real problem here, folks. You got roaches everywhere—deli, bakery, even the meat coolers. And with all the steps the state mandates to bring it up to code, you're probably looking at ten days before you can open again."

As if to emphasize the severity of what they were up against, a cockroach skittered across the floor. Gary stomped on it.

Bernadine blew out a breath.

The inspector shook his head. "I've given Mr. Clark the names of a couple of local fumigators and cleaning agencies. Sorry to do this. I know you all just opened, but I have to shut you down."

"We understand," Bernadine said. "Thanks for your time."

After he departed, she told Gary, "Go ahead and call the fumigators. I'll call Barrett and have him pull the videos from the surveillance cameras for the past few days."

Gary stepped on another of the insects and said angrily, "These things had to have been brought in, Bernadine."

"I agree, and I'm sure the cameras will let us know who's responsible."

"And when we find out, they'd better leave town," Lily said.

That evening, Bernadine called an emergency town meeting for the adults. Everyone knew about the infestation at the store, and they were pretty angry.

"All Gary's hard work down the drain," Genevieve said furiously. "Do we know who did this?"

Bernadine said, "Yes. Let Barrett finish setting up the video first."

Once he was done, they dimmed the lights and fed the surveillance video through one of the big-screen monitors.

"One of the reasons I went with this camera system was because of the way it's camouflaged," Barrett said. "If the bad guys think there are no cameras, then we can catch them doing this . . ."

And on the screen was Tommy Stewart, pushing a grocery cart. It was early in the morning, and there were not many people inside the store. He stopped at the deli, picked out one of the prewrapped sandwiches, and placed it in his cart. From there, he and his cart meandered their way to the door of the men's bathroom. He glanced around as if to see who might be near. Seeing no one, he and his sandwich slipped inside. Because there were no cameras in the restroom, it was impossible to see what he might be up to. A short time later he exited.

Jack asked, "Who takes a sandwich into the restroom?"

"Someone who's planning to sue us for having cockroaches in that sandwich."

"What?" Reverend Paula asked.

She gave them a quick rundown on her meeting that morning with him and his lawyer, and who she believed was the brains behind Stewart's stupidity.

"Wow," Clay exclaimed. "So she's an extortionist now, too."

As the video continued to play, Stewart placed the sandwich back in the cart and moved on.

"Now watch closely," Barrett encouraged.

Stewart was alone in the aisle that held the bread, chips, and cookies. He looked around cautiously, then withdrew a midsize manila envelope from inside his coat. He took another quick glance at his surroundings, then up at the ceiling.

Barrett said, "Making sure he's not on camera."

"Idiot," Trent declared disgustedly.

The envelope was quickly opened, and the contents—dozens of cockroaches—emptied onto the floor and the shelves holding the food.

Cries of outrage and disgust filled the room.

They all watched as he emptied the contents of

three other envelopes in various aisles around the store before pushing his cart nonchalantly to the cashier stations. He was next seen trying to hit on Gemma, but she wasn't buying. She rang up the few items on the belt and sent him on his way. The last shots were taken by the parking lot cameras. They showed him smiling proudly as he walked to his old Ford and drove from sight.

Everyone began talking at once.

"Where'd he get that many roaches?" Lily wanted to know.

"Probably from the Franklin feed store," Trent told her. "They sell them to people who own birds and reptiles."

"Gary said all our turkeys are being thrown out," said Rocky, "so I've no idea what we'll be eating for Thanksgiving."

"Oh, dear," Sheila cried.

Gary added, "I've called suppliers from here to Topeka and back, trying to get more, but all their turkeys have been promised to other customers, so looks like we're out of luck. Sorry, everyone."

Tamar said, "Not your fault. I'll take care of the turkeys. It'll take more than cockroaches to spoil our Thanksgiving."

"Are you sure?" Bernadine asked. "We could maybe fly some in from somewhere."

"No. I have it covered," Tamar assured her.

"Too bad it wasn't Astrid on the video. Then

maybe we could press charges and put an end to her madness once and for all."

Lily said, "She'll get hers. Karma's only a bitch if you are, and right now, Astrid is in the cross-hairs."

"I hope so. I hate that she's sitting over in Franklin, gloating and toasting the closing of our store."

Everyone else did, too. Astrid 2, Henry Adams 0.

On her way back to the Power Plant, Bernadine got a text from Roni, informing her that the DNA test results were back. The celebrated rocker Conor Sullivan was indeed Zoey's father. Bernadine was glad to finally have something to smile about.

After dinner, Roni and Reg decided to break the news to Zoey about the test. Cass was in the guest room, so they'd have privacy. She'd rejoin them when the time came to hook up with Conor and their mother on Skype.

Roni said, "We need to talk to you about something, Zoey."

She looked away from the Nascar DVD on the living room's big flat-screen and into their faces. "Am I in trouble?"

"No," Reg reassured her. "Not even a little bit."

She exhaled audibly. "Good."

They sat down.

Reggie took the lead. "Remember the test we had you do with the cheek cells a few weeks back?"

"Yes."

"Well, we lied about what it is was for. It wasn't for your cousins, but for a paternity test."

Confusion knitted her brows. "Like the ones rappers have to take for their baby mamas?"

Roni chuckled, and Reg nodded. "Someone was claiming to be your bio dad, and if it turned out not to be true, we didn't want you to be hurt."

Zoe's eyes widened. "Was he telling the truth? Who is he?"

"He was telling the truth. It's Cass's brother, Conor."

Zoey's hands flew to her mouth, and tears filled her eyes. "For real? He's my dad?"

They nodded.

"Oh god," she whispered.

"Is that okay?" Roni asked. "If you don't want to be part of their family—"

"No. I do. I do." Then she paused. "I don't have to go and live with him, do I?"

They laughed. "No."

"Good, because I don't want to leave you guys."

Tears filled Roni's eyes. "That's nice to hear."

"As Amari says, let's not get this twisted. So, that makes Cass my aunt?"

"Yep."

"Oh, wow! Now, that's sick. Crystal is going to be so jealous."

"And," Reggie added, "you have four little sisters."

"Get out!" Her jaw dropped.

"True," Roni said, tickled by the utter awe on her daughter's face.

"I'm the oldest? What're their names? Do they live in Ireland, too?"

"How about we have Cass come in and get your dad on Skype, so they can fill you in on everything you want to know."

Tears ran down Zoey's cheeks again. "I thought nasty Aunt Yvette and her kids were my only other family outside of yours."

"Nope. You have lots of other people to love now."

She came over and gave Reg a big long hug and a kiss on the cheek, and did the same with Roni. "Thank you for finding my dad."

"You're welcome, but thank Cass. She was the one who figured it all out."

"Can I go get her now?"

"Go right ahead."

She took off running. "Auntie Cass!"

Roni looked at Reg. "It worked out."

"Indeed it did."

They shared a hug and a kiss and left the living room to join Cass and Zoey.

●●●

Over at Bernadine's, the doorbell sounded. When she answered it, she was surprised to find Austin Wiggins and a tall, beautiful young blonde standing on the porch under the light. Was this his daughter?

"Hi, Ms. Brown. Hate to bother you, but can we come in for a sec?"

She hesitated, wondering if Astrid was somehow involved in the visit, but then stepped back to let them enter.

As she closed the door, Wiggins said, "I just wanted to stop by before I leave town. This is Lindy. Lindy, this is Ms. Bernadine Brown."

"Pleased to meet you, Ms. Brown," the blonde said in her baby-doll voice.

"Same here, Lindy."

"I've filed for divorce. Lindy and I are on our way to Vegas. We'll get married as soon as I'm free."

Bernadine picked her jaw up off the floor. "Congratulations. I hope you'll be very happy."

Lindy volunteered the answer to the question burning inside like a lit match.

"Wiggy and I met a little over a year ago. I was runner-up in the Ms. Heifer contest at the county fair, and he was one of the judges."

"You were robbed. You should've won."

Lindy giggled and kissed his cheek. "Isn't he sweet?"

The encounter was so bizarre, Bernadine didn't know what to say, so she settled for smiling.

Wiggins said, "I just wanted to stop in and say good-bye and apologize for the hell Astrid's been causing. When she told me I couldn't run for reelection, that was it."

"I see."

"Well, guess we'll be going. Make sure you see the Franklin paper Thanksgiving morning."

"Astrid's going to be so surprised," Lindy said.

"Oh, okay. Thanks for the tip."

A second later they departed, leaving a very confused Bernadine standing in her foyer.

CHAPTER
24

Two days before Thanksgiving, the guests began flying in. Bernadine had Nathan rent a few more town cars and hire a couple more drivers so he wouldn't kill himself driving back and forth.

That evening, the residents and guests met up at the Dog for a preholiday get-together. As she made her way around the place, she met Jack's parents. His mother was so enamored with Henry Adams's quaint charm she declared she wanted to build a house and move in. Eli, Jack, and Jack's dad choked on their sodas. Rocky, sitting with them, laughed.

Bernadine's heart swelled with love upon seeing Diane sitting with her kids. She had her granddaughter on her lap. Even her son Marlon and his partner Anthony were at the table. Although they were bunking at her house, seeing them seated as a family was wonderful.

While the jukebox blasted out "One Nation Under a Groove" by George Clinton and his Funkadelic gang, she stepped aside to allow the harried Crystal to pass by, carrying a piled-high tray of orders. "Hi, Mom. 'Bye, Mom."

Bernadine stopped next to speak with the Garlands. Zoey looked so content seated beside her grandma Jasmine, grandfather Charlie, and the rest of her large extended family. Zoey asked excitedly, "Ms. Bernadine, did Mom tell you I have two dads now?"

"Yes, she did."

Cass was seated with them as well.

"And," Zoey added, "he's a rocker!"

Reg was grinning. Bernadine was happy that he didn't seem to be having issues with adding the Sullivans to his daughter's life. "I heard that. Are you going on tour?"

"No. You know I have school."

"Oh, that's right."

Roni and the others at the table grinned.

Next stop, the Paynes. Bernadine was so taken

aback by the sight of the woman sitting with them, she had to catch her breath. Preston's bio mom, Dr. Margaret Winthrop, stood and gave her a huge hug. "Thanks so much for putting me in touch with Preston." A beaming Preston looked on.

"So glad to have you here."

"Of course Mother wasn't invited. I wanted my first Thanksgiving with Preston and his family to be perfect, and so far, it has been that and more."

Bernadine was touched by Margaret's sincerity, and apparently Sheila was too, because she picked up a napkin and wiped at her teary eyes. Bernadine was asking Margaret about her flight into Hays when the music died and the interior of the Dog suddenly went deathly quiet. She turned to see a few people run to the windows and peer out. In the center of the room stood Griffin July, in all his handsome glory.

"Dad!" Amari cried.

Bernadine, like everyone else, stood tensely waiting for the entrance of the over-the-top Oklahoma Julys, but Griffin raised his hand reassuringly. "Relax everybody. It's just me. The rest of the family's in Florida for the holiday."

Tamar could be seen chuckling.

Griffin added, "I come bearing—" He glanced around. "Rocky, where are you?"

She stood.

"I come bearing . . . turkeys!"

Pandemonium erupted, and shouts of "Griffin! Griffin!" filled the place. The guests looked on, bewildered, but Bernadine was sure their family members would explain.

"They're in my truck. Amari, Trent, Mal. Need some help bringing them in."

So they hurried outside to help.

The morning of Thanksgiving dawned cold and bright, with two inches of snow. As Bernadine and the other parade goers stood dressed warmly but still freezing along the route in downtown Franklin for the annual Thanksgiving parade, she prayed for summer. It was a typical small-town event. There were fire trucks and politicians in classic convertibles. Astrid waved from the seat of an old restored Caddy. Decked out in her black fur, she bore a striking resemblance to Cruella de Vil. Upon seeing Bernadine, Astrid blew her a big kiss. Bernadine countered with a silent curse. The Franklin high school marching band came down the street next, playing "Santa Claus Is Coming to Town" while the majorettes in their short-skirted uniforms and white tights and boots twirled alongside. Mal and the Buffalo Soldiers wearing their parade blues rode their mounts proudly, and everyone cheered. As they passed on, Bernadine looked up the street. The only thing left now was Santa, who was usually played by Austin Wiggins. She wondered if anyone else knew that he and Lindy had lit out for Vegas.

Apparently not. As they waited and waited for Santa to show, Astrid could be seen stomping angrily back down the parade route. In the end, she had to get on the microphone and tell the children that Santa had called in sick. She declared the parade over and sent everyone home.

The Thanksgiving dinner was a huge affair. Everyone was dressed in their Sunday best, and there were mountains of food. Reverend Paula stood to bless the food, but a tremendous noise outside stopped her, and people rushed to the windows to determine the source.

"It's a helicopter!" Amari cried. "Wow! That's sick. It's landing right outside."

Seconds later, a man with long dark hair, dressed in leather, entered along with a beautiful woman in a nice blue dress. He called out in an Irish accent, "Sorry we're late."

Bernadine watched Zoey's mouth drop. Cass stood and laughed. "It's just my mum and brother, everyone. Reverend, carry on."

As Conor and Fiona made their way to the Garlands' table, Paula said the prayer, and then Marie shouted, "Let's eat!"

And eat they did.

After the meal there was dancing and mingling

and all the things small-town folks did best. Bernadine, standing with Mal's arm around her waist, said, "You know, this isn't a bad place to live."

"I like it. Like you, too."

She gave him a quick kiss.

Lily called out, "Soul Train line! Everybody line up!"

Bernadine looked up at the man she loved. "Ready to bust a move?"

"Am I a July?"

Laughing, they got in line.

By the time Bernadine got into bed, it was past midnight. What a day. She picked up the Franklin paper that had been delivered while she was at the Dog. The headline read: "Mayor Wiggins Divorces Wife! Confirms He Was Paid to Marry Her!"

Giggling, Bernadine set the paper aside. She'd read all the dirty details in the morning. Certain that Astrid was home spitting nails, she snuggled down into the comfort of her bedding. Squirrel Head 1, Seabiscuit 0. She was still smiling when she drifted off to sleep.

DISCUSSION QUESTIONS

1. Talk about the many family-related issues found in *Heart of Gold*.

2. Bernadine did her best to incorporate Reverend Paula's theme of kindness over rightness into her life. Was she successful? How difficult would it be to incorporate that theme into your life?

3. Through Diane, we know a bit more about Bernadine's childhood and the issues she faced growing up with her mother. Does this new knowledge alter your perceptions of who you thought Bernadine was?

4. Did you approve or disapprove of the way Bernadine handled Crystal's return?

5. Discuss the growth and maturity shown by Amari and Preston since *Bring on the Blessings*.

6. What's up with Devon?

7. What should Bernadine do about Astrid Wiggins?

8. What do you think the future holds for Zoey Raymond Garland?

AUTHOR'S NOTE

Heart of Gold is our fifth visit to the small town of Henry Adams, Kansas. As with the previous books in the series, Zoey's story widened our view of many characters and answered some questions, but also paved the way for new ones, such as: What is Bernadine going to do about Astrid Wiggins? Will Kiki and Bobby really move to town, and how many more beatdowns is Devon going to need before he gets a clue? In my travels around the country promoting book four, *A Wish and a Prayer*, babies were frequently brought up. "Henry Adams needs babies!" or "Lily needs to have a baby!" or "Bernadine needs to marry Mal and have a baby!" Folks, Lily would probably rise up off the page and smack me into next week should I even think about making her pregnant. After all, she already has Davis, and now Amari and Devon! She's also past her childbearing prime, so no babies for Lily. As for Bernadine, she's over fifty-five. No babies for her either. As for marriage to Mal: readers under the age of forty desperately want them to marry. Those fifty and above simply shrug. Like Bernadine and Mal, they don't see the need to make the relationship any more formal than it is, but we'll see what the future holds.

Heart of Gold was a joy to write. The first draft differed greatly from the final one—scenarios changed and characters appeared, disappeared, and were replaced by others. Cassidy Sullivan walked into this story unannounced. I had no idea she was waiting in the wings. One of the joys of writing by the seat of my pants is that characters like Cass appear out of nowhere bearing magi-type gifts that make a writer smile.

I want to thank Dr. Paul King of Atlanta for taking time out of his busy day to answer my questions about Zoey's care. Any mistakes I may have made in the writing are mine—not his. Big thanks to my editor for granting me the time I needed to give *Heart of Gold* the TLC it needed. Her patience is exceeded only by her editorial savvy—both of which make me a better writer. As always, many thanks to my agent, Nancy Yost of NYLA. Sixteen years and counting! She's the best. I also want to thank Avon/Harper. Who knew when my first novel, *Night Song*, was published in 1994, that twenty years later, I'd still be an Avon Lady and that my fictional town of Henry Adams would still be alive and kicking. I'm blessed to have such a remarkable publishing house behind me. From marketing to publicity to art, a writer couldn't ask for a better team. I couldn't ask for better readers either and to them I bow because without you, I'm nothing. Your encouragement, praise, and blessings fill my heart.

See you next time!

B

ABOUT THE AUTHOR

Beverly Jenkins is the author of twenty-five historical and contemporary novels, including four previous books in her beloved Blessings series. She has been featured in many national publications, such as the *Wall Street Journal*, *People*, the *Dallas Morning News*, and *Vibe*. She lives in Michigan.

Center Point Large Print
600 Brooks Road / PO Box 1
Thorndike ME 04986-0001 USA

(207) 568-3717

US & Canada:
1 800 929-9108
www.centerpointlargeprint.com